A CHANCE ENCOUNTER

Slapping his crop against his thigh in frustration, Peveril saw no way to claim the Beauty's attention all to himself. He clamped his teeth shut on an oath.

"A lovely autumnal afternoon, is it not, Lord Lindford?" a female voice said at his shoulder, taking him by surprise.

"Wha—? Oh, yes. 'Afternoon, Miss Marlowe," Peveril greeted her a bit off-handedly, lifting his hat and giving her a slight bow when he finally noticed her standing near him.

"What a coincidence, you riding here just at this hour, my lord," she said.

Peveril was disconcerted to see a gleam of amusement in her wide eyes, even as she gave him a warm smile. Not used to this sort of teasing from a young lady, he looked at her more closely for a moment before saying with an engaging grin, "Lord, ma'am, should've thought you couldn't help but *expect* to see me here, after the hint you gave me."

The generous smile remained on Mary's face. Peveril had dismissed her as a little brown squab, but as he looked down at her he saw that he had been too hasty in his judgment. He was reminded of his earlier notion that she was a soft little dove, not a brown squab at all, and his attention was momentarily diverted from the Beauty, Belinda. Something appealing about Miss Mary Marlowe stirred him—though he couldn't decide what. There was something in her eyes that he couldn't identify; as he had no experience with quick-witted females, it was no surprise that he didn't recognize intelligence when it was staring him in the face . . .

Other Zebra Regency Romances by
Meg-Lynn Roberts:

An Alluring Lady
A Perfect Match
A Midnight Masquerade

Christmas Escapade

Meg-Lynn Roberts

ZEBRA BOOKS
KENSINGTON PUBLISHING CORP.

ZEBRA BOOKS are published by

Kensington Publishing Corp.
850 Third Avenue
New York, NY 10022

First Printing: December, 1994
Printed in the United States of America

Charms strike the sight, but merit wins the soul.

The Rape of the Lock, Canto V, 1.34
Alexander Pope

Chapter 1

"Caught up with you now, Pev. We're the same age," the Honorable Percival Throckmorton asserted with great glee to his friend, Peveril Standish, Viscount Lindford, as they strolled along Piccadilly in the early hours of a misty October morning.

The two fashionable young bucks had just emerged from a select gentlemen's gathering where they had been celebrating the Honorable Percival's twenty-third birthday in rather uproarious fashion, with wine, cards, and song. Their progress down the empty street was a trifle erratic, and they listed noticeably from side to side as they made their way to the viscount's lodgings in Jermyn Street. Both gentlemen had consumed an excess of spirits, as the occasion had demanded, with the perfectly understandable result that they were feeling more than a little up in the world.

"Dash it all, Percy, you ain't the same age as me! I'll be four-and-twenty before the month's out," the viscount replied quarrelsomely, but with irrefutable logic, as they strolled arm and arm along the dark, deserted street where a light mist was gathering unnoticed about their ears. "You're almost a whole year younger. You can't catch up."

Percy came to an abrupt halt in the middle of Piccadilly. He lifted his curly-brimmed beaver hat and scratched his head in puzzlement. "Beats me how we can both be three-and-twenty and not be the same age, Pev!" he cried in bewilderment.

"Rabbit it!" exclaimed the viscount as he tripped over the curbstone and struggled to maintain his balance. His friend had stopped directly in his path and, as Peveril was feeling none too steady on his pins, he landed in the gutter, liberally spattering his legs and feet with mud.

"You shot the rabbit, Pev?" Percy questioned, squinting up at his much taller friend.

"Shot the cat—not the rabbit, Percy," corrected Peveril, stopping to brush at the sleeves of the exquisite evening jacket he wore. "And no I ain't—leastways, not yet, but if you don't stop jostling me about, I swear I shan't answer for the consequences."

"Heh? Shot a cat. You don't mean it, Pev!" The smaller man put a hand on the viscount's arm. "M'mother has cats," he said in a woeful voice. "Three of 'em. She won't like this at all." He shook his head sadly. "Not at all!" He looked accusingly at his companion, and gave a most undignified hiccup after his weighty pronouncement.

"Well, if that don't beat the Dutch! Here I was celebratin' with you and you accuse me of shootin' your mama's cats! Damme, if you ain't all about in your head, Percy!"

"Mama wanted me to come home to celebrate m'

birthday, but what's the sense of that, heh?" Percy asked, ignoring his companion's outburst. "Can't dash off to Wiltshire one day, then dash back here the next for that curst curricle race 'tween Rolly Squires and Feckless Fakenham. Got a monkey ridin' on Feckless to win, you know."

"You'll catch cold there, Percy. Fakenham's a ham-fisted driver, if ever there was one," Peveril warned.

" 'Sides, the little season ends in a few weeks anyway," Percy continued, taking no notice of his friend's words. "Be goin' home for Christmas with a party of friends. Can celebrate then."

"I'm one of your friends, Percy. You ain't invited me."

"Did too. You can't make it. Goin' on a repairin' lease after your last bout at the gamin' tables, Pev . . . dibs ain't in tune. Pockets all to let, you said."

"Well, I can go on a repairing lease in Wiltshire just as well as in Hertfordshire, can't I, Percy? Better even—farther away."

"As long as you promise not to shoot any of m'mother's cats, Pev."

"Devil take it, Percy! I don't have any interest in shooting any of Lady Bramble's over-fed felines. Where's the sport in that, heh?"

The viscount glanced down to inspect the damage to his evening shoes and the fashionable clocked stockings he wore with his silk evening breeches. He saw that the gilt buckles on his shoes bore not a semblance of the shine so lovingly bestowed on them before he had gone out that evening by his devoted valet, Wagstaff, and that the shoes themselves were caked with mud and grime. To add to that indignity, the stockings he wore over his well-muscled calves were spattered with effluence from the gutter he had just trod in.

His vivid blue eyes were narrowed in disgust as he inspected the damage to his clothing. "Ruined, beyond a doubt! Wags will have an apoplexy, as sure as check!" he muttered, thinking of his exacting valet. Careless as he was about most things, Peveril was always turned out in the highest style, thanks to the exacting attentions of Wagstaff.

Uttering a colorful oath, Peveril took hold of Percy's arm again and the two young bloods proceeded to wind and weave their way arm-in-arm down the damp, ill-lit street. Puffs of pale mist blown along by a light breeze drifted across their path from time to time and lent an eerie quality to the darkness of the night.

A woman's piercing scream rent the foggy night air.

"What the blazes?" The viscount stopped in his tracks, nearly knocking over the unsteady Percy who held to his arm. "You hear that, Percy?" Peveril asked, shaking his head, trying to clear away the brandy fumes that bedeviled him.

"What, Pev?" Percy asked, squinting up at his friend as he tried to regain his balance, using his gold-tipped malacca cane to hold himself upright.

The shrill shriek came again.

"That! Sounds like some female screechin'."

"Whew," Percy whistled between the gap in his front teeth. "Devilish, ain't it?"

"Help! Help! He's twying to steal my locket!" The

distant, barely distinct, words were born on the breeze. And now sounds of a distant struggle reached their ears, too.

"Blister it! Some female's in trouble. Think we should dash to the rescue?" Peveril asked.

He didn't wait for his friend's answer, but began to stride off in the direction of the fracas. The sounds of the struggle had grown in volume and seemed to involve several persons. The viscount's long legs carried him at a brisk pace in the direction of the Green Park just off Piccadilly.

"Heh? Ain't at all sure—" Percy tried to protest but he was pulled along willy-nilly by his much stronger friend, who had an iron grip on his elbow. Percy, half a foot shorter than the lanky viscount, had to run to keep up.

"Leave us alone, you cowardly brutes!" shouted a diminutive young woman in a dark cloak as she laid about her with a small, frivolous, gold-fringed fan. "Watch! I say, Watch! Help! We are being set upon by footpads! Come quickly!" she called, hoping to summon one of London's famous night watchmen to her aid.

The brave lady was battering a rough-looking assailant about the head and shoulders as he tried to grasp a diamond necklet with a large golden locket hanging from it—and possibly a kiss for his pains—from her companion, another young lady whose ostentatious headdress of plumes had come unpinned from her hair and was hanging askew over one shoulder. A riot of shining blond ringlets tumbled down round her shoulders, gleaming in the faint lamplight. The girl braced herself against the body of a gilded coach and screamed fit to wake the dead as she tried to fight off her attacker and protect her precious necklace.

"Marwy, Marwy, he's twying to steal my golden locket! Stop him!" she screamed in the piercing, high-pitched voice that had attracted Viscount Lindford's attention. "Help! Help! Somebody save me!"

Peveril and Percy arrived on the scene at a dead run, both breathing heavily.

"Blood and thunder! Do you see that, Percy? Those footpads are trying to steal that lady's jewelry!" Peveril shouted, taking in the murky scene of confusion before his eyes at a glance.

The viscount didn't wait for his friend's response. He was off, throwing himself into the midst of the fray with relish—and with little regard for the likely consequences to the fine clothes he wore. He set about him with his fists, slamming his knuckles into the chin of the footpad who threatened the young lady, sending him sprawling on the ground.

Another large, rough-looking man emerged from the park's undergrowth. With a loud, menacing growl, the scoundrel put his shaggy head down and his long, beefy arms out in front of him and charged like a bull toward the viscount.

Peveril turned quickly to counter the attack of this new assailant as the fellow charged forward, head first. Using his finely-honed athletic ability, Peveril neatly sidestepped the ferocious charge, and kicked the footpad in the midsection as he roared past, doubling him up.

Two smaller footpads—boys really—dressed in rags and cursing in the cant favored by the habitués of a certain, notorious den of thieves in the city, seeing their burly leader on the ground, immediately released their hold on the coach horses, ran over and set upon the viscount, hanging onto his arms for dear life and trying to land blows to his back and shoulders to prevent him from attacking their cohorts and foiling the robbery.

"We'll have yer cobbler's awls, guv'nor!" one of the young scamps declared in a bloodthirsty threat. "Bash 'is bowsprit in, Nobby!"

"Shut yer gob, 'Enry!" his companion ordered. "I'm a gonna darken this 'ere gentry cove's daylights for 'im!"

Sobering quickly, Percy looked on the scene of chaos with trepidation. He was horrified by Peveril's headlong rush into the thick of the action. He gulped. Despite his decidedly peaceable nature, he saw there was nothing else for it but to go to his friend's assistance. Yes, and by Jove, there were two damsels in distress, fashionable ladies by the look of them, who required his help, too!

Finding sudden inspiration in necessity, Percy took his malacca cane in his hands and used it to hit the man doubled up by Peveril's punch who had straightened up and was preparing to attack the viscount from behind.

Percy whacked the burly fellow smartly over the head. Seeing that the blow knocked the footpad to the ground, Percy swung around on his toes, ready to tackle the next assailant.

"Oh, well done, sir!" congratulated the darkly-clad young lady. She stood supporting her taller companion with one arm about her waist, trying to comfort the weeping girl while she watched the two fashionably-dressed young gentlemen attempt to beat off the footpads. She saw that one of them was a young exquisite in a satin coat trimmed with gold braid stretched across his shoulders. Undoubtedly a *ton* dandy, she decided, and a most unlikely hero.

With some difficulty the viscount was able to shake off the pesky children who clung tenaciously to his back and shouted curses in his ear while they beat him with their small fists. As the two boys scampered away from his swinging fists, he turned again to take on one of the larger thieves.

"Nothing like a good mill to clear one's head," he growled menacingly and swung with the full force of his body. There was an ominous ripping sound when he landed the satisfyingly crunching blow to the burly man's face. The seams of his beautiful jacket split asunder with the effort.

"Run for it, lads," ordered the ruffian whose chin had just suffered intimate contact with the viscount's fist, to the eternal detriment of several of his teeth. "This 'ere gentry cove looks like a la-de-da dandified fop, but 'e's a reg'lar devil with 'is pops."

The other scoundrel, who was lying on the ground after Percy's attack, scrambled to his feet, and all four footpads ran off and disappeared into the dark, foggy night, leaving behind two shaken ladies and two disheveled, distinctly winded, and now quite sober, gentlemen.

The ladies stood in front of an elaborately decorated town coach, painted a bright blue and richly embellished with gilt trim on its lamps, door handles and metal work. It had been pulled off the main road bordering the Green Park and now stood along the shadowy little lane beside the park paling. Several of the hexagonal ornamental coach lamps had been smashed by the thieves. Dim light shone from the solitary lamp that remained burning and lit the misty scene with an unearthly light.

The four perfectly-matched grey coachhorses harnessed to the vehicle stood restively pawing the ground and rocking the coach from side to side. Incongruous white-feathered plumes waved over their heads, and their golden bridles gleamed in the illumination of the coach lamp. They looked quite eerie in the scant light—like ghost horses.

Neither the coachman nor any other attendants who by rights should have been accompanying the ladies were anywhere to be seen.

The two young ladies looked at their gallant champions with vastly different expressions on their faces.

The blond lady whose screams had summoned the gentlemen still looked somewhat frightened. She blushed rosily when she encountered the viscount's piercing gaze, and her long, gold-tipped lashes swept down modestly to cover sparkling green eyes that were still moist from her recent tears. She busied herself rearranging her voluminous cloak, pulling it forward to cover the sleeves of her evening gown and smoothing it down over her waist.

The smaller, more self-possessed, of the two ladies—the one who had bravely tried to beat off the attackers—looked first to her more fashionably-garbed companion to see that she had stopped wailing and could stand on her own without swooning now that their attackers had fled into the night. Then she reached up to straighten the hood of her serviceable grey cloak over her short, dark hair before she came forward with one hand outstretched to thank the unknown gentlemen.

"Oh, sirs! How can we ever thank you enough for coming to our rescue so bravely? It was very risky. You could have been hurt. But I don't know how we would have managed to drive the blackguards away without your help. You've not only saved us from those dreadful thieves, but you've prevented the theft of a fortune in jewelry, as well," she told them with heartfelt gratitude. "Thank you! It is wonderful to know that chivalry is not dead in England, thank goodness!" A generous smile stretched across her piquant little face, lending a bright sparkle to her grey eyes as she came toward them.

"I am Mary Marlowe," she continued, "and this is my charge, Miss Belinda Ramsbottom, who will thank you herself when she has a chance to recover somewhat from the fright she's had."

Mary looked back at Belinda who stood beside the coach dabbing at her eyes with her lace-edged handkerchief, then turned again to face their benefactors. "I'm afraid she is still somewhat overset by the dreadful experience. I hope neither of you gentlemen suffered any hurt during the encounter?"

"No," Peveril answered distractedly. He had automatically taken the small hand that had been outstretched to him and had shaken it briefly, but had not glanced at its owner. His eyes were riveted on her companion. He stood transfixed, gazing awestruck upon the vision of celestial beauty before his eyes, obviously not hearing a word that Mary said.

Seeing the direction of the tall young gentleman's gaze, Mary smiled ruefully. She was well accustomed to Belinda's holding every man's eyes, for the girl was without doubt the most beautiful creature Mary had ever seen.

She looked more carefully at their dashing rescuer. He was a most striking gentleman himself, she decided, despite his now thoroughly disreputable appearance, bruised and dirty as he was from the recent skirmish. He was wonderfully tall and lean, with broad shoulders and long, well-shaped legs.

She saw his thick, dark hair was worn long. Now disheveled from his exertions on their behalf, it curled down to his collar in a most romantic manner. He had firm, well-cut lips, a jutting chin that betokened some stubbornness, and a crooked nose—surely broken sometime during his career—that could only be described as aristocratic. With the bravery and athletic ability he had just demonstrated, Mary was not surprised that he had driven away the footpads.

"And thank you, sir," Mary said with an equally bright smile as she held out her hand to the second gentleman who stood surveying the scene with the gold knob of his malacca cane pressed to his mouth.

"Pleased to be of service, ma'am," Percy answered

bashfully, releasing his cane and lifting his head in embarrassment. He gave her a small, awkward bow.

"I don't know if you should be pleased, sir, but we certainly are," Mary said with a relieved smile.

Taken unawares by her quick wit, Percy blinked and said, "Assure you, no trouble at all, ma'am."

"Oh, I doubt that, sir!" Mary laughed. "To whom may we address our thanks?"

"Oh, sorry, ma'am. Percival Throckmorton, at your service." Percy bowed again.

"I am so pleased to meet you, Mr. Throckmorton. And your valiant friend is—?"

"Heh? Oh, that's Pev, er, Peveril Standish, Viscount Lindford, you know."

"Viscount Lindford. Hmm. No, the name is not familiar," Mary said after a moment's consideration. "He must not be on Mr. Ramsbottom's list."

"Beg pardon, ma'am?"

"Oh, nothing of consequence, Mr. Throckmorton."

"How did you come to be set upon, Miss Marlowe?"

"We were very late returning from a party, partly because the footman who had accompanied us was nowhere to be found when we were ready to leave. Jordie, the coachman, decided to take a short cut through the park here. He spotted what looked to be a body lying at the side of the road, clad in the livery of one of Mr. Ramsbottom's footmen, and he stopped to investigate. He called to me that he feared our missing footman had met with foul play. When he got down from his perch, those footpads accosted us," Mary explained.

" 'Egad, ma'am! Someone was murdered, you

say!" Percy looked around wildly, expecting to see a dead body.

"Oh heavens! I hope not!" Mary exclaimed, going over to investigate the bundle that lay half under a pile of leaves at the side of the pathway. "Oh, look, Mr. Throckmorton! It's only some bits and pieces of old livery that have been stuffed with straw to make it seem that a body lay here in the road. I suppose in the darkness, Jordie mistook it for the livery of Mr. Ramsbottom's household staff. It was all a dastardly trick, of course, to get any coach that came along to stop so that the footpads could set upon the unsuspecting occupants."

"I say! Think you have the right of it, ma'am. These togs must've been stolen," Percy opined, poking the livery with his walking cane. "What a deuced plaguey trick!"

Mary prodded the straw bundle with her foot and the head rolled off. "This could have been almost anyone's livery. Jordie was fooled, though. And once he had leapt down from his perch, the gang of footpads set upon him and knocked him unconscious."

"Where is he, ma'am?" Percy peered into the darkness for a sign of the missing coachman.

"Oh, good heavens! I suppose they must have dragged him off into these trees," Mary said as she looked around for Mr. Ramsbottom's coachman. "Jordie, Jordie? Where are you?" she called.

She was answered by a moan coming from among the trees and undergrowth at the side of the lane. She set off in the direction of the sound and Percy, after a brief hesitation, hastened to her side and offered his arm.

* * *

Viscount Lindford paid no attention when his friend and the somberly-clad Miss Marlowe disappeared into the night. He was too busy devouring the vision before him. His jaw hung slightly ajar as he gaped at Miss Ramsbottom, the most exquisite incarnation of feminine beauty he had ever had the good fortune to behold in his young, but not inexperienced, career.

In the dim light he could just make out that the young lady was dressed in a bright blue velvet cloak, lavishly trimmed and lined with ermine. The hem of her white silk gown, embroidered with pink roses, showed beneath her cloak. There was a sparkle of diamonds at her throat and in her ears. The flash and glitter of expensive gems could be seen covering her wrists, too, where the ermine-trimmed edge of her cloak fell back from the sleeves of her gown as she clutched the cloak to her and stared back round-eyed at him. She wore a fortune in jewelry, but that was not what held his wondering attention.

Peveril's gaze moved up from an inspection of the young lady's expensive, fashionable clothing to her heart-shaped face. She was standing directly under the remaining coach lantern and he could see her features clearly. Her hair, a divine shade of yellow gold, now in charming disarray, was thick and naturally waving. It gleamed brightly in the faint light. A hint of delicate roses bloomed in her cheeks, otherwise her complexion was a finely tinted porcelain. Her large round eyes were a stunning emerald green, fringed with long golden lashes and framed by perfectly arched dark golden brows. She had a little nose that was in no way snub, and her bow-shaped lips, neither too large nor too small, were of a dark rosy hue and looked as though they had been formed to be kissed.

Even as he devoured her with his eyes, her little pink tongue darted out to lick off the light film of moisture that had gathered on her dew-kissed lips from the misty air and her recent tears. The unconscious gesture sent Peveril's temperature soaring another degree. He longed with an emotion hitherto unknown to him to press his own lips to that tender kissable mouth.

He felt a ringing in his ears and a tingling in his toes, not to mention a warmth coursing through his blood as he completed his inspection. Devil take it! He had never seen such ravishing beauty! And the innocent look in the girl's wide eyes fairly cried out for a man's protection. His protection, he realized, his chest swelling with possessive jealousy.

Seemingly of their own volition, for his dazed mind was strangely detached from his body, his lips silently formed the word "angel."

Belinda stole a look under her eyelashes at one of her rescuers who was standing staring at her with a moonstruck look on his handsome young face. He was certainly an attractive young gentleman, she saw. Why, he had all her other suitors beaten to a stand with his dark good looks and tall, slender, yet well-muscled body, she decided with a tiny shiver of anticipation. Even his eyes were striking. They were of such a clear, piercing blue, and surrounded by such thick, dark lashes, that she experienced a pang of envy—why, they were quite as beautiful as her own dazzling emerald eyes, she realized with dismay.

Ever vain of her appearance, Belinda had become an expert at reading admiration for herself in a gentleman's eyes and she immediately brightened when she saw such an expression in her rescuer's vivid gaze. She recovered her spirits somewhat and deigned to bestow a smile of bewitching splendor on the young man, then blushed becomingly. She looked down, the long sweep of her lashes hiding her mesmerizing eyes for a moment, before she peeped up again to encounter the gentleman's burning gaze. Two perfectly shaped, crystal tears formed in her emerald eyes and slowly trickled down her cheeks in perfect unison.

She pressed the backs of her little hands to her cheeks and brushed at the tears in an appealing, childish gesture.

Peveril, who had been standing like a stock, was suddenly propelled into motion as he realized the poor girl was still overset by the recent incident. He lurched forward, knelt down on one knee in front of her, and proffered up his handkerchief, then changed his mind and offered his services instead, mopping at her checks, drying the tears that had begun to stream copiously.

"Oh, thank you, sir," the angel said in a tearful voice. "Thank you for wescuing us fwom such a terwible pwedicament. I was so vewy fwightened, you know." He was so brave, she was sure he could protect her from a hundred footpads.

"There, there. Don't cry, child. By Jove, I've got

you safe now. What's your name, sweet angel?" Peveril asked hoarsely.

"Bewinda," she said shyly, giving her name a childish pronunciation. In times of tiredness or great stress, her pronunciation, never a strong point, slipped even further.

"Belinda—that is a dashed beautiful name for a beautiful angel like you. Those curst villains didn't harm you, did they? For if they did, you can be devilish sure I won't rest until I see the blasted rogues in their graves!" Peveril swore melodramatically.

Belinda shivered at his fierce tone. "Oh, no. But I was afwaid those horwid men would take my earwings and my locket. It's gold, you see, and I wear it on my diamond necklet," she said in her childish voice as she lifted the heavy golden locket resting safely around her neck and showed it to Peveril. "My papa gave it to me."

"Beautiful," he said, planting a little kiss on her fingers as she lifted the locket for his inspection, never taking his eyes from her face to inspect the geegaw. His heart was pounding like a drum in his chest at the contact with his lovely vision. "Bless me, if you ain't just like an angel!"

"Oh! Your lip is bweeding, sir!" she cried in horror when she saw her own fingers smudged with blood. The young gentleman's lip was still oozing a trifle from a slight cut he had suffered during the recent free-for-all.

Peveril handed her the damp handkerchief he had used to wipe away her tears and she dabbed gingerly at his mouth. He gazed at her admiringly as she went about her task in a rather squeamish manner.

"Pleased to spill a bit of claret on your behalf, ma'am. Daresay my lip will be miraculously healed now you've tended it, Angel Lady." He reached for her fingers and kissed them tenderly as they gripped his hand most trustingly.

"Oh, you are silly, sir!" Belinda giggled. "What's your name?" she asked when she had finished her work.

"Peveril Standish, er, that is, Viscount Lindford, at your service, Miss—? How the deuce should I address you, beautiful angel?" At her look of bafflement at this query, Peveril asked, "What's your surname, my dear Belinda?"

"Wamsbottom," she told him with a small giggle as he rose from his knee at last, still holding to her little hand that was curled possessively around her locket.

"Ramsbottom? No! Devil take it, that can't possibly be right! Sure to be something heavenly, such as Miss Cloud, or Miss Divine?"

"No. It is Wamsbottom, and it is a sad twail to me. I hope to change it soon," she said coyly, peeping up at him.

"You do? What to?" Peveril asked, taken aback by this pronouncement.

Belinda laughed flirtatously. "Well, that all depends on which one of my admiwers I choose to mawy."

"Oh, don't say such dashed unspeakable things in my hearing, my angel. Blister it, you'll break my heart, if you marry some confounded admirer before you've given me a chance to get to know you!" Peveril averred, tearing at his gold-braided jacket to bare his now torn and grimy white silk shirt and pressing his hand to his affected organ. "By Jupiter, I'll plant those curst admirers of yours a facer or two before I'll let one of them carry you off!"

"Oh, my lowd, you must not be so fiewce! You will fwighten me."

"What's that you're saying about being frightened, Belinda?" Mary asked, coming back from her mission of mercy and hearing the last bit of nonsense spouted between the pair.

Immediately dropping Belinda's hand, which he had been caressing, Peveril turned a somewhat sheepish look on Miss Marlowe as she came up to them, feeling he had been caught out behaving a trifle foolishly. Miss Marlowe had about her the look of a governess, he thought, eyeing her a bit shamefacedly—but not too fierce a dragon, for all that, he decided, regarding her with his head a little to one side.

"We must ask Viscount Lindford and Mr. Throckmorton's assistance in seeing us home now, Belinda, for Jordie is in no condition to drive us."

"Oh, yes, and Viscount Lindfowd has been so bwave, Marwy, I want him to come to see me tomorrow," Belinda said forwardly before the viscount could request permission to call.

"By Jove, *yes,* Miss Ramsbottom! Wild horses couldn't keep me away from—" Peveril began, but Mary cut him short and addressed herself to her charge.

"I'm sure, if Viscount Lindford were to present himself at your house when Mr. Ramsbottom returns from his business trip, your papa would permit him to call, and Mr. Throckmorton, too," Mary said in a friendly voice with a nod to the viscount, who scarcely heeded her words.

Mary knew that she and Belinda stood greatly in debt to the two gentlemen, but she was also mindful of her employer's instructions to guard his daughter from unscrupulous gentlemen. She would have to take care that the viscount and his friend were not overmuch in Belinda's company until Mr. Ramsbottom approved them.

Mary shuddered inwardly. Should Belinda form an attachment to one of Mr. Ramsbottom's hated fortune hunters while the girl was in her charge, Mary would be immediately dismissed from her position as Belinda's companion. And that position was all that stood between her and an unpleasant future. The unwanted match with a distant kinsman that would then be her fate was to be avoided at all costs.

"Lord Lindford, could you just step off the lane into those trees and lend Mr. Throckmorton your assistance?" Mary asked briskly, putting aside her own worries for more immediate cares. "I'm afraid poor Jordie—our coachman, you know—was knocked unconscious by the footpads. He's still quite groggy and cannot walk unaided. I fear he is far too heavy for Mr. Throckmorton to manage on his own."

"Lord, yes, ma'am! Should've called me before. Unless your coachman's a midget, Perce ain't likely to be able to carry the fellow on his own." With that careless answer, the viscount immediately went in search of his friend and the groggy coachman.

Belinda smiled and waggled her fingers at him as

he glanced back once in her direction with a perfectly besotted look on his face.

For his part, Peveril had trouble believing the girl he had just encountered was real. By gad, he'd never seen her like before! Perhaps she was only a figment of his still-intoxicated brain, he thought with a rueful grin as he tramped into the undergrowth.

In a short while, the gentlemen placed the coachman inside the carriage with the two young ladies. Percy climbed in, too, to lend his assistance in supporting the woozy man.

After assuring Miss Marlowe that it would be no problem at all for him to tool the coach and four, Viscount Lindford mounted the steps of the absurdly gilded vehicle, gathered the reins of the plumed horses, and drove away in the direction of Curzon Street where Mary told him the Ramsbottom residence was located.

Chapter 2

Mary saw the still shaken Belinda, who foolishly expected to see thieves and footpads hiding in every corner of her father's imposing house, safely delivered into the hands of her abigail, Bessie. Bessie promised to put her nervous young mistress to bed and sit with her all night, if necessary, to calm her fears.

Mary then went off to her own room, her mind full of the recent stirring events, and it was a long time before she could calm herself enough for sleep. She changed into her night rail without assistance and paced over to the window to look out onto the dark square in front of the Ramsbottom house.

How fortunate they had been that the young gentlemen had appeared on the scene when they had, she thought gratefully. If Belinda's necklace and other jewelry had been stolen by the footpads, Mary would not have been surprised if Mr. Ramsbottom had blamed her for the loss of the costly gems and dismissed her from her post. Then she would have been in the suds for sure, she thought, raising her slim hands to her face and closing her eyes briefly.

Managing to impose some calm on her agitated mind at last, she got into bed. Sleep, though, was a long time coming as she thought back over the circumstances that accounted for her being in her present position.

It was her refusal to give in to her imperious grandfather's order that she marry his heir, her distant cousin, Sir Cedric Ledbetter, that had led to her present position as Belinda's companion. For close on a year, her grandfather, the Earl of Wyndham, had ranted and raved, fumed and shouted, bullied and sulked, and refused to allow her the income left her by her mother, who had been his only child, unless she complied with his wishes and agreed to the match with Sir Cedric.

Since the death of her parents when she had been quite young, she had always lived happily with the earl at his estate, Wyndham Park, before this matter caused a breach between them. Her early years had been quite uneventful. She had loved her studies and had enjoyed working with the gifted governess her grandfather had hired to tutor her. Then, when she had turned eighteen, she had had a season in London. The earl had not accompanied her to town, using his perpetual gout as an excuse, but he had arranged that she be sponsored by one of their relatives, a tonnish society hostess, Caroline, Lady Tate—or Aunt Caroline, as she had asked Mary to call her. The Tates, a family of distant cousins, had entertained Mary royally when she was in town.

She had taken well enough during the season, with

her sweet nature, lively personality and charming, but not spectacular, looks. She was a petite girl, standing not much over five feet two in her stocking feet. Her Aunt Caroline had said that her long, dark tresses were too heavy for her and recommended that she have her hair cut short. Mary had done so and the resulting cap of curls framed her little face becomingly, drawing an observer's attention to her beautiful, long-lashed, grey eyes.

She had drawn her fair share of admirers, but when the season came to an end in June, she had found that there was not a single gentleman she could like well enough to marry, even though she had had three offers. She had gone home to Wyndham unattached and carefree.

The following year when she was nineteen, the earl told her that she need not have another season since he had made other arrangements for her future. When he told her he had contracted a match for her with Sir Cedric Ledbetter, she had been stunned.

After she recovered somewhat from her surprise, she had promised to consider the match, saying she wished to become better acquainted with the young man. The earl had been annoyed at this early spark of defiance and grumbled that he should have thought she was well enough acquainted with her cousin already.

At the time, Mary remembered Sir Cedric only vaguely. She had met him briefly at Wyndham Park once or twice when she was quite young and occasionally when she had visited in the homes of her various relatives when she was older. He had seemed years older than she, even though he was only six years her senior. He had never put himself forward to win her friendship or even her good opinion when they had been together. Indeed, he had taken no pains to converse with her at all, beyond the exchange of conventional greetings and leave takings. So, despite having spent several weeks under the same roof with Sir Cedric on more than one occasion, she was not at all well acquainted with him.

They never had become formally betrothed. Cedric had been in mourning for his father when Mary was nineteen. The following year his mother died, and he had written to the earl saying he did not consider it appropriate to court a young lady at such a time. While she acknowledged that his sentiments did him credit, his letter was couched in such overblown, flowery prose that it had made Mary's eyes roll when her grandfather showed it to her.

He had eventually arrived to spend several months with the earl at Wyndham Park when Mary was turned one-and-twenty. She found him to be a humorless young man of fair beauty and noble mein, but no personality to speak of. He had not two words to say for himself that weren't pompous in the extreme.

After just a few weeks of his company, Mary was convinced she could never tolerate being married to such a prosy, pompous gentleman. She soon found she could not be in the same room with him for two minutes together without wanting to laugh in his face when he began one of his long-winded speeches. In her opinion, Sir Cedric Ledbetter was a perfect block, and she could no more see herself his wife than she could imagine herself growing another six inches!

When she informed her grandfather that she considered a match with his heir to be impossible, he had exploded. "What's that you say, girl? I'll have no missish protests, now, Mary. You'll do as you're told! It's all arranged."

She had not expected such a reaction and had been taken aback at first, but when the earl had persisted in his determination that she marry Cedric, she had been equally adamant in her refusal. Mary was small in stature, but she was the earl's equal in determination.

Oh, she had no doubt that her grandfather loved her, after his fashion. Indeed, he had ranted on about how the marriage would be for her own good. He told her how this arrangement would insure that she would become the next Countess of Wyndham, her future would be secure. He had declared that he wanted her to have his house and all his worldly goods, but with the "damned laws of primogeniture" it was impossible unless she married his legal heir.

He had dug his heels in deeper each day, vowing he would not tolerate her defiance in this matter. He was determined that she knuckle under to his will. And he had no doubt that she *would* knuckle under—eventually.

Her nature was not such that she enjoyed the state of strife between them. And so, finally, with much sadness, Mary had decided that she could no longer make her home under her grandfather's roof, but when she had applied for her inheritance from her mother, he had refused to give it to her. Mary considered herself a reasonable person, but she would not tolerate being forced into a loathsome marriage. She resolved to find a way to support herself without his help.

At two-and-twenty, she was past the age when she needed to live with a companion. But she had no funds with which to set herself up on her own and she didn't wish to batten herself onto one of her many kind relations. The earl wielded considerable power and influence over the family, for he could buy and sell the pack of them together, and Mary knew that he would have been able to compel her return, if she had dared go to one of them. They all loved her dearly and would gladly have taken her in, but she would not put them in the position of having to defy the powerful earl, when they might suffer the consequences of his ill-will.

She had finally fled to the nearby town of Oxford and applied for a position at a young ladies' seminary there that catered to the daughters of minor landowners and wealthy merchants. With a glowing reference in her pocket from her neighbor, the kind and influential Lady Mentmore-Jones, daughter of the Duke of Cheddington, she had been accepted as a junior mistress, where her primary job seemed to be to keep a lot of silly girls, including Miss Belinda Ramsbottom, in order while she tried in vain to introduce them to the rudiments of poetry and the finer points of English grammar.

The earl soon learned of her whereabouts, of course, but he did not try to force her to return home. He thought she would soon tire of her game, see reason, and agree to the match with Cedric. The stalemate continued, but Mary suspected that her grandfather's patience would soon give out and that he would pounce any day.

The daring hero of the night's dramatic action took himself and his companion back to his comfortable bachelor lodgings in Jermyn Street, smiling in wonder at his recent, extraordinary encounter.

Peveril dismissed the minor injuries to his face, his cut lip and the bruises on his lean cheeks, and the even more considerable damage to his clothing when he reached home. Leaving Percy in the cluttered sitting room, with orders for Wagstaff to make the gentleman comfortable, he walked through to his bedchamber, absently brushing down the sleeves of his now ruined jacket. He didn't notice that the jacket was rent in two along the back seam nor that his shirt cuffs were all bloody and torn. He kicked off his muddy evening shoes with not even a curse for the ruin of a perfectly good, and quite expensive, suit of clothes.

"Oh, my lord, not your gold braid jacket! Split at the seams! Ruined beyond any hope of repair. Oh. And your cuffs, torn to ribbons!" Wagstaff moaned as he helped his master out of the ruined clothing and disposed of it sorrowfully.

"Throw them all out, Wags," the viscount said nonchalantly.

Lord, but he had never seen such a perfect little beauty, Peveril thought dreamily, gazing unseeingly at the silk-hung walls of his bedchamber and completely ignoring his valet's mournful words and the pained expression on his face.

After Wagstaff had helped him on with his dressing gown, Peveril stretched and yawned and took himself off to bed with the same bemused look on his face he had worn for the past hour to dream of a beautiful blond angel who had dropped wondorously in his path out of the mists of the night.

Peveril Standish was a good-hearted but volatile young gentleman, not much different from the other heedless young blades loose on the town, always on the lookout for a lark, ready to kick up a dust over some trifle or other.

In his younger days—all of two or three years ago—he had not been above boxing the night watchmen, or catching the spurs he wore specially for the purpose under the petticoats of a pretty young thing when he was strolling down a fashionable street just to get a glimpse of a pair of trim ankles, and engaging in other such frivolities that idle young men were prone to. While he would own without embarrassment to having committed these and other outrageous follies in his time, these days, at the mature age of almost four-and-twenty, he considered himself beyond such foolishness. Indeed, he would have insisted to anyone audacious enough to ask, that *that* sort of behavior was well in his past now.

Had he been asked what he did to entertain himself these days, he would have answered "nothing out of the ordinary," and would have been surprised if anyone thought there was anything particularly remarkable about his daily routine. His life of idle pleasure was just such as many another young buck loose on the town pursued.

During the day he might visit Weston, his tailor, or Lock, his hatter, or perhaps Hoby, his bootmaker, for his clothes were always in the mode. And although he wore them somewhat carelessly, being loose limbed and not caring for the tight fit that some fashionable gentlemen demanded, he was a credit to his valet who always saw that he was turned out in the first stare of fashion.

After such sartorial chores, the viscount might frequent his club and blow a cloud with his friends where he would certainly look over the betting book and possibly even stake a wager of his own on some foolishness or other. Or he might go to a salon where he could spar with another gentleman boxer or, more daringly, sport his canvas against a professional pugilist and risk a split lip or a trip to the floor on his backside from a crushing blow to the chin.

He might then look in on the horseflesh for sale at Tattersalls, or drive his sporting curricle at a spanking pace through the streets of London and increase his speed once he was out on the open roads of the countryside. Or perhaps he would ride his well-set-up bay hack in the park, where occasionally he would accept a challenge from one of his cronies and engage in a forbidden race in the early morning before most of the fashionable world was up and about.

In the evenings, he might go to the theatre to ogle any new actresses come to town, and perhaps look in on the green room after the performance, or he might attend a cock fight where the wagers flew about as thick and fast as did the feathers of the unfortunate cockerels. Afterward, as like as not, he would meet some of his friends for a late meal where they were sure to crack open more than one bottle of a good vintage wine.

And then he and his friends might decide to try their luck at one of the new, private gaming hells that had sprung up all over Mayfair recently, never giving a thought to the fact that many of these fashionable high-stakes establishments existed expressly for the purpose of separating young sprigs of the nobility from any blunt they might possess. There he would play cards without any great skill or concentration, or try his luck at some other game of chance, carelessly wagering his money for the sport of it—money he couldn't really afford to lose. He would have been extremely surprised to know that more than one sharp gamester who had played a hand or two of cards with him took him for an easy touch, and sought him out for the express purpose of taking advantage of his inattentiveness.

And just occasionally, he looked in on a fashionable little ladybird, especially if she were young and jolly, to sample her wares. However, he had yet to feel the need to keep a permanent mistress as did so many gentlemen of his acquaintance.

Many society matrons deplored Viscount Lindford's shocking way of life, giving it as their opinion that he was likely headed to the devil with all possible speed. But privately, many of them acknowledged that he was a charming scapegrace whom they would not disdain to see gracing their ballrooms or their sitting rooms dancing attendance on their daughters, nieces, or other eligible young female relations.

"That Peveril Standish is a hellion," opined one such matron of good standing in the *ton.*

"Yes, but so charming!" enthused another. "And so outrageously handsome!" She sighed. "He will warm some lucky gel's bed for her when he's caught in parson's mousetrap one of these days."

"I would say he would be too hot to handle for a young gel fresh from the schoolroom," added a third, her eyebrows raised haughtily.

" 'Tis not to be wondered at with his breeding! Old Lindford, his father, was accounted a very devil and his mother was a beautiful, flighty peagoose, you know."

"Psha! If he'd have lived thirty years ago, young Lindford wouldn't have been considered too hot to warm *my* bed," cackled a faded Georgian beauty, who liked to shock these prudish modern matrons with tales of her roguish youth. "Ah, if only I were twenty years younger," she lamented, disregarding the fact that she was seventy if she was a day, "I'd make a push to engage the rascal's attention." Her eyes gleamed devilishly.

Such gossipmongers didn't bother the viscount, or put a cramp in his easy-going style. He took no notice of them.

If his behavior had earned him the reputation of being wild to a fault, then perhaps his critics were in the right of it. He *had* gone through life heedlessly, as careless in the way he squandered money on fripperies, gaming and horses, as he was offhandedly generous to his friends, making loans when he himself didn't have a feather to fly with to fellows whom it was unlikely would ever have the wherewithal to pay him back. And as for society's strictures about proper behavior, in common with his young friends, he didn't pay a great deal of attention to such things.

But though they might not credit it, there was more to the viscount than his critics supposed. Their sons and nephews could have told those who censured him that, in addition to his natural flair and style and his athletic ability, Lindford was a great gun. Generous to a fault to his friends, good-natured, if somewhat impetuous, in his dealings with his fellow man, the viscount had a great deal of casual charm that earned him many friends and admirers. Wild, careless and heedless he might be, but there was not an ounce of real harm in young Peveril Standish.

Chapter 3

"Wasn't it lucky Viscount Lindfowd came along to wescue us last night, Marwy?" Belinda breathed dreamily as she languished in bed enjoying her cup of chocolate the morning following the incident in Green Park. "So bwave! So tall! So fiewce!" She shivered deliciously at the memory.

"Yes, indeed. And we owe our thanks to Mr. Throckmorton, too," Mary reminded her. "I fear the viscount, brave as he was, would have been overcome by those ruffians, if his friend hadn't been on hand to lend his assistance, as well."

"Umm," was all Belinda replied to this observation. It was clear to Mary that the girl had decided to ignore the rather unprepossessing Mr. Throckmorton and give the flamboyant viscount all the credit for their dramatic rescue.

Mary was sitting near the bed with Belinda's engagement diary in her hands, ready to go over their agenda for the day. She had been up for several hours and had already been out for an energetic walk three times around the park-like square in front of Mr.

Ramsbottom's solidly-built, three-story red brick mansion on Curzon Street. She had lived in the country all her life, except for her brief season in London four years previously, and she missed the open space of her grandfather's large estate where she was used to taking long walks in all weathers. She looked forward each day to her morning's abbreviated exercise.

Belinda was rarely up before noon. She always insisted that a girl couldn't get too much beauty sleep. It never ceased to amaze Mary that anyone could sleep half the day away, letting precious hours of time and youth slip by so mindlessly, but Belinda was an indolent creature, not overly fond of walking, unless she had an eligible gentleman to escort her or a new gown or bonnet she wished to show off.

"Oh, Marwy, don't you think Viscount Lindfowd is vewy womantic-looking? I think he looks just like a knight in my book. See." Belinda lifted the brightly-colored book she had been looking at to show Mary the picture of a fairy-tale knight rescuing a damsel in distress. The maiden in the tinted illustration, with her cornsilk yellow hair and impossibly bright grass green eyes, bore a striking, if highly stylized, likeness to Belinda herself.

Belinda often called Mary's attention to the illustrations of fictional heroines, such as those of Queen Guinevere and Enid, in the childish books she liked to look at as a break from studying the fashion magazines. She always insisted that the cartoon-like pictures were just like her, for she liked to see herself as a maiden from one of these fairy tales. Mary tried to disabuse her of this nonsensical notion from time to time, but the girl was too immature, or too silly to pay much heed.

"Hmm. Not *very* like a knight in shining armor," Mary murmured with amusement when she looked at the gentleman in the picture. She concealed her merry smile with difficulty as she looked at the picture. The hero had been painted in the highly colorful garb of the Elizabethan age with doublet and hose, a wide ruff at his neck, and short velvet cloak. He sported a black goatee and mustache. He was making a leg to his lady-love and doffing a tall-crowned hat with a long feather plume attached to the brim.

Mary stifled a laugh. To think that the aged Elizabethan rogue in Belinda's picture looked one whit like the smooth-shaven, dark and disheveled young gentlemen clad all in the current mode who had come to their assistance last night was ludicrous in the extreme.

"I think I'll allow him to couwt me."

"Who? The viscount, or this gentleman?" Mary teased, tapping her finger against the picture on the page.

"Lindfowd, silly. He'll make ever such an exciting beau!" Belinda went on weaving a fairy-tale romance for herself, just like the ones she liked to hear Mary reading to her.

"Indeed, and so you said about Sir Thomas Nichols, and the Duke of Exford, and Mr. Peregrine Fowler, and a hundred other gentlemen you've met since you came to town," Mary said. "Why, ever since we attended the assemblies in Sidmouth last summer before we came to London, you've been expressing undying admiration for one gentleman or another."

Belinda made a little moue of displeasure when Mary reminded her of her interest in certain other gentlemen. "Well, maybe I did like them once upon a time, but this is diffewent. Lindfowd is so tall. So handsome. And his hair—so vewy dawk and thick and shining. And such, blue blue eyes!" she gushed. "And so stwong and fowceful to beat off those howid footpads. Even you must admit how handsome he is."

"I could not say," Mary prevaricated. "It was quite dark last night, you know, and there were a hundred things to distract us. Are you sure the young man was all you imagined him to be?"

"Yes, he was," Belinda insisted stubbornly. "He was quite, quite perfect!"

"Perhaps when you see him in the light, you will discover a flaw or two. Should you not wait and judge him over the course of a few weeks before you make up your mind so positively?"

"Oh, Marwy, you're so stwaightlaced and unwomantic! I've alweady quite made up my mind to allow him to couwt me. You can't talk me out of it this time!"

"Oh? And what if the gentleman is indifferent?"

"No such a thing! I know he loves me quite fewociously alweady," Belinda asserted confidently, lifting the long-handled mirror edged with silver-chasing from her bedside table and gazing at herself in its reflecting surface. She twitched her fair curls into place around her face. "He was quite weady to make me a declawation last night."

"No! You don't say so? Why, how could you trust

someone who behaves so rashly? But then, he was not quite sober, you know. I daresay that accounts for it."

Belinda looked at Mary, her green eyes narrowed in suspicion. "How do you know that?"

"I detected brandy fumes on his breath and on that of his friend, Mr. Throckmorton, too. When gentlemen are abroad so late, they have invariably been out roistering, you know."

"You're just saying that because you don't want me to be happy. You know papa wants me to marwy that dweadful old Mawquess of Dulwich." Belinda thrust out her lower lip in an unattractive pout.

"I believe your father favors the Duke of Exford at the moment," Mary corrected calmly. "He would like to see you a duchess, you know."

"Well, I would like to be a duchess ever so much, but I don't want *Exfowd.* He's *old!*"

"You've liked him well enough until now," Mary reminded her. "Why, I can recall times out of mind when you've positively lavished praise on him for his many kind attentions and all the presents he sends you. Why, you were in transports of delight over the last poem he sent you—the one that likens you to divinity. How did it go?

> Oh, fairest Belinda, thy glorious locks of shining gold beckon me
> To adore thine eyes of emerald green, that shimmer like the sea
> To worship thy cheeks as white as the purest bank of snow,

To pay homage to thy lips, formed by Cupid
into a perfect bow.
How I delight in gazing upon thy Divinity,
E'en though thy beauty greatly disturbs my serenity!"

Belinda was not to be mollified by Mary's recitation of the duke's fatuous ode to her beauty, even though it was her favorite. "Papa's ordered you to talk me out of what I want to do," she complained, giving Mary an accusing look from those jewel-like eyes, cold and hard.

"Now, Belinda, you know that I would not try to force you to do something against your will. Your papa is not even here right now. Besides, what is between you and your father is none of my concern."

"That's not twue. Papa hiwed you to look after me, to take me to pawties and to intwoduce me to society. He pays your salawy and you must do as he says. But you are *my* companion, and I want you to do as *I* say," Belinda insisted petutantly, her little pink lips trembling in agitation. Soon tears gathered in her lovely green eyes and she began to cry in earnest.

Mary, used to her tricks, nevertheless soothed her charge's overwrought feelings as best she could, promising to speak to Belinda's father when he returned from his business trip and to detail Viscount Lindford's heroic deeds of the previous night so that the young man might find favor in Mr. Ramsbottom's eyes.

But she knew that before Lindford would be allowed to call on Belinda, her employer would thoroughly investigate his family background and financial resources, as he had that of each gentleman who had shown an interest in Belinda. What methods he used, Mary had no way of knowing. He had learned of her own background before he hired her through such mysterious means.

She could not predict what such an investigation of Lord Lindford would produce. She had not heard of the viscount when she had been in London for her season some four years previously, nor was the Standish name at all familiar. She was certain she knew none of his family. But, if his finances weren't in order, no number of heroic deeds would render him eligible, no matter that the viscount's social standing was superior to that of Mr. Ramsbottom and his beautiful daughter.

Belinda's maid, Bessie, came in to help her mistress dress for the day and Mary was able to make her escape. She went away shaking her head over the girl's foolishness. But she had to admit Belinda's point. It was true that Mr. Ramsbottom had hired her to keep an eye on his daughter.

Mary well remembered the day she first met Mr. Ramsbottom.

Belinda had been sent to the seminary where Mary was a junior mistress to acquire some social polish. Toward the end of the summer term, after five months at the school, Mary was called into the headmistress's office where she was informed that Belinda's father wished to speak to her.

She had then been ushered into a private room on the ground floor where she saw a large, florid gentleman standing by the window, gazing out on the school lawns. He had turned and regarded her for a moment, standing with his feet wide apart, his jacket open and his thumbs hooked in the pockets of his waistcoat. As she stared across the room at him, she wondered how such a burly, red-faced man could have sired a beauty like Belinda.

"Good day to ye, Miss Marlowe. Stanley Ramsbottom, at yer service, ma'am. Have an advantageous proposal to lay before ye," he had said without further preamble.

Mary had suppressed her gasp of outraged horror, but Mr. Ramsbottom saw the false conclusion she had reached reflected in her eyes and in the stiffening of her spine and had laughed heartily, his burly frame shaking with his mirth.

"No, no! Put away yer alarm, missy," he had said in an accent that marked his northern, working-class origins. "Don't want a mama for my girl precisely, but a companion. A lady of good breedin' to show her the ropes. This school's been well enough, but my girl's turned eighteen and it's time she was introduced to society. She's gradely enough to be a princess, no one can deny, but don't want any of those spendthrift Hanoverians for a son-in-law, with a hand forever in my pocket!" He had laughed hugely at his own joke.

Mary had swallowed hard and tried to sort out what the gentleman was asking of her. "And you think I would be a suitable companion for your daughter?"

"Granddaughter of an earl, ain't ye?" he had

asked, and Mary had been taken aback that he knew her background.

"I do not at all think—" she had started to refuse his offer.

"Had a fallin' out with ole Wyndham, didn't ye?" he had asked, regarding her with a sharp gleam in his small, bright eyes.

"How did you know?" Mary had gasped.

"Got my ways, got my ways. Stanley Ramsbottom didn't get where he is today without some careful studyin' of the markets, and careful studyin' of people. I've made inquiries, missy, made inquiries. Ye'll do, ye'll do. Quality like ye ain't usually school mistresses."

"Really, sir! I must beg you to excuse me!" Mary had said in a furious voice.

"Here. Come down from yer high-ropes, missy. Sit yerself down here comfortable like and listen to my proposal before ye go flouncing out of here in a high-bred temper," he had responded, taking the air out of her sails, just as she was about to launch into what she thought about the vulgar manners of persons who busied themselves about other people's business. "It might just be to yer advantage."

Mary had remained standing where she was and stared coldly across the room at her visitor.

"Ain't ye curious about what I have to say?" he had asked with a broad wink.

And Mary had ruefully acknowledged that she had indeed been curious enough to listen to his proposal that she take on the job of companion to his daughter. Not only had Mr. Ramsbottom known about her family and connections, but he had also known the fact that she had had a season herself four years ago when she was eighteen.

"Fallen on hard times, ye have. An unmarried spinster lady, ye are now," he had said baldly.

At first Mary had been insulted, but upon consideration, she realized that that was what she was—an unmarried gentlewoman fallen on hard times. After giving him a hard stare, she had raised her chin and said, "Go on."

"But there ain't any need for ye to bury yerself away in this school. What ye want is to go to London," he had continued temptingly. "Move about in society some. See the friends ye made four years ago."

He went on to explain that Mary's job would be to secure invitations for herself and Belinda from her connections among the *ton* so that his daughter could be introduced to the highest reaches of society. He didn't seem to think that Mary's relative youth was any bar to the position. It was her high birth and the *entrée* she could give his daughter into polite circles he was interested in.

He promised her a chance to gain a thousand pounds—a more than generous financial remuneration for her services, he had told her with one of his sharp looks. He reckoned the interest from such a princely sum would enable her to keep house for herself for several years, if she were careful with her money and made sound investments. In addition, he would provide her with room and board and a modest allowance for her wardrobe while she was in his employ.

To earn the money, Mary was to help him achieve

his goal of marrying Belinda to one of the denizens of the *haut ton.* But not just any denizen. Mr. Ramsbottom wanted a title, and not a "rubbishy baronetcy or even a viscountcy, either," he had declared forcefully. He wanted an earl or marquess at the least, and preferably a duke, if one were available. Making no bones about it, he admitted he wanted "the best money could buy" for his beautiful only child, for he had ambitions to connect himself with the highest and mightiest in the land.

Even though Mr. Ramsbottom was obviously from that class of persons the aristocracy referred to as "cits"—persons who had not been born to money or family name, but who had made their own way in the world and acquired the necessary financial resources to be able to live in the highest style—Mary thought it was quite possible that he would achieve his goal with very little trouble.

She guessed that he was a wealthy merchant, but even so, he might well find himself with a plethora of purse-pinched nobs clamoring for Belinda's beautiful hand, and even more handsome dowry, for such gentlemen were notoriously expensive, and Belinda was lovely enough to set any man's heart to beating faster. The girl was an incomparable beauty, a real diamond of the first water, and only just turned eighteen, ripe for the London marriage market.

And as Belinda would be quite a considerable heiress one day, and, even now, would bring a dowry of over a hundred-thousand pounds to the man she married, her father fully expected to be able to achieve his goal. But he warned Mary that he wouldn't tolerate any out-and-out fortune hunters, even for a title.

He couldn't tolerate a man who had no head for keeping his money safe, and swore he wouldn't have any man playing fast and loose with Belinda's inheritance.

Mary was very tempted by Mr. Ramsbottom's offer even though Belinda had not been one of her favorite pupils. But then the lot of them were empty-headed ninnyhammers, as far as she could tell.

She had by then become heartily bored by the tediousness of the routine of the school and the silliness of the girls she was ostensibly instructing. After some deliberation, she found she could not refuse the opportunity to further assert her independence from her stubborn grandfather. She wondered what the earl would do when he learned she had taken employment with a cit, and what his next move would be in trying to get her to agree to marry the dreadfully dull Sir Cedric.

"I say, Pev, there seems to be a bruise on my chin," Percy said, wincing as he gingerly fingered the tender spot on his face while trying to disentangle himself from the jumble of sheets and blankets on the viscount's sofa where he had made his makeshift bed.

He had spent what remained of the previous night at Lindford's lodgings in Jermyn Street, just off St. James Street. It was a convenient location for a young bachelor, situated as it was near several of the fashionable men's clubs.

"Comes from displayin' your sport against a pack of thievin' footpads, Perce," Peveril pointed out with a grin. "A small price to pay for rescuing ladies in distress."

"Ladies in distress? Thought I must've been dreamin'. You mean we really did meet up with two chits bein' set upon by a gang of ruffians in the park last night, Pev?"

"That we did, Percy. Greatest piece of good fortune to come my way this age. Wonder what our reward will be?" the viscount said with a reminiscent smile playing about his mouth. He was thinking of the divine Miss Ramsbottom. No, he amended, the divine *Belinda.*

Peveril sat sipping a cup of coffee, clad only in a splendiferous midnight blue satin dressing gown decorated with a Greek key motif picked out in gold embroidery along the collar, lapels, and hem. There was a faint bruise under his eye, his lips were slightly swollen, and he had a cut at the corner of his mouth, but those were the only visible signs that he had enjoyed a mill the previous evening, or rather in the wee hours of that morning. Not for anything would he have admitted that his fists were raw and quite sore and that his back ached where the two young hellions had pounded him for all they were worth.

He was stretched out in his favorite old leather chair with his feet crossed at the ankles and resting on the arm of the sofa where, from the look of the tangled bedclothes, his friend Percy had made a most uncomfortable bed the previous night. A newspaper was strewn about the cozily cluttered room, along with Percy's discarded clothing, giving the chamber a well-lived-in air quite apropos for a fashionable young bachelor on the town.

Percy, still worried by the pain in his chin, stuck his tongue into his cheek and tested the spot. He peered around apprehensively at his things scattered about his friend's comfortable but somewhat shabby sitting room. Seeing that Pev was glancing through a section of the paper in a desultory fashion, he surreptiously lifted the corner of the blanket that was covering him from neck to feet. He breathed a sigh of relief. He was not after all in the buff, as he had feared. He must've borrowed one of Pev's night-shirts. The thing was yards too long, but at least he was decently covered, he thought.

Peveril was holding his coffee cup precariously in one hand and staring off rather dreamily into space. The newspaper he had been glancing through slipped unobserved to the floor as he spoke to his friend. "She was an angel right enough, Perce. An angel descended from heaven, come to earth to steal my heart." He heaved a sigh. "Ten to one says I'll rivet her attention all right and tight within a fortnight," Peveril wagered confidently.

Percy saw the bemused smile on his friend's face with amazement.

"Eh? An angel? You saw an angel, Pev? With wings and all? Didn't see any such a thing, m'self."

"Don't be jinglebrained, Percy. It's a manner of speaking. I'm talking about the divine Belinda."

"Who?"

"One of the young ladies we rescued last night. By gad, she was a beauty! Didn't you remark her, Percy? A face like a goddess—all wide green eyes and blonde ringlets and a figure like an hourglass—leastways, she was covered up by a deuced evening cloak, but she must have a figure like a real little pocket Aphrodite. To match her incomparable face!"

Percy scratched his head in an effort to recall the events of the previous night. "Can't say as how I remember much. Were celebratin' m'birthday. Had taken on a deal of brandy. Both a bit the worse for wear, don't y'know. Was walkin' home with you to wear off the effects, and there was a devilish sound. Almost split m'eardrums, it did. Then there was those two females. Lord, was your angel the one with the devilish screech, Pev?"

"She has a voice like an angel, Percy," Peveril contradicted with a hurt look. He didn't know how anyone could find a flaw in such a diamond of the first water. "Just like the rest of her."

"Noisy chit, and vaporish, too," Percy insisted. "Was cryin' fit to burst . . . now, her friend, Miss Marlowe was a sensible lady, I remember. Rescued her coachman, set us all to rights, and had us all safely home in jig time."

"Didn't get a good look at her, Percy. An older lady, was she? Belinda's companion, I think she said."

"Older lady? No such a thing. Right takin' little thing, herself."

"What? Do I detect a note of admiration for the little squab?"

"No, no. Ain't in the petticoat line," Percy protested in alarm. "Not a ladies' man in the least, Pev!"

Peveril laughed, then went on to catalog the list of Miss Belinda Ramsbottom's perfections.

"I say, Pev. You thinkin' of droppin' the handkerchief?" Percy asked, agog with surprise. Peveril had confided his *tendres* before, but this sounded something beyond the short-lived infatuations that frequently afflicted the notoriously fickle viscount. Percy was a good deal shaken by the idea that his friend had been fatally wounded by an arrow from Cupid's quiver. And at such a tender age, too. The same age as he was, by gad!

Peveril nodded his head solemnly. "Think I've been hit at last. I'm fair dished this time, Percy," he said with a soppy smile on his face.

"You ain't even spoken with her properly yet, Pev!"

"What's that to say to anything? One look was enough to know that she's the one, Percy. Ain't never felt like this before. See, even my hand ain't quite steady." Peveril held out a long, slender-fingered hand for his friend's inspection.

Percy could see that it shook slightly. "Effects of our carousin' last night, Pev," he said, nodding his head sagely.

"No," the viscount insisted. "The fair Belinda fair bowled me over as soon as I clapped eyes on her . . . I'm in love, as sure as check, this time, Percy."

"You really thinkin' of takin' up a leg-shackle, Pev? Can't believe it of you!" Percy exclaimed.

"Course I am. Goin' to put my fate to the touch and pop the question soon as I talk to her papa."

"But . . . you ain't got any funds to set up your establishment. Thought you was badly dipped. Pockets to let and all that . . . said you was goin' on repairin' lease. Heard you distinctly!"

It was the viscount's turn to scratch his head as unwelcome memories of his financial embarrassments intruded. "Well, but I can't leave town now! You must see that, Percy . . . Tell you what—I'll be damned if I don't turn over a new leaf! I ain't coxcomb enough to ask a lady to marry me and then not be able to take care of her. Make a recoup somehow. Still got the Acres, after all."

Percy was familiar with his friend's careless way of referring to High Acres, his family's country estate in Hertfordshire. The place was huge, but empty of all furniture and fittings—and the roof was falling down, if he didn't mistake. The estate had been left to go to rack and ruin for more than a score of years while a succession of its owners had enjoyed themselves in London and on the continent.

"It ain't much, but if she'll have me, I'll hire a first-rate bailiff to manage the Acres and I'll turn a profit, see if I don't! Suppose we'll have to give up the pleasures of London for a year or two. But, lord, with such a capital little beauty at my side, it'll be no penance to stay in the country. Damme, it'll be a right cozy set-up," Peveril predicted dreamily, leaning his chin on his fisted hand and contemplating the joys in store during a rosy future with the exquisite Miss Ramsbottom.

Percy shook his head at the turnaround in his friend's outlook. Lindford was ever a rash and daring sort of fellow, but this was something out of the ordinary, even for him.

Peveril suddenly jumped to his feet. "What the blazes are we doing wasting time here? Burn it, I must call on Belinda! Introduce myself to her papa and take her out for a drive. Tell you what, Percy, she'll do me credit," he declared proudly as he left the room to dress.

Chapter 4

"I am so sorry, Lord Lindford. Both Belinda and I stand greatly in your debt for your quick thinking and brave actions last night, but it is not my place to allow you to call on her or take her driving," Mary stated in a firm voice, but with inward misgivings, as she faced the viscount in the drawing room of Mr. Ramsbottom's elegant Mayfair townhouse.

She stood before him with her hands folded tightly in front of her and her chin held high as she carried out her employer's orders. Her duty made her uncomfortable and, under the circumstances, she did not feel she could bid the gentleman to take a seat.

"But, confound it all, ma'am!" Peveril exclaimed, holding out his strong, graceful hand toward her in frustration. He had been impatiently pacing there in the drawing room since arriving in haste a quarter of an hour ago, and now to be denied a chance to see Belinda sent his quick temper flaring. "Why not?"

"My employer, Mr. Ramsbottom, is out of town at present and I'm afraid you will have to wait until he returns and gives his permission before you may call on his daughter, my lord." Noting how anxiety lent a boyish appeal to the viscount's handsome features, she sighed over her unhappy duty of denying him his wish.

"You don't understand, Miss Marlowe. I *must* see her." He drew a deep breath. "Deuce take it! I came expressly to ask her to drive out with me. I—I'm thinkin' of payin' her my addresses, you see, ma'am."

"So are any number of other gentlemen," Mary answered dryly.

A demon of jealousy raged in Peveril's breast at these words. "Devil take it, she's not betrothed already?" he demanded loudly. He clenched his hands into fists at his side and took a step toward her.

"No, my lord, she is not yet engaged. Her father wishes her to have an opportunity to meet many gentlemen before she bestows her hand. But she has many suitors."

It was Mary's opinion that Mr. Ramsbottom had cannily kept all Belinda's suitors hanging fire thus far, casting his net wide, trying to land the highest title on the market. But she had no intention of mentioning such a thing to the importunate, rather dangerous looking, young man who stood not a foot away glowering at her out of narrowed eyes.

"Looking for the best buyer, is he?" Peveril snapped, a scorching light in his blue eyes blazing down at the petite little lady who stood calmly before him.

"Oh no, my lord. That is not the way of it at all!" Mary declared. It seemed Lindford had not yet heard of the Ramsbottom fortune and had jumped to the wrong conclusion. And it seemed that Belinda's enormous dowry was not his objective. He had fallen headlong into love with her beautiful face without knowing anything of the fortune that would accompany her lovely hand.

Peveril was frowning heavily at Mary, trying to decide how he could overcome the obstacles to seeing the divine Belinda she had placed in his path. For a mad moment, he was almost overcome by a wild desire to put his hands on little Miss Marlowe's waist and lift her out of his way, so that he could rush upstairs and feast his eyes once more upon the enchanting vision he had seen last night.

"I am sorry, my lord," Mary replied, her eyes full of regret. She was indeed sorry she had upset their intrepid champion of the previous evening. She liked the young man. Her voice was sympathetic as she advised. "You will have to be patient and wait until Mr. Ramsbottom returns and speak with him then."

"Burn it! How do you have the authority to deny me, Miss Marlowe?" Peveril ground out, his volatile temper getting the better of him as he challenged her authority.

Mary looked up to see a fiery glint in Lindford's vivid blue eyes. She had thought him a brave but gentlemanly enough young man the night before, but now she found his physical presence almost overpowering. Heavens! He had looked tall and lean last night, but now as he towered over her, she saw that he had the breadth of shoulder and build of a born athlete. She clasped her hands more tightly in front of her and resisted the urge to take a step back from him.

"I'm acting on Mr. Ramsbottom's orders, my lord, and it would cost me my situation to gainsay them," she informed him, proud that her voice held steady under his burning glare. Her soft grey eyes pleaded with him for understanding of her difficult position.

Peveril realized that he was scowling down at the poor young woman and softened his angry expression. "Sorry, ma'am. Had no right to speak to you that way. Accept my apologies, Miss Marlowe."

He ran a hand through his dark curls and took a turn about the room before returning to face Mary. "Spoke before I thought," he admitted with a disarming lopsided grin. " 'Fraid I'm not very successful at governing my temper sometimes."

This blunt admission found favor with Mary. She liked him better for candidly acknowledging his fault.

She smiled at him with a sweet expression in her eyes. "I understand, my lord. We are, both of us, in difficult situations at the moment."

He smiled back, ruefully. They looked assessingly at one another for a long moment.

"Lord Lindford—" Mary began diffidently.

"Ma'am?"

"Until Mr. Ramsbottom approves, you may not *formally* call on his daughter, but there is no reason you may not speak to Belinda when we are out in public. If you happen to find yourselves at the same entertainments, then of course, she would wish to acknowledge the gentleman who so valiantly prevented the theft of her jewelry," she told him, giving him as bold a hint as she could without absolutely defying her employer's dictums.

Peveril stared into her wide eyes, trying to make

sense of the woman's seemingly contradictory statements. It dawned on him that little Miss Marlowe was not an unreasonable old dragon as he had thought her a moment ago, but a lady of sense and some sensibility, who was trying to be fair, without jeopardizing her position as companion to Miss Ramsbottom.

He looked at her more carefully, seeing the understanding in her rather pretty grey eyes set in her pleasing little oval face, and observed the friendly smile curving up her soft lips. Her clothes bespoke a woman of no consequence who liked to fade into the background. She was certainly dressed dowdily enough in a serviceable grey morning dress with only a little white lace at the collar and cuffs to add any interest to the gown. But there was that about her presence that bespoke a friendly, down-to-earth nature.

It suddenly occurred to him that she probably had nowhere else to go, if she lost her place in the Ramsbottom household. And she looked as though she needed the position to survive, too, for she was just a little slip of a thing. A girl really. Not an older woman at all, as he had thought last night.

She looked like a soft, little grey dove, he thought inconsequentially, and wondered in surprise where such a nonsensical notion had come from.

He grimaced, trying to clear his head, and ran a careless hand through his once carefully arranged curls, further disarranging his valet's painstaking work. Wagstaff would likely cut up stiff at the result. "Never seen a more beautiful girl, Miss Marlowe! Knocked me all to flinders, at first glance. Top-of-the-trees. Diamond of the first water doesn't begin to do justice to her beauty! Why, she's an out-and-out angel! Can hardly believe she's real!"

"Yes." A smile quivered on Mary's lips as she spoke, "Belinda has been hailed as the Incomparable of Incomparables, you know!"

"By Jove! And so she is!" Peveril agreed fervently. "You'll not stop me speaking to her, you say, should I meet her outside this house?"

"Of course not. We stand greatly in your debt, my lord. And as soon as Mr. Ramsbottom returns and gives you his approval, you may call here as often as you wish, you know." Mary smiled up at him, a bright, cheerful smile full of sympathy and understanding.

Peveril noted the sweetness about Mary's mouth when she smiled, and calmed down. He flashed her a boy's bright, irresistible grin. "Thank you, ma'am. I make no doubt we'll meet again soon."

"No doubt, my lord," Mary agreed with a wry smile.

He gave her a slight bow and took his leave.

When he quitted the room, a huge grin lit Peveril's lean boyish face. He would soon see the divine Belinda again. His heart sang! Could he live till then? he wondered.

He clapped his curly-brimmed beaver hat on his head, a frown of concentration replacing the smile on his face as he descended the steps of the Ramsbottom residence. He would make damned sure he found out where the Beauty went each day. He would have Small, his groom, watch the house.

If necessary, Small could worm his way into the

good graces of an accommodating housemaid in the household to find out what Belinda planned to do each day. If Small's charms fell short, the viscount would have no hesitation in resorting to bribery. No doubt Ramsbottom's servants could be persuaded to open their mouths for a meager coin or two, he decided with his typical insouciance.

After Lindford took his leave, Mary shook her head regretfully. There was no doubt he was anxious to join Belinda's herd of adoring admirers, trailing after the girl like a moonstruck calf. Well, they all made cakes of themselves over her foolish but beautiful charge when they fell under her spell. Even stolid, mature men like the Duke of Exford were given to stormy displays of jealousy, and childish rantings and ravings.

And, for some unfathomable reason, Belinda's admirers felt compelled to commit their overblown paeans of praise to her beauty to paper. Only today she had received another.

Thy golden locks my eyes do dazzle.
Thy melodious voice my ears never frazzle.
Be not deaf to all my pleas,
Only grant me one smile, Fair Divinity, please!

In Mary's opinion, such sophomoric efforts left much to be desired as love poetry. Unfortunately, it was her task to repeat these ramblings, full of excruciating similes and torturous rhymes, to her charge, for Belinda herself could barely read. She dreaded the thought of reading such rubbish from the viscount and wondered uncomfortably when his poetic offerings would begin to find their way to Belinda's doorstep.

It was really too bad that Lindford was caught in Belinda's toils, Mary reflected with a sigh. She liked him. He reminded her of Theo—Theodore Tate, one of her second cousins. Theo had a certain hey-go-mad exuberance for life and was always off on some mad lark or other, but there was no harm in him, only a great deal of charm and fun and the heedlessness of youth. Being of an age, she and Theo had a special friendship.

She had often worried that Theo would come to some harm before he matured enough to act sensibly, but he had recently joined the cavalry unit he had had his heart set on. He would look quite splendid in his scarlet regimentals, she thought with pride, then sobered when she remembered that he was due to leave for Portugal within the month to join Arthur Wellesley's army that was opposing the French upstart, Napoleon. With the tremendous responsibility that would shortly descend on Theo's broad young shoulders, he would be a man before the winter was out, she thought, trembling for his safety.

Mary smiled slightly and shook her head again, wishing she could make the viscount open his eyes and see Belinda for the silly, frivolous ninnyhammer she was. Ah well, she thought, perhaps he was as foolish a young gentleman as Belinda was a young lady.

She would certainly be glad when Mr. Ramsbottom returned and accepted the suit of one or another of his daughter's admirers. It would be a relief when she had earned her thousand pounds and could afford to set up her own establishment. Life with Belinda was not dull precisely, but her charge was often tedious in the extreme. However, not for a minute did she regret her decision to accept the position, for it was only a temporary expedient. Marriage to Cedric would have meant a lifetime of tedium.

Mary made her way upstairs, thinking she would have to endure a storm of tears and recriminations from Belinda when she learned that Viscount Lindford had called and been denied a chance to speak with her. Luckily, she found her charge occupied in trying on some new gowns just arrived from her modiste.

When Mary joined her, Belinda was standing in front of an ornate pier glass, framed with elaborate gilt carving, happily admiring her own reflection. She did not think to quiz Mary about why she had been called down to the drawing room.

When Belinda, accompanied by Mary, departed on an excursion to Hyde Park with a gentleman caller in an elegant open barouche the following afternoon, the viscount's groom Small was already on duty at his post, keeping watch outside Mr. Ramsbottom's house. He was able to follow the barouche and apprise his master of the young lady's destination.

Small ran back to the viscount's lodgings in Jermyn Street as fast as his legs could carry him to tell his master where the ladies were bound. He found his lordship pacing agitatedly about the cluttered sitting room.

"Got a gent with 'em, m'lord," he said out of breath, and in some trepidation as to his employer's reaction to this piece of news. "As is how they got there, in 'is carriage."

"What! Out with one of her blasted suitors already!" yelled the viscount, directing a burning look of injury at the hapless messenger. The trusty Small took a step or two back before his impetuous master could vent his fury on him by taking hold of his collar and giving him a good shaking.

"Blast it all!" Peveril exclaimed, slamming his fist into the palm of his other hand. "Who was it? Anyone I would know?"

"Can't say as how I seen the gent afore. Well set up ginger-pated cove. Team a bit showy and mismatched. Tailorin' of the best, though. Shoulders out to 'ere." Small spread his arms to their full extent.

"Padded with buckram most like," Peveril muttered dismissively as he headed out the door to the mews behind his lodgings where his mount was stabled.

He saddled his favorite hack, Ajax, a large, powerful bay gelding, himself and rode straight to Hyde Park where he soon spotted his quarry.

He guessed Belinda's presence before he saw her by the mob of men gathered round a beautifully appointed, gleaming black barouche pulled off to one side of the drive so as not to block the other carriage and horse traffic in the park at that fashionable hour. "Blister it, knew she'd be wildly popular, but this beats all!" he muttered to himself. He clamped his jaw shut on an oath, determined to cut a swathe through her throng of admirers and gain her notice.

He turned his big bay and cut across the park to the disapproval of several observers. He narrowly missed oversetting a very plump lady whose little pug lap dog had gotten away from her. The pug was racing right at the feet of Peveril's mount, barking and trying to nip the horse's heels. When the woman came screaming and running after her dog, she threw herself across Peveril's path and he had to take heroic action to avoid her. He didn't spare a backward glance to see the woman looking daggers at him while she clutched her little dog to her ample bosom with one arm and shook her fist at him with the other.

When he arrived in a great cloud of dust amid the crowd gathered around Belinda, he was greeted by a particular friend of his, Jeremy Fletcher. "I say, Pev, not at all the thing to be galloping across the park with all the crowds about. Dangerous thing to do. Even for you."

"Deuce take it, Jer! It was all the fault of that overfed pug. Ajax would never have taken it into his head to behave so in a crowd, if the nasty pug hadn't been pesterin' him."

"Still and all, Pev. Best take care what you're about in future."

A nerve of temper jumped in Peveril's cheek but he decided to ignore his friend's lecture, instead saying, "Didn't expect to see you here, Jer. You enamoured of the divine Belinda, too?"

"You know me, Pev. Never one to be out of the fashion. Looks to be the mode to trail after the incomparable Miss Ramsbottom." He shrugged.

"Something to liven up the little season. Still, don't look as though I'll succeed in getting in her good books this afternoon. I'm off to the club. Care to join me, Pev?"

"I'll look in later, Jer," Peveril promised, turning his attention to the young lady as his friend turned his horse about and rode away. He gazed upon her peerless countenance and swallowed. His half-remembered vision became stunning reality. Lord, but in the few hours since he had first seen her he had forgotten just what a perfect beauty she was!

"'Afternoon, Miss Ramsbottom," he greeted her loudly, raising his hat in a polite salute and wondering how the deuce he was to fight his way to her side through the press of horsemen and pedestrians surrounding the barouche. "Pleased to see you in such prime twig after your fright last night," he congratulated her, at once accomplishing two things. The young lady's eyes were immediately riveted on him as she was reminded of his heroics of the previous evening, and he let the other gentlemen gathered around her know that he had some particular claim to her attention.

"Oh, hello, Lowd Lindfowd! It's vewy nice to see you again!" Belinda cried with pleasure, giving him a dazzling smile and waving her dainty little gloved hand at him. "Viscount Lindfowd was my savior last night, you know," she announced dramatically to her throng of admirers.

"Indeed!" exclaimed the heavy-set, red-haired gentleman who sat next to her in the barouche with a cynical twist of his heavy, red lips. "And what did the fellow do that was so extraordinary as to earn *your* gratitude, my dear Miss Ramsbottom?" the man asked with a sharp glance at the viscount from his hooded, close-set eyes.

Recognizing Peregrine Fowler as the gent sitting up beside Belinda, the viscount instantly bristled up. So, that blasted blackguard Fowler would cast doubts on his heroic deeds of the previous evening, would he? Peveril grimaced and shot him a fulminating glare, but was unable to take any effective action.

"Oh, Mr. Fowler, Lowd Lindfowd saved me from horwid footpads who twied to steal my jewelwy," Belinda said with a simper, turning her bewitching green eyes on the man sitting next to her and laying a little gloved hand on his arm.

"I feel safe now Lowd Lindfowd is here to pwotect me," she said gaily to the assembled group with another radiant smile in Peveril's direction. "And if any of you should twy to steal my locket, he will deal with you most dweadfully!"

"Pleased to deal with any *scoundrels* for you, Miss Ramsbottom," Peveril declared meaningfully, with a challenging glare at Fowler. Though reputedly a well-to-grass gent, there was something decidedly smokey about Fowler, Peveril knew. Rumor had it he had repaired his fortune through various nefarious means that included fleecing young greenhorns newly come to town at cards.

"Ah, but the beautiful neck that graces the locket is much more worth guarding than a mere gaudy trinket, however, expensive," Fowler murmured ingratiatingly, ignoring Lindford's provocative words and turning Belinda's attention back to himself. He leaned near her, picked up her gloved hand and bestowed a lingering kiss on it, to Peveril's impotent fury.

Belinda chose to be insulted. "It's my favowite piece of jewelwy," she contradicted, fingering the item round her neck while her bottom lip protruded out at Fowler's perceived insult to the precious locket. She turned her frowning eyes away from him.

"If only I had been on the scene, I would gladly have lain down my life for you, my dear Miss Ramsbottom," averred Crispin Taylor, another of her admirers who stood beside the barouche. He was a pale young gentleman with flaxen locks who wore a rather colorful silk scarf artistically draped around his neck instead of the usual white neckcloth.

Belinda giggled through her fingers and when someone asked what had happened, she held all eyes as she told a much exaggerated version of the story, attributing to herself certain brave deeds that should have been credited to Mary.

Mary, who had earlier stepped down from the barouche to exercise her legs a little, was making her way back to the barouche when she saw the viscount sitting his mount near Mr. Fowler's vehicle. She saw that he was looking upon the proceedings with a face like a thundercloud, twitching his crop back and forth in an agitated manner, his moody gaze fixed on Belinda.

Slapping his crop against his thigh in frustration, Peveril saw no way to claim the Beauty's attention all to himself. He clamped his teeth shut on an oath.

"A lovely autumnal afternoon, is it not, Lord Lindford?" a female voice said, taking him by surprise.

"What? Oh, yes. 'Afternoon, Miss Marlowe," Peveril greeted her off-handedly, lifting his hat and giving her a slight bow when he finally noticed her standing near him.

"What a coincidence, you riding here just at this hour, my lord," she said.

Peveril was disconcerted to see a gleam of amusement in her wide eyes, even as she gave him a warm smile. Not used to this sort of teasing from a young lady, he looked at her more closely for a moment before saying with an engaging grin, "Lord, ma'am, should've thought you couldn't help but *expect* to see me here, after the hint you gave me."

He dismounted, thinking to ingratiate himself with Belinda's companion.

Mary laughed. "*Touché,* my lord. I see you mean to put my hint to good advantage."

"Just so ma'am. But it's devilish difficult getting near enough to speak to her," he said with a frown before turning his eyes back to Belinda, who was speaking of him, if not to him.

Mary touched him lightly on the arm. "Do not look so displeased, my lord. This is how Belinda loves to carry on. She so much enjoys all the attention she is receiving. You would not deny her such a treat, would you?"

Peveril's face immediately softened. "Not for worlds," he replied, not looking at Mary. "She's uncommonly beautiful, isn't she, ma'am?"

"Oh, yes, very. I've never seen a lovelier girl and I have several second cousins who were hailed as Incomparables when they were presented, yet not one of them could hold a candle to her."

"Lord, I'd readily believe it!"

Something she said penetrated his preoccupation and slowly registered in his mind. "You have cousins who were presented? Did you enjoy a presentation yourself, ma'am?" he asked, mildly wondering what her background was.

"Yes. I had one season when I was eighteen, but I didn't take. And then my grandfather decided against another. He had made other plans for me, you see," she explained dryly.

"Egad, ma'am, you must've been dashed disappointed."

"Oh, no. Not at all!" She laughed. "I'm a country girl at heart, used to plain, honest dealing. I'm afraid I didn't much like being on display and always having to behave like a meek, docile young thing. It would have been a severe strain on my nerves to go through all that again."

Peveril lifted his black brows. "A hoyden are you, ma'am? A little thing, like you? I'd not credit it!" He grinned down at her roguishly, his beaked nose looking more prominent in his boyish face as he smiled.

Seeing the generous smile remain on Mary's face, the viscount looked at her more closely. Why, she was too sweet to be a termagant, was the thought that popped into his mind from nowhere.

He had dismissed her as a little brown squab, but as he looked down at her he saw that he had been too hasty in his judgment. Her short dusky curls were almost hidden under the hood of the too-large iron grey cloak she wore, but they looked soft and inviting as they framed her piquant little face. Her wide eyes were sparkling up at him with something devilish intriguing in their grey-blue depths while her soft mouth was curved up in a playful smile.

He was reminded of his earlier notion that she was a soft little dove, not a brown squab at all, and his attention was momentarily diverted from Belinda. Something appealing about Miss Mary Marlowe stirred him—though he couldn't decide what. There was something in her eyes that he couldn't identify; as he had no experience with quick-witted females, it was no surprise that he didn't recognize intelligence when it was staring him in the face.

At any rate, Peveril felt he would have nothing to fear from Miss Mary Marlowe in his pursuit of her companion. Such a sweet little lady wouldn't throw a rub in his way, he felt sure.

He turned his attention back to the Beauty. Through the simple expedient of asking her, he was able to learn her plans for the evening.

"Oh, I'm pwomised to dine and dance at Lady Bewyl Clawemont's tonight. Isn't that wight, Marwy?" she asked her companion.

Mary confirmed that such was the case.

"Lady Bewyl's the Duke of Exfowd's sister, you know," she said to the group at large. "It will be the squeeze of the little season. Will you be there, Lowd Lindfowd?" she asked, batting her long lashes flirtatiously.

"Wild horses couldn't keep me away!" he promised with his hand over his heart, hoping he could cadge a last-minute invitation to the affair. "Beg you to save a set for me, Miss Ramsbottom!"

"Of course. Because you wescued me just like one of those knights of long ago, I will save you two!"

she promised blithely. At her words, her other suitors set up a clamor, begging that she promise them two dances, as well.

Mary cringed at Belinda's bold words. The girl had absolutely no regard for the proprieties and no conception that this forward behavior would be considered fast by the high sticklers. She resolved to take Belinda aside when they returned home and put a flea in her ear. Again. Much good it would do, though, she thought with resignation. Belinda had no more idea of proper behavior than a cat. Less even. It was another of the reasons it had been so difficult for Mary to secure invitations for her to polite circles.

"So you're dining with Exford's sister tonight, eh? Ain't got the duke in her eye, has she?" Peveril looked at Mary with a worried question in his eyes.

"I really could not say, my lord," Mary prevaricated, not meeting his eyes. She suspected that Mr. Ramsbottom did indeed have the duke very much in his eye, but Belinda blew hot and cold about the Duke of Exford, and whether his grace's consequence would ever permit him to offer for the daughter of a merchant was something that remained to be seen.

Peveril knew the present Duke of Exford vaguely. He was a stewed prune of a man, much given to old-fashioned political pronouncements of the Tory conviction. "Fellow's a confirmed bachelor, from all I've heard. Not much given to looking about him for a duchess. 'Sides, he's old enough to be her father and a devilish dried up old stick to boot!" he concluded disgustedly.

Oh, dear, Mary thought, Viscount Lindford sounded exceedingly jealous already. She hoped he was not given to enacting scenes, but remembering his impetuous actions of two nights ago, she knew she could not count on any such thing.

"And what are your plans for tomorrow, Miss Ramsbottom?" Peveril called out, seizing the chance to learn all he could about the incomparable's movements.

"Oh, I never know where we'll be going. Ask Marwy. She keeps our engagements stwaight in her little wed book," Belinda answered with a wave of her hand before her attention was claimed by Fowler once more.

"Miss Marlowe?" Peveril turned to Mary, his brows raised in query.

"Now, Lord Lindford," Mary answered with a twinkle in her eyes, "you cannot expect me to be your collaborator, you know."

He laughed. "Was afraid not. Such a deuced proper little guardian as you are," he teased, reaching out to tweak a stray curl that peeked out from under her hood.

His finger brushed her soft cheek as he did so and Mary was disturbed by his touch.

"You know very well that would be violating my duty, my lord," she said a bit breathlessly, feeling the hot color flood her cheeks. She was relieved when he turned away a moment later to mount his horse. He rode away with a careless wave, leaving Mary puzzled at her reaction to his teasing gesture.

As Peveril rode off he resolved with renewed determination to win the delicious Beauty for himself. It seemed he was to have formidable competition from Fowler and the Duke of Exford, but both were older men. The others surrounding her today were mere puppies, with the exception of his friend, Fletcher. But he was sure Jeremy was not seriously pursuing this latest Incomparable. After all, Jer was in his late twenties and a confirmed bachelor, set in his ways, and not likely to let some chit disturb his comfortable existence.

Peveril was not vain, but he thought he would be preferable in looks to the gouty, undistinguished-looking duke or to the rather ugly Fowler whose cold black eyes set in his red face sent a shiver down even his spine. The ginger-haired fellow's habitual disagreeable expression was sure to depress a gay young thing like Miss Belinda. Then there was Fowler's unpleasant temper. Peveril was sure Belinda wouldn't want Fowler.

He felt instinctively his age was an advantage. What young girl would want to be tied to an old codger with one foot in the grave? he wondered with the supreme confidence of youth. And then, too, he could give her a title—she would be Lady Lindford if she married him. He brightened for a moment, then remembered that she would be a duchess if she accepted Exford's suit. Glumly, he wondered how he could make a viscountcy more attractive to her than a dukedom.

Chapter 5

"Oh, Lowd Lindfowd, I'd be ever so gwateful if you would fan me," Belinda uttered in a breathless voice. "It's terwibly hot in here, isn't it?"

Peveril stood beside his angel lady in Lady Claremont's stuffy, overcrowded ballroom, determined to stick close so that he could claim a good share of her attention.

Belinda waved her own little hand in front of her face to indicate how warm she was, causing the spangles sewn into the white gauze overdress she wore over her ecru colored gown of watered silk to sparkle in the candlelight.

"I shall be happy to do that for you, my dear," piped up the Duke of Exford who stood at her other side, glowering at the viscount. The duke reached for the fan dangling from a silver satin ribbon at her left wrist even as he spoke.

"Here, I say, Exford! Miss Ramsbottom asked me to see to her comforts," Peveril snapped belligerently. "Go offer your services to some other lady."

"I'll thank you not to address me in that tone,

Lindford," the duke replied pompously, drawing himself up and trying to look down his nose at his youthful rival. He was singularly unsuccessful in this foolish effort—standing on his dignity afforded him little advantage as the viscount stood half a foot taller than he did.

Belinda's eyes swiveled back and forth between the two men and glowed with excitement. She put her hand on the duke's arm and looked up at him meltingly.

"Oh, your gwace, I am so vewy thiwsty. It would be ever so sweet of you to get me a dwink of lemonade," she said archly, playing off one suitor against another with aplomb. Her technique would not have shamed a much more experienced belle.

When the duke stomped off with a heavy frown on his splotchy face to see his rival left in sole possession of the field, Belinda handed Peveril her ivory-handled fan and he began to comply with her request.

"I weally am ever so hot," she murmured, blinking up at Peveril, and almost swaying against him. He put a hand under her elbow to steady her and ceased his fanning motions, snapping the fan shut.

"Tell you what! Take you out on the balcony for a breath of air. Be just the ticket, if you're feeling over warm."

"No, it won't, Pev. Not the thing at all. Think I should fetch Miss Marlowe," Percy interjected, overhearing their conversation as he came up behind them. "Stands to reason. Lady's feeling faint. Needs her companion."

"No, no, Mr. Thwockmowton. I don't want you to find Marwy, just yet. Lowd Lindfowd will take care of me," Belinda insisted with a little moue at the thought of having her plans unraveled by such a negligible gentleman as Percival Throckmorton.

"Here's Miss Marlowe now!" Percy exclaimed thankfully, as he spotted Mary making her way toward them. He didn't like the look in Peveril's eyes above half, for it promised a reckoning later for breaking up his *tête à tête* with the Beauty.

"Come along, Belinda. I believe you are promised to Sir Thomas Nichols for the next set," Mary reminded her as she came up to the little group.

Belinda frowned, and barely resisted the urge to stamp her slippered foot in vexation as Mary led her away. She had wanted Lindford to take her out on the balcony, just to see what a sensation it would cause.

Earlier as she had stood in a little curtained alcove in the ladies withdrawing room while Mary and a maid pinned up the torn skirt of her gown, she had overheard several girls talking about the viscount. Mr. Throckmorton's vivacious little cousin, Emmy Belfours, had been among them.

"Oh, yes, Lindford's a *particular* friend of my cousin Percy," Miss Emmaline Belfours was saying to four or five other young ladies who were gathered round her.

"Oh, how fortunate you are, Emmy! Actually to be acquainted with such a wild young blade! You must know, he's accounted a great daredevil. My brother Harry says Lindford's a devil of a fellow with his fives, that he's a regular top sawyer and drives a bang-up curricle. He's up to all the rigs, you know," repeated Sally Bristol, a lively, curly-haired, freckle-faced young lady who thought herself greatly daring for using the slightly vulgar cant currently popular among young sprigs of fashion. The young gentlemen had picked up the slang from their servants and the lower orders of London society. The wiff of wildness was enhancing to one's reputation as a fashionable young blood out on the town.

"Yes, Lindford's a great rip, my brother Sep says. Though Sep's too quiet and studious to run with the viscount's crowd, I believe he's admired Lindford from afar ever since he came up to town," Miss Virginia Smythe added in her deep, throaty voice.

"Ohh, it's quite glorious to see him close-up at last!" sighed Elspeth Winterhaven, a timid, washed-out blond. "He's more handsome than I thought, even with his crooked nose," she added with a giggle.

"Oh, I know why his nose isn't straight," Emmy told them with the air of one imparting a great secret.

"Do tell, Emmy!" two of the young ladies cried at once.

"It was broken in a cricket match when he was at Harrow. I believe he was only in his early teens at the time. He was thought very daring for insisting on playing silly mid-on when his team were in the field. You know how close mid-on stands to the batsman. Well, the ball came so fast at him once that he didn't have time to catch it. It hit him square in the face and put paid to his nose. He was famous for his batting, too, Percy says, though he was out too often for flashing outside his off stump . . . actually, we're fortunate he's here tonight. Pev's not one to frequent parties for the younger set," Emmy continued confidentially, assuming an air of intimate acquaintance with the viscount's likes and dislikes, comings and goings.

"No, I've not seen him about before tonight. I believe this is the first party he's attended during the little season." Sally giggled.

"I'm afraid he thinks we're too dull for him," Emmy added with a sigh.

"My mama doesn't speak well of him. She says he isn't fit company for delicately-nurtured females," asserted a prudish, platter-face girl with frizzy blond hair.

"Fiddle!" exclaimed Anne Fitzhugh, a hard-to-please brunette beauty who was to embark on her third season in the spring. 'I don't give a snap of my fingers for what my mama says about him. I think he's ever so handsome, despite his broken nose."

"What does your mama say, Anne?" Emmy questioned, wide-eyed.

"That he's wild to a fault, and 'handsome is as handsome does.' *And* that he drinks too much and thinks too little."

"Oh, stuff! That description would fit most men!" declared Sally, with all the worldly wisdom of a young lady of nineteen.

The viscount's mildly disreputable, and considerably exaggerated, reputation for dashing behavior, together with the air of wildness that hung about him, not to mention his tall person and boyish good looks, rendered him exceedingly attractive and intriguing to these impressionable young ladies. He had not come much among them before, as he generally considered dancing parties for hopeful young ladies decidedly flat, complaining to Percy that such parties inevitably forced one to waste a perfectly good evening among "a deuced pack of dowds and hopeful chits" who were nothing more than "green schoolgirls not yet up to snuff, puttin' on airs."

"*I've* heard he's all to pieces from playing ducks and drakes with his fortune—which wasn't much to begin with," said Susan Jenkins, the platter-faced girl with a toss of her frizzy head.

"No!" cried Emmy, shocked. "I can't believe he's that badly dipped! I know he likes to place a wager or two, now and then. All gentlemen do, you know, Susan."

"If he's under the hatches, maybe that's why he's hanging about that underbred heiress," Susan snapped bitingly.

"No. That can't be it. There have been scads of heiresses on the market ever since he came up town when Percy did, almost four years ago, and he's never shown the slightest interest," Emmy defended her cousin's friend and one who appeared to her in the light of a demi-god.

"Well, I'm an heiress, too," stated Sally, "and I wouldn't mind in the least if he were to dangle after me. I would pick up his handkerchief the moment he dropped it at my feet and gladly hand over my dowry."

"Yes. How I envy Miss Ramsbottom for capturing his attention. She is indeed fortunate." Anne Fitzhugh sighed enviously.

"I wonder if he's kissed the Incomparable yet?" Sally asked daringly, and they all dissolved in giggles.

"He must know how to kiss for my brother says he

frequents the company of *chères-amies,*" whispered Elspeth in a shocked voice, blushing furiously.

"Oh, there's nothing in that. Men *will* behave so. It doesn't put them beyond the pale, you know," drawled Virginia, who at one-and-twenty considered herself considerably more sophisticated than these girls just out of the schoolroom. She was a spectacular brunette, who liked to think herself worldly wise and quite up to snuff in such matters. She glided away from the group and returned to the ballroom, leaving them to their schoolgirl chatter.

Belinda had put a hand up to her mouth behind the curtain to stifle her giggles when the girls first began to talk about the viscount. She heard all their lavish praise and positively swelled with triumph. It seemed all her peers were sighing and languishing for Lindford, such a handsome and daring young blood, who could be counted on to get up to all kinds of devilment at the drop of a hat. And how they envied her to attracting his interest!

Lindford's natural physical attractiveness was enhanced in her eyes and her determination to have him at her feet increased with every word the girls had uttered. When she heard them discussing his amatory exploits, the thought entered her head that she would dearly love to find out what it was like to be kissed by such an exciting blade. She determined to take the first opportunity that presented itself to find out, vowing she would get Lindford to kiss her before the night was over.

Mary's heart sank when she heard the girls' chatter and saw Belinda's gloating smile and the glow of triumph in her eyes.

As alarming as it was to hear that the viscount had dissipated his fortune, Mary knew better than to credit casual gossip. Yet if there were any truth in it, Mr. Ramsbottom would ferret it out and the viscount would be forbidden to come anywhere near Belinda. What would the volatile gentlemen do then? And what would her capricious charge do? Mary wondered in trembling and trepidation.

"I say, Mar, is that you? Fancy seeing you here!" a young gentleman exclaimed on spotting Mary in Lady Claremont's supper room.

"Oh my goodness, Alex! You're in London?" Mary exclaimed with a glad smile, rising from the table she had been sharing with Belinda and her supper partner, the Duke of Exford, and giving her young cousin her hand.

"As you see, Mar," Alexander Tate said with a grin for his favorite relative, spreading his arms wide at his side.

"How are you, my dear? and how are Aunt Caroline, and your sisters?"

"We're all in prime twig," Alex replied.

"And has Theo been posted yet?" Mary asked anxiously.

"He set sail for Portugal two weeks ago. Too early to expect a letter yet . . . the old gentleman know you're here in London, Mar? There was a devil of an uproar at Wyndham when you ran away, you know. Mama's been in a quake and none of the family will go near the old goa—, er, Great Uncle Wyndham since you left, Mar."

"Oh dear, I'm sorry grandfather is in one of his angry moods. But I could not bear to stay under his roof a day longer!"

"Angry? That's a deuced understatement, if I've ever heard one. The earl's in more than an angry mood. Almost had an apoplectic fit, from what I hear," Alex said with more than a touch of irony.

Mary looked alarmed. "He's—he's not unwell, is he?"

"Lord, no! Just mad fit to burst at your defying him that way. I've heard he's sent for Cedric, though."

"Sent for Cedric, has he? Whatever for?" Mary asked, anger burning in her anew.

"Wants him to carry you back to Wyndham and marry you out of hand, Mama says."

"I will refuse to go with him, Alex," Mary replied, her jaw hardening. "You may as well tell them all that I do not intend to knuckle to Grandpapa's Turkish treatment." She had felt sorry for her grandfather at Alexander's first words, but this news only served to firm her determination to defy him.

"Why don't you go to Mama, then? You know she'd be more than pleased to have you. In fact, think she'd be tickled pink, white and blue! She didn't come up for the little season this year, or she'd have insisted you go to her as soon as she learned you were in town. Goin' home to Kent tomorrow. I'll carry a message to her for you, if you like."

For a moment Mary was tempted by this idea. She knew Aunt Caroline would gladly defy the earl on her behalf—and possibly suffer for it. And there was her own commitment to Mr. Ramsbottom.

"Your mama is kind, Alex, but you know she could not withstand the earl's demands that I go home to Wyndham. It's wonderful to know that I would be welcome at your mama's home, should I need to go there, but I'll not burden Aunt Caroline with my presence just now."

"What! You wouldn't be so cowardly with me there to defend you from the earl, would you, Mar?" he teased. At Mary's smile, he began to quiz her on just exactly what she had been up to since leaving her grandfather's house. Upon learning of her residence with the new Beauty, he begged for an introduction. Mary obliged him and Alex joined their party, much to the duke's disgust and Belinda's delight.

After dancing with her cousin, Mary watched as Alex went off to dance a cotillion with Belinda. Judging by the bemused smile on his face, he seemed to be falling under her charge's spell, just as most men did. Alex was a personable young man, though Mary doubted he could pass Mr. Ramsbottom's stringent test of acceptable suitors for Belinda. But Alex had said he was leaving town on the morrow, she remembered with relief. Thank goodness he would not have the opportunity to join Belinda's cadre of suitors. She would hate to think him caught in the toils of her foolish charge.

Oh, the room *was* overheated, Mary thought. And her dance with Alex had been quite energetic. She wandered over to an open window for a breath of air. She leaned her elbows on the wide embrasure, was partially hidden behind the heavily embroidered green and gold draperies that hung from ceiling to floor. Suddenly she became aware that two ladies stood on the other side of the curtains gossiping. They were speaking of Belinda. It would have been most embarrassing to reveal her presence at that juncture, so she didn't move and was an unwilling eavesdropper on their conversation.

"My dear, Lillibet, that Ramsbottom creature is a very hussy!"

"I couldn't agree more, Selina. You will never see her in *my* ballroom!"

"Nor in mine, I assure you. How came she to be invited here tonight?"

"Why, Beryl Claremont told me that Exford *insisted* she be invited. Imagine! Her own brother, the Duke of Exford, interested in such a creature!"

"Surely, *surely,* Exford would not be so remiss in realizing what's owed his name as to offer for an underbred cit, Lillibet! Imagine such an unsuitable creature as the Duchess of Exford! Oh, it doesn't bear thinking of!"

"No, indeed. Such a mésalliance would be positively indecent! And to think, Selina, that the Earl of Wyndham's granddaughter is the girl's companion. I have never heard of such a shocking thing!"

"Mary Marlowe has no more business setting up as a companion than my own Susan. She should be having a season of her own and contracting a suitable alliance, for, if I mistake not, she'll soon be on the shelf. I can not imagine what Wyndham can be thinking of to allow such a shocking arrangement!"

"Oh, I quite agree. And for the granddaughter of

the Earl of Wyndham to put herself at the beck and call of a cit! Why, I can't for the life of me think what the gel's about!"

"No. And now that wild Peveril Standish is hanging around the Ramsbottom hussy, too!"

"On the catch for a fortune, I suppose, for the Standish blunt is long since gone and the house and estate in ruins, from what I've heard."

"Yes, spared by King Harry during the Dissolution, but brought to rack and ruin by those spendthrift Standishes! But for a Standish to marry a cit would be almost as bad as Exford doing so."

"My dear Selina, how dreadful! That I should live to see the day the Standishes were sunk so low as to contemplate such a shocking mésalliance! My spirits are quite overset by the dreadful prospect, I assure you."

"I had almost decided to make a push to capture young Lindford for my Susan."

"Oh, no, my dear Selina! He is so wild, he's past redemption."

"Well, I don't know, Lillibet. I've always said that a little resolution will work wonders with these young scapegraces. My Susan is a strong-minded gel. I believe she could reform him in next to no time."

The ladies wandered off and before Mary could move away two gentleman strolled into the alcove to take their places.

"My God! never seen a more glorious creature!" one of them remarked in a raspy voice.

"No, by Jove. The Incomparable of Incomparables. No other chit can hold a candle to her. Girl's a regular peagoose, from what I've seen, but did you ever see a more glorious figure? My fingers itch to twine themselves round that trim waist."

"Umm, yes, and the bosom ain't half bad either, for a mere chit. Father's a cit from what I've heard. Think there's a chance she would accept a *carte blanche?"*

"Don't be more of a fool than you can help, Oldham! The girl's a damned heiress. Father's rich as Golden Ball! On the catch for a title, I've heard. And, from what I hear, old Ramsbottom ain't overly fond of those whose dibs ain't in tune. On his guard against fortune hunters."

"Worse luck for me then, devil take it!"

"And for me. I could just do with such a ripe, little ladybird to warm my bed—and my pockets as well."

"Funny little dragon who guards her though. Looks respectable enough. Where did old Ramsbottom find the filly?"

"Wyndham's granddaughter, don't you know."

"By Jupiter, you don't say so! Fellow's pockets must be demmed deep, indeed, to be able to buy the granddaughter of an earl as a companion for his daughter."

When the gentlemen had moved away, Mary made her escape and wandered back along the edge of the ballroom. The comments she had overheard left her ears burning, but she wasn't surprised by them. Although Belinda's beauty and fortune assured that she would be wildly popular among the gentlemen, her exquisite face struck terror into the breasts of anxious matchmaking mamas with chicks of their own to launch, and a fierce jealousy in the hearts of some of the other young ladies her age. And gentlemen of all ages looked upon Belinda with just such rapacious eyes as the two she had just overheard.

Belinda had been the subject of such wildly clashing opinions since she had made her first appearance in a social setting. Some three months previously in Sidmouth, one of the fashionable watering places on the south coast of Devon, she had first dipped her toe in what was a small pond of high-born society, before plunging headlong into the treacherous waters of a London season in full sail.

The Sidmouth campaign had met with mixed results. Mary and Belinda had attended the assemblies in both Sidmouth and Exmouth, another elegant seaside town just along the scenic coast where she had first encountered the Duke of Exford. With her extraordinary beauty and her unending supply of expensive gowns, all quite *à la mode,* Belinda was at once heralded as an unparalleled Diamond of the First Water among the gentlemen. Among the ladies she was immediately acknowledged as an unparalleled threat, both to the hearts of their menfolk and to their daughters' chances of attracting the interest of eligible gentlemen when she was by.

Belinda had caused a similar sensation when they had arrived in London a few weeks previously. Gentlemen of all degrees had fallen at her feet at first glimpse of her exquisite profile and ripe figure.

But Belinda's foray into London society was not the unqualified success her father had desired. Mary had tried her best to secure invitations to tonnish affairs from her London acquaintances, but had had only limited success. Many of society's influential hostesses had refused to extend invitations to the heiress, despite their previous acquaintance with the well-connected, unexceptional Miss Mary Marlowe. Both the competition Belinda offered to their daughters, sisters, and other female friends and relations, as well as the fact that she hailed from that resented class of persons known as cits, were against her, despite Mary's best efforts.

Mary found it rather hypocritical that persons who had acquired their money through their dealings in merchandise, rather than from the land, were often resented, despised and looked down upon by those persons, who through no effort of their own, had acquired a recognized place in society by the accident of birth. But she was powerless to change this snobbish thinking. It was too ingrained.

However, despite the snubs Belinda had received from the female denizens of the *ton,* their gentlemen relations frequently demanded that she be included in entertainments their ladies sponsored—as was the case tonight.

And despite the ladies' snubs, several prominent gentlemen seemed ready to sue for Belinda's hand, including three of her most persistent admirers who had followed her to London from Sidmouth—among them, his grace, the Duke of Exford, as well as Mr. Peregrine Fowler, and Sir Thomas Nichols, all gentlemen of some financial substance and social standing who had been given Mr. Ramsbottom's seal of approval. Though, of course, Mary knew with certainty that the Duke of Exford would receive Mr. Ramsbottom's most effusive blessing if he ever actually declared himself. The lure of a dukedom would be irresistible to the merchant's ambitious soul.

Chapter 6

Mary had walked halfway round the ballroom when she spotted Lindford leaning negligently against the wall near the door, his arms folded across his chest and his legs crossed at the ankle. She smiled and moved in his direction, thinking to speak with him for the first time that evening, but stopped short when she noticed the jealous, sulky expression on his face. He was watching Belinda dance with her cousin. He looked as though he would like to step forward and snatch Belinda out of Alex's arms.

Oh dear, she thought apprehensively, I hope he isn't about to create a scene.

The Duke of Exford, who was dancing with Emmy Belfours in Belinda's set, was casting a fulminating eye upon Alex as well, Mary saw with concern.

Heavens! Belinda will enjoy this, she thought with vexation.

Mary had learned that not only did Belinda bask in the admiration of her many beaux, but that she found childish excitement in pitting one of her besotted admirers against another. The girl had a perfect genius for granting her favors to more than one gentleman at a time and delighted in having the gentlemen vie for her attention. Her flirtatious manner inevitably aroused jealousy among her competing swains and often led to quarrels, and it had been Mary's unpleasant duty to step between two angry gentlemen to soothe down their tempers on more than one occasion. And though she always took Belinda to task for her outrageous behavior afterward, she could sense that the girl enjoyed stirring up these quarrels and would like nothing so much as to provoke two of her suitors into fighting a duel over her.

Mary glanced warily at the viscount as the set drew to a close and took note of his fashionable garb for the first time. No one could have faulted the correctness of his evening dress, black knee-breeches and cutaway jacket of blue superfine worn over a shirt of the finest white lawn. His snowy white cravat was arranged in intricate folds about his neck, but his over-long dark locks were brushed carelessly into no particular style at all.

He wore his clothes with the same natural flair and off-hand nonchalance that characterized his speech and manners, she decided. Altogether the impression he gave was one of unstudied elegance, which, she reluctantly admitted, was really quite attractive. Once again, she was reminded of her cousin Theo.

In her mind's eye she saw Cedric all pokered up, stiff and unbending, standing ramrod straight, worrying if the tiniest crease was visible in his jacket, or if one hair on his head was out of place, and felt all her old revulsion at the idea of ever becoming his wife.

Her resolve never to give in to her grandfather's wishes redoubled.

Lindford's very nonchalance was part of his charm, she decided. Remembering the conversation she had overheard earlier in the ladies' withdrawing room, she wondered if he were at all conscious of the impact he had made on the hearts of so many impressionable young ladies.

Before the couples could even leave the floor at the end of the dance, the Duke of Exford had claimed Belinda's hand for the ensuing set and walked off with her to the other side of the room. Peveril grimaced as he watched them, then turned to look about him. He caught Mary's eye on him, and sauntered over to her.

"Care to dance, Miss Marlowe?" he asked rather casually.

"Thank you, my lord. That would be delightful," Mary said, smiling sweetly up at him and noting the frown between his eyes. He looked like a thundercloud with his stormy blue eyes boring down into hers. She wished she could banish the unhappy look from his face.

As Peveril led Mary through the steps of the country dance, he was forced to tear his eyes away from Belinda to take some notice of his partner. When Mary smiled up at him, he grinned back into her eyes, losing his preoccupied look.

"Look up to all the rigs tonight, Miss Marlowe," he complimented, smiling at her approvingly and thinking that she looked more attractive than he had yet seen her. He was surprised to note that she was dressed in a very fashionable gown of soft, pink velvet that suited her pretty grey eyes and soft, dark curls very well. But of course there was no comparing sweet, little Miss Marlowe with a real diamond of the first water like the divine Belinda, he thought, glancing back to the Beauty.

"Why, thank you, Lord Lindford. May I return the compliment and say that you are looking considerably more the thing this evening, after the other night's unfortunate contretemps."

He gave a crack of laughter. "Was a right dust-up, wasn't it? Wags, my valet, had twenty fits at the state of my gear when I got home. Daresay it broke his heart to throw away a set of clothes."

"I'm so sorry your garments were ruined. I'm sure Mr. Ramsbottom will reimburse you for them when he returns. And Mr. Throckmorton, too."

"Think nothing of it, ma'am. Was all in a good cause," he said, his eyes straying back to Belinda.

"She is very beautiful, is she not, my lord?" Mary asked, divining his thoughts easily enough, for they were writ clearly upon his open, expressive face.

He nodded absently, then sighed and looked down at Mary, saying, "Lord, I've never seen a more beautiful girl! Guess her face is her fortune, eh?"

"Oh no, Belinda has more than her face for her fortune, my lord. In fact, you might say that her fortune matches her face."

"What? You don't mean to say old Ramsbottom has money?"

"Oh yes, indeed, Lord Lindford. Miss Ramsbottom is a considerable heiress."

"The divine Belinda a great heiress! Well, I'll be damn-jiggered!" Peveril exclaimed, his eyes wide in amazement. He gave a strangled cough. "Your pardon, ma'am," he apologized. "Took me by surprise."

Mary smiled her forgiveness just as the pattern of the dance separated them.

He was anxious to question her further when they came together again. "Any word on old Rams—er, on Mr. Ramsbottom's return, ma'am?" he asked directly when his hand met hers in a figure of the dance.

Mary felt the pressure of his hand warm on hers. "No. My employer doesn't inform his household staff of his movements, but comes and goes just as he pleases. He could be back tomorrow, or weeks from now. Lord Lindford . . ." she began diffidently, wishing to forewarn him of the shoals ahead. If what she had overheard earlier about the state of his finances was true, all would not be clear sailing for his courtship of Belinda.

He looked down at her inquiringly.

"I must tell you that my employer is a difficult man to please."

She fairly caught his attention with these words. "The devil he is!" Peveril exclaimed. "How so, ma'am?"

"He, ah, has certain requirements he expects those who aspire to his daughter's hand to meet." From the little Mary already knew of the viscount, she thought he and Belinda would not suit. But, if he had indeed fallen into an infatuation for her charge, he was likely doomed to a severe disappointment. She wished to spare him with a timely hint of how the wind blew.

"Does he, by Jupiter! What sort of requirements?" he demanded keenly.

"Shall I be frank, my lord?" Mary asked, giving him a hesitant look.

"By God, I wish you would!" Peveril stopped dancing, carelessly disrupting the pattern of the dance and leaving the set short of the required number of couples. He took Mary's arm and guided her off the dance floor and out of the room to a well-lit chamber off the passageway adjacent to Lady Claremont's ballroom.

"Mr. Ramsbottom is a very wealthy gentleman. He desires his daughter to make a match with the highest and mightiest in the land," Mary told him as Lindford led her across the room to stand in front of the blazing fire burning in the grate.

"Fair swimming in lard, is he?" Peveril let go of her arm and turned to face her.

Mary nodded and looked up at him with a gleam of humor in her eyes. "Swimming in coal, would be a more accurate metaphor, my lord," she said dryly, familiar with the cant of her young male cousins and understanding him well enough.

"Coal? You don't mean to tell me the fellow's a deuced coal merchant?"

"He is, my lord."

"Good God, the divine Belinda's the daughter of a cit!" Peveril exclaimed in amazement. As he was not in the habit of frequenting *ton* parties, he hadn't heard the current gossip circulating among the tabbies about the Beauty's less than refined background, nor the fact that she was a considerable heiress.

Mary nodded, struggling to maintain her dignity at the comical look of disbelief on his face.

Peveril could not stand still. He began to pace about the large room.

"A damned coal merchant!" Peveril shook his head as he walked. "Well, if that don't beat all!"

"I believe, Mr. Ramsbottom is a very successful supplier of coal, among other things," Mary added, managing to hold on to her gravity. "I gather that he made his original fortune as an owner of a coal mine in the North."

"Original fortune! Do you mean to say that he's got more than one?" He stood stock still and stared at her.

Her lips quivered, but she swallowed her laughter at his look of amazement and continued, "Yes, I believe so. He seems to have an interest in an astonishing number of ventures all over the country."

Peveril's jaw had been hanging open. He suddenly clamped his lips shut as the implications hit him. "And this deuced cit has the effrontery to judge me! And demand his daughter wed a nob! Why, if that ain't the outside of enough! Damme, the fellow's a damned nail! A jumped up mushroom to have such cheek!" he thundered, forgetting to moderate his language in Mary's presence.

Mary decided to give him the truth with the bark off. "Mr. Ramsbottom also has a vast dislike, a morbid fear you could almost say, of fortune hunters, or those whom he perceives as fortune hunters. He has given me to understand that he will only approve a suitor for his daughter, if that gentleman's own financial house is in order."

"The deuce you say. Blast it all, this is a fine kettle of fish!" Peveril had a sudden presentiment that

Belinda's father would never approve of his suit when that gentleman returned and discovered the widely-known state of his finances. There was certainly nothing secret about his dealings with the world—he was forever behindhand. He took another turn about the room and rubbed his hand through his hair.

"A cit to deny me!" he exclaimed in unthinking anger, giving Mary an idea that all was not well with the state of his finances, after all. "Burn it, I ain't some shocking loose screw like some I could name, you know! Have a title and a house in the country. Family name goes back generations. You ain't hinting old Ramsbottom won't approve of me?" Peveril demanded fiercely.

"My lord, I have no idea if Mr. Ramsbottom will approve your courtship of Belinda, or not. But I thought, after your brave deeds on our behalf the other night, I should warn you of what to expect." Mary desperately wanted him to understand why she was telling him what she had. She merely wanted to spare him disappointment and pain, if she could.

"Grr." Peveril made an inarticulate noise in his throat, not much mollified by her explanation. "Fellow ain't got a title. No one's ever heard of him," he complained with a slight frown. "Man's a clunch to think I'm a fortune hunter. Why, I didn't even know his lay when she bowled me ov—er, that is, when I decided to court Miss Ramsbottom."

Mary gave him a bright look. She believed him entirely. He was not a fortune hunter, only a very free and easy and quite heedless young gentleman.

While Peveril was in this rare contemplative mood

another thought struck him. "The old skint don't mistreat you, does he?" He stopped before Mary and looked down at her in narrow-eyed concern. She was just a little thing. Sweet. He wouldn't put it past such a nasty old clutch-fisted geezer as she had described to use her like a damned drudge.

"No, no, my lord. He only hired me to see that Belinda was introduced to the *ton.* He pays me well and it is not an onerous duty, for the most part."

"And you're no relation to the family?"

"Oh no, indeed not," Mary denied with a wry look.

"What's a little thing like you setting up as a companion for, anyway? Said you had a season. Must have connections with the *ton.*" Miss Marlowe had piqued his interest. He peered down at her, trying to understand her. "What's happened to your family?"

"I'm afraid I'm on my own now, Lord Lindford. My parents died when I was quite young," she answered warily, at the same time feeling unaccountably pleased by his concern.

"Why aren't you staying with your relations then? Must have some. Had a come-out, after all. Can't you go to any of these relations who sponsored you when you came up to town to make your bow?"

"Er, I have several relatives I *could* go to, but I don't choose to at the present time."

"Cast you out for some reason, have they?" Peveril began to feel a concern for Belinda's companion which surprised him.

"No, indeed. It is just that I am at loggerheads with my grandfather at present."

At his look of inquiry she continued, "He desires me to make a match I want no part of. I am asserting my independence, you see," she told him with a disarming smile and a gleam of laughter in her eyes, "and making my own way in the world."

"The deuce you say! This sounds very bad to me," Peveril asserted with feeling. "Young chit like you out on her own, working as a drudge in some deuced old skint's household."

"No, no, my lord. Mr. Ramsbottom is a generous employer—he doesn't stint me in wages and other perks. I have been enjoying myself since we came up to town at the beginning of October. I've never been in London during the little season before."

"Belinda stands your friend though, I'll be bound. She would, wouldn't she? She's such a glorious creature. Heart's bound to be soft. An angel, after all!"

"We rub along tolerably well together," Mary hedged, not liking to mention that she found her charge a brainless peagoose, stubborn and demanding one moment, a wilting watering pot the next, who hardly knew her own mind. She hoped the viscount would soon discover for himself that Belinda was a spoiled beauty who was foolish almost past bearing.

Peveril was in no mood to question Mary further. He went off in a dream of capturing the beauty's hand, despite this new difficulty. He stared straight ahead at the painting of a buxom Lady Claremont portrayed as an alluring Aphrodite hanging over the Adam mantlepiece in front of him. In his abstraction, he took no note of the outrageously flattering portrait.

"What am I to do to win her, Miss Marlowe?" he asked in an anxious voice.

Mary was not immune to his plea, but she didn't wish to raise false hopes. "Convince Mr. Ramsbottom that you are no fortune hunter, that you will never ask him for money, and that you will be able to provide well for Belinda and give her the social position he desires."

"Thunderation! Is that *all?"* he asked sarcastically. "A mere bagatelle!" He snapped his fingers, but his features were grim and his eyes blazed with a hot light. It seemed he would need an amazing turnaround in his luck at the gaming tables to stand a chance of capturing the Beauty's hand.

"Perhaps if I explain to Mr. Ramsbottom how you and Mr. Throckmorton beat off the footpads, he will look on your suit more favorably."

"You'll stand my friend with old Ramsbottom, then?" he asked Mary with an entreating look in his blue eyes as he came to stand before her. "And my ally with Miss Belinda?"

He asked so winningly, Mary couldn't refuse. He was so like Theo.

"Of course, my lord," she said, her generous smile lighting up her face. "It would be the least I could do, after the way you and Mr. Throckmorton rescued us, putting yourselves in danger on our behalf."

In a fit of spontaneous gratitude in keeping with his nature, Peveril seized Mary by the waist and twirled her about, giving her an exuberant hug and planting a kiss of gratitude on her soft cheek as he set her on her feet. "You're a bang-up good sport, Miss Marlowe!" he exclaimed gratefully. "A real Trojan!"

An electric jolt shot through Mary as she felt Lindford's strong hands at her waist and the light touch of his lips against her face. She blinked at him in surprise but he had turned away, anxious to return to the ballroom and Belinda.

Later, as Mary lay in bed thinking over the events of the evening, she smiled, then sighed as she recalled the viscount's friendly embrace. He was an engaging young man, all right, and she had been charmed. Thoroughly reckless, of course. Foolish Belinda was no fit wife for an impulsive young gentleman like Lindford, though. She hoped he would soon get over his *tendre,* for his pursuit of Belinda in any case was like to prove futile. She would be sorry if such an appealing, friendly gentleman were to be made unhappy.

"Goodness! Do I actually envy Belinda his regard?" she asked herself in guilty surprise—and blushed as she gazed up at the canopy covering her bed. She admitted to herself that she did find him attractive and enjoyed being in his company. But such lovelorn thoughts would never do! "Don't be a goosecap, my girl," she admonished herself, vowing to put such nonsensical ideas from her mind, before she should find herself with a severe case of the blue devils. "He's naught but a charming, heedless boy."

"Trotting pretty hard after the new heiress, ain't you, Pev?" asked his friend Jeremy Fletcher as he sat with Peveril and Percy in Brook's, their gentlemen's club, at number Sixty, St. James Street.

The viscount and his cronies had retired to the club to indulge in a pint or two of good ale to slake their thirst after the hard work of Lady Claremont's ball.

"Hang it all, Jer! Didn't know till tonight that old

Ramsbottom has a fortune he intends to leave the chit!"

"Where've you been, Pev? On the moon?" Jeremy asked in surprise. "Old man's rich as Golden Ball. Gossip's been all over town for the past fortnight and more since the Beauty first appeared. She's attractin' suitors like bees to honey. Seems Exford followed her to town from Sidmouth, or some such place. Wager-in's been heavy that he has the inside track, from what I hear. Not that he needs the blunt, what with that enormous pile of his down in Devonshire filled with treasures and all the income from the dukedom."

"Exford! That dry old stick! He's old enough to be her father. That curst Fowler and Nichols, too, been hanging' around her. She wants none of them, though. Think she favors me. Told me I was like some dashed fellow in one of her story books," Peveril told them proudly.

A reminiscent smile played about his lips as he thought back to the ball. After his dance with Mary, he had returned to the ballroom and found Belinda all glittering smiles for him. She had favored him for the remainder of the evening and he had even managed to kiss her when they had succeeded in slipping behind the window curtains unnoticed. Well, the kiss had been a mere peck, he admitted. But still and all, surely the divine Belinda didn't grant her favors indiscriminately. He considered it a positive sign that she returned his regard in equal measure.

"You from a book, Pev? Don't seem likely," Percy said with a bewildered look on his face.

"Probably means the hero in one of those dashed marble-backed novels all the ladies are readin' nowadays. M'mother's forever got her nose in one, though she denies it and calls them rubbish. Forbids my sister, Ellen, to look at them, too, but I think Ellie's taken a peek at one or two of Mama's cast-offs." Jeremy laughed as he recalled the guilty look on his sensible mother's face when he had come upon her unexpectedly one afternoon when she was devouring the newest release from the Minerva Press.

"Picked up one of those dashed books by mistake once," Percy admitted sheepishly. "Couldn't get the hang of it at all, what with ladies faintin' all over the place and devilish loose screws tryin' to take advantage of 'em. Couldn't see the sense in it. Gave up after about ten pages. Don't see how you'd fit into one of the dashed silly stories at all, Pev."

"You didn't continue reading long enough, Percy," Jeremy advised him. "You didn't get to the hero. He comes in and saves the maiden from the disasters that have overtaken her."

"Eh? You sayin' Pev is like one of those heroes, Jer?"

"Well, I suppose Miss Ramsbottom must think so."

Peveril looked pleased that Belinda thought him like a hero in a novel. "Mean to drop the handkerchief, Jer," Peveril confessed.

Jeremy whistled between his teeth. "So you're serious. Guess this calls for a toast then," he decided, raising his glass in a salute. "To the Beauty."

"The Incomparable Beauty," Percy and Peveril repeated as they all raised their glasses, then drank deep.

"And to your happiness, Pev," Jeremy continued. "May the divine Belinda make a conformable wife and be as easy to live with as she is to look upon . . . and may her temperament be as beautiful as her face and form!" Jeremy toasted. "Hope that beauty of hers ain't only skin deep," he mumbled under his breath.

"Hear, hear!" joined in Percy, tapping his hand on the table to second Jeremy's toast, though he suspected the hope that Miss Ramsbottom would be conformable was futile. He had seen the flash of temper in her eyes and her pouting lips directed at him tonight when he had broken up her *tête-à-tête* with Pev. He gave a little shiver at the memory. Likely to turn into a termagant, if he knew anything about it—one of those women who scared him silly and had him running for cover with their constant complaining and carping.

"When do you mean to pop the question, Pev?" Jeremy inquired.

"Soon's old Ramsbottom returns to town."

"Wonder when he's gonna turn up?" Percy asked, looking down owlishly at the dregs in his glass.

"Wish I knew, Percy. Hope it'll be soon. This waitin' to know my fate is a devilish business. Wouldn't wish it on my worst enemy. Can't keep kickin' my heels here much longer, at any rate, once the Beauty's accepted me." Peveril continued. "Must go home and see about putting High Acres in order. Got to find a way to make my ancestral estate profitable so I can provide for a wife and family."

"You ain't thinking of turnin' respectable, are you, Pev?" Perce asked, shocked to the soles of his feet at such an unprecedented idea.

The viscount grinned ruefully. "Guess that's just what I'm gonna do, Percy."

"Damme! Never thought I'd live to see the day you talked about becoming a farmer, Pev!" Jeremy exclaimed. "Sounds devilish dull to me."

"Can't be helped, Jer. I've outrun the bailiff once too often. Got to make a recover somehow. Otherwise, don't stand a chance with the Beauty. Her skint of a father will be sure to turn me off. Going to have to try my luck in the hells, as it is, to pay off the worst of my debts. Got to have some ready cash, as well, and, by jingo, I've got to buy Belinda an engagement ring, too! Going to have to be a diamond of the first water, worthy of her beauty, too, not some trumpery thing."

"Might try the Club House," Percy said suddenly, naming the fashionable new gaming club that had recently opened its doors a little further along St. James Street at Bennet Street. "Dashed select establishment. Could be just the place to make a quick recover."

"That's a deuced good idea, Perce!" Peveril exclaimed, not used to ideas of any sort, good, bad or indifferent, coming from his slow-witted friend.

"I don't know, Pev," Jeremy warned cautiously. "Play's devilish deep there. Might get yourself deeper in dun territory. Why don't you talk to your man of business first, and see what he can suggest."

"Talk to old Canning? You can't be serious, Jer! He'll give me such a bear garden jaw my ears will be sore for a week, and he'd likely pack me off to Hertfordshire before I could turn around, much less have a chance to fix my interest with the Beauty! No, thank you. I'd rather take my chances at the tables."

* * *

"Nice little thing, Miss Marlowe," Percy remarked absently as he sat in the viscount's sitting room the following morning, enjoying a late breakfast.

"You think so, Percy?" Peveril answered without considering the matter. He was in a buoyant mood this morning. He had been uncommonly lucky at the gaming tables at the Club House whither he and his friends had repaired for what remained of the previous night. Percy had gone along to urge him on, Jeremy to try to restrain him. He was particularly pleased that he had made a packet at piquet from one of Belinda's most persistent suitors, Peregrine Fowler. The man had shown some animosity toward him and made one or two ugly comments, but Peveril had shrugged them off. He was pleased with all the world this morning. All seemed to be in better train for his courtship.

"Yes, I do. Danced with her last night, you know. A sensible chit. Not at all puffed up in her own esteem, like some I could name. Easy to be with."

Peveril looked keenly at his friend. It was unlike Percy to show so much admiration for a female. An idea occurred to him. "Been thinkin', Percy," he said meaningfully, laying his knife and fork down and tilting back in his chair.

"Eh?" Percy exclaimed in astonishment. "What do you want to do a deuced rum thing like that for at this time of the morning, Pev?" Percy yawned. "Dangerous thing to do. Ain't even properly awake yet."

"Want you to call on Miss Marlowe, Percy," Pev

continued, unfazed by Percy's gabble. "Ask her to go out driving with you, or some such thing."

"Here, I say, Pev! Ain't in my line!" Percy protested, looking ready to strangle on his neckcloth. His cheeks were beet red.

The viscount waved off his friend's heated objections. "I ain't allowed to call on the divine Belinda, but you might call on her companion with no thought of being turned away. Would be a way for me to get a foot in the door."

"No, no. Not your man, Pev. Do better to ask Jer."

"Do it for a friend, Percy?" Peveril wheedled. "How else am I to get near enough to fix my interest with the Beauty and beat out all her other admirers?"

The amiable and accommodating Mr. Throckmorton reluctantly agreed, knowing there was no point in arguing with Pev once he'd set his mind on a thing.

Chapter 7

" 'Morning, Miss Ramsbottom! You look like a ray of sunshine this morning! Just the ticket to warm us all up on this dashed chilly day!" Peveril, wearing a flirtatious smile on his face, hailed Belinda just as she and Mary were about to ascend into the Ramsbottom town coach that stood in the street in front of her father's house. Percy, standing behind his friend, mumbled a greeting to the ladies, too.

"Oh gwacious, Lowd Lindfowd! Here you are again!" Belinda exclaimed with a giggle, accepting the outstretched arm of the viscount when he had turned from greeting Mary and clapped his curly-brimmed beaver hat on his head once again.

"This yeller thing you're wearin' is very fetching. Don't recall seeing it before. Is it new?" Peveril asked, appreciatively eyeing her bright yellow three-quarter length pelisse trimmed with soft white ermine fur.

"Oh, yes. I saw it in a shop when I was out with Dukey and I weally had to have it." Belinda twirled about, showing off her outfit, taking care to allow the long white feather in the matching casquet she wore over her bright ringlets to remain at just the right angle as she moved.

Percy silently mused that the Beauty must have selected her headgear to match the plumes her father's coach horses wore over their heads.

"Most becoming," the viscount complimented her again, though he was not best pleased to hear she'd been out with Exford again.

"How did you know just when we would be leaving, my lowd?" Belinda asked with a coquettish lift of her brows.

"Must've been fate!" he replied with a grin for Belinda and a sidelong look and wink at Mary. "Always conspiring to throw us together."

Belinda promptly invited the gentlemen to accompany her and Mary on their shopping excursion to New Bond Street, saying they would come in useful. "For I'm planning to buy ever so many shawls and hats and wibbons. You can carwy all my packages for me," she said happily, as though conferring a treat of the highest order.

Mary smiled ruefully, thinking that the viscount and his ever-present companion, Mr. Throckmorton, had appeared on the scene as if on cue yet again. After the ball at Lady Claremont's, she and Belinda could not take a step out of the house without encountering Lindford. As often as not, Mr. Throckmorton, was with him, too.

During the day, she and Belinda might come upon the two gentlemen in the park or in Gunter's or perhaps in one of the exclusive shops along Bond Street. And in the evening, the viscount and his friend were sure to be in attendance at any entertainment on offer, be it the theatre, the opera, or a private soirée, on the few occasions when Mary had been able to secure invitations to such exclusive gatherings.

Belinda accepted Lindford's appearances on the scene unquestioningly, seeing them as delightful coincidences, but Mary thought these innocent meetings too numerous and too well-timed to be accidental. Her suspicions centered upon a little man whom she frequently saw peeping from behind the trees and lurking about in the square in front of the Curzon Street house. Once she had seen him in conversation with one of Mr. Ramsbottom's housemaids. She was sure the fellow was in the employ of the viscount. However, she didn't know how to stop the man's spying, or indeed if there was any reason she should attempt to do so.

Mary didn't chide Belinda for her invitation to the gentlemen today. Strictly speaking, she felt that these informal meetings did not violate her employer's orders. Her conscience was clear. Lindford did not *formally* call on Belinda nor act as her official escort on the occasions when they were together.

Meantime, the viscount's friend, Mr. Throckmorton, had suddenly taken to calling on *her*. He had begun issuing garbled invitations to come out driving with him and asking her to allow him to escort her to some entertainment or other, always hinting that he would not be averse to Miss Ramsbottom's accompanying them, too.

Mary was hardly flattered, instead choosing to be vastly amused by his unexpected attention. She didn't have to cudgel her brains too strenuously to know that he came at Lindford's bidding and that his visits were another ploy on the viscount's part to be near her charge. She refused Percy's invitations for the most part, explaining that her time was not her own, but she took great care not to hurt the kind gentleman's feelings in the process.

Once or twice, she had gone out for a brief drive with him when Belinda was busy with her modiste or her hairdresser. Percy was a pleasant, easy-going gentleman, and although it seemed he was unused to entertaining ladies from his many slips of the tongue and lapses into unintelligible cant phrases, Mary thoroughly enjoyed herself when she was in his company, always finding his unorthodox conversation highly entertaining.

"Belinda, Percy. Over here!" Emmy Belfours called out a greeting when Mary and Belinda alit in Bond Street for their shopping expedition that morning with the two gentlemen.

Emmy was standing across the street with her mother, Lady Belfours. The two parties merged to exchange compliments. Belinda was not a favorite with most young ladies, but she got along well with Emmy. When the two young ladies met, they would put their heads together and giggle as they exchanged confidences and the latest gossip.

An inch or so shorter even than Mary, Emmy was a vivacious bundle of energy. Her dark blond hair was cut short and worn in a halo of curls about her always-smiling elfin face. Emmy reminded Mary of nothing so much as a dark-eyed sprite, always ready for mischief.

"Oh, you must come shopping with us, Emmy," Belinda invited the girl to join their party.

"May I, Mama?" Emmy asked. "Please?"

"I daresay it will be quite proper. Here's your own cousin, Percy, to take care of you. Though why I place any reliance on his sense, I know not."

Percy gave his aunt a wounded look. "Dash it, Aunt Belle. I ain't some shocking loose screw, you know. Know how to do the pretty well enough," he complained. "I'll take dashed good care of Emmy."

His aunt patted his arm. "Yes, I daresay you will, now I've put you in mind of your duty. And here's our dear Miss Marlowe. I place all my trust in her good sense. She'll make sure you young rapscallions don't land the girls in any mischief," Lady Belfours replied, trusting to Mary to impose some sense and propriety on the party.

The young people strolled off, Belinda on the viscount's arm, while Percy escorted Mary and his cousin.

The gentlemen soon grew tired of shopping and balancing an ever growing number of parcels in their arms. Peveril convinced Belinda that she would like nothing so much as some refreshment. He held out the temptation of one of her favorite treats—an ice at Gunter's Tea Shop. She clapped her hands and agreed that that was just what she wanted, no matter that it was not exactly the weather for ices. The party all cheerfully repaired to the popular establishment.

"Mama has finally agreed to hold a holiday ball. I've been teasing her to do so *forever,*" Emmy announced to them when they were all comfortably seated round a table.

"That's famous news, Em!" Percy exclaimed. "Aunt Belle gives dashed good parties! Hope she'll have those lobster patties your cook makes. I'm devilish fond of 'em."

"Oh, I'm sure she will, Percy. She always does. All of you are invited, of course," Emmy said gaily, knowing that her mama, unlike many other hostesses in town, had no objection to having the beautiful cit under her roof for an evening.

"Oh good! I love pawties!" Belinda exclaimed, clapping her hands. "When is it to be, Emmy?"

"Oh, a definite time hasn't been fixed yet, but as we're to spend the Christmas holidays at home in Wiltshire, it will have to be soon. Mama's already begun to write out lists and lists of things that must be done, so things are well in train. I'm to be in charge of making a kissing bough, so I will ask you to procure me some mistletoe, Percy," Emmy said with a mischievous look.

"Pleased to oblige, Em. Er, that is, if you'll tell me where I can find the dashed stuff," Percy said, looking perplexed.

They all laughed at his comical look.

Peveril turned to Belinda with an entreating look. "Let me be the first to request a dance with you at this party of Miss Belfours', Miss Ramsbottom, before any of your other dashed beaux beat me to it!"

"Well, if you are vewy nice to me, Lowd Lindfowd, pewhaps I'll dance with you *once* at Emmy's pawty." Belinda looked coyly up at him through her lashes.

"And what constitutes being very nice, Miss Ramsbottom?" Peveril asked with a naughty grin, making great play with his own eyes from under sleepy lids.

"Well, you might let me dwive your curwicle—" Belinda began in a wheedling tone, leaning toward him over the table so that they were gazing right into one another's eyes.

"That will do, Belinda," Mary interrupted them hurriedly. Their exaggerated flirtation had begun to attract embarrassing attention from surrounding tables. "I know you are eager to learn to drive but you must consult your father first about his wishes in the matter," Mary said firmly. "Even were Lord Lindford kind enough to offer to teach you, I'm afraid you could not accept."

"Lord! Don't want Pev to teach her anyway, ma'am. A cow-handed whipster. Rides well enough, but not handy with a team. Wouldn't have him in the FHC, you know," Percy confided in a voice loud enough to be heard by the whole room. "Jer's your man for the job, if you want to drive."

Peveril shot his friend an injured look. "My driving ain't that bad, Percy!" he complained.

"Yes, it is, Pev. No use denying it. Take the time you got your wheels caught in the side of a haywain—"

"Alright, I admit it." Peveril cut him off before he could relate all the embarrassing details. "Dash it! That story don't redound to my credit. Do much better to ask Fletcher, Miss Ramsbotom, as Percy says. 'Fraid patience ain't one of my virtues."

"Oh, but I'd so much rather *you* teach me,"

Belinda complained with a little moue of disappointment.

"Sorry, my dear. 'Fraid it just ain't on," Peveril apologized with a placating smile.

As the viscount wouldn't budge, even at her pretty pleading, Belinda soon turned her attention back to her sugared ice.

"Miss Marlowe, ma'am, pleased if you'd agree to go for a drive with me in the park this afternoon. And Miss Ramsbottom, too, of course," Percy spoke up after receiving a kick under the table and a significant look from the viscount.

"Well I . . ." Mary began. Percy had put her in an uncomfortable position. She really *must* stop allowing Belinda to be so much in the viscount's company, she thought guiltily, or her employer could rightly accuse her of disobeying his explicit instructions.

"Oh, do say yes, Marwy. We don't have any other plans and I'm sure Papa won't mind," Belinda prodded her.

Mary was afraid that Mr. Ramsbottom *would* mind, but she agreed nevertheless. It seemed that once she had relaxed her guard and allowed this easy camaraderie to develop between the viscount and Belinda, there was no putting a barrier up between them again and warning him off. Besides, she could not forget her promise to him at Lady Claremont's ball that she would stand his friend.

And so it was fixed that Percy would take up Mary and Belinda for a drive that afternoon. Mary had no doubt at all that the viscount would be in Percy's carriage when he called for them.

* * *

Lindford's star was still in the ascendant after the trip to Gunter's and their subsequent drive. With all the attention she received from so many eligible gentlemen, Mary was surprised that Belinda continued to favor him, but her decided penchant for his company had not flagged from their first dramatic meeting. It seemed she still retained the impression of him she had formed that first night. Namely, that he was just like a knight in shining armor whose timely and most romantic arrival on the scene of the attempted robbery was a sure sign that they were meant to be together. And if that were not enough, her information from Emmy that she was the envy of all the other unattached young ladies who had remained in town for the little season had only served to heighten Belinda's interest in the viscount, as did his reputation for wild, daring behavior. She considered it a decided feather in her cap to have captured his attention and to be so envied by her peers.

"He's all a gentleman should be!" Belinda remarked to Mary late the next morning. They were seated in Belinda's dressing room, waiting for her maid to help her dress for the day. "He's so handsome! So bwave and exciting! And *young*. Not a dull old dog, like Dukey."

Mary noticed that Belinda had recently taken to using this foolish diminutive to refer to the Duke of Exford. Before Lindford's arrival on the scene, his grace's exalted position had made him Belinda's favorite escort, but his star had slipped of late.

And, if her recent behavior were anything to go by,

Mary could almost credit that Belinda had actually fallen in love with the carefree young gentleman. She watched them carefully whenever they met and observed that they certainly behaved like a pair of billing and cooing lovebirds, batting adoring eyes at one another or flirting outrageously.

But often after praising Lindford to the skies, Belinda would stop, put her head on one side and her finger on her chin and enumerate all the advantages of becoming a duchess as opposed to a viscountess, and Mary would doubt the girl's ability to remain constant to any one man as yet, no matter how exciting and handsome. She thought Belinda was too flighty, too immature, to really know her own mind, and concluded that her charge wasn't really in love with Lindford, but just with the excitement of attracting the attentions of a popular, devil-may-care young man.

"If I marwy Pevewil, I'll be Lady Lindfowd," Belinda giggled, twirling round the room in her frilly dressing gown.

"Heavens, Belinda! Has Lord Lindford proposed without waiting to ask your father's consent first?" Mary exclaimed in surprise.

"No, silly. But he says I'm the most beautiful girl in the world and he can't live without me. So I think he *means* to ask me. Don't you, Marwy?"

"That very much remains to be seen. I hope you have not led Lord Lindford to believe you are free to engage yourself to him without your father's permission, Belinda."

Belinda tossed her head and turned to gaze at herself in a nearby looking glass.

"Oh dear, Belinda, I beg you not to set your heart on this match before your father returns and gives his consent," Mary said, hoping to make her charge see reason. "You would not want to risk disappointing both yourself and the viscount, would you?"

"Fiddle! I'm sure once Papa returns, he'll agwee to my betwothal. He won't wefuse, when I tell him it's what I want," Belinda declared with assurance. Her eyes were focused far away, as she dreamed of herself in her silk wedding gown. "Papa always lets me have my own way, in the end."

Mary didn't take such a sanguine view. Belinda's memory was not quite accurate. Mr. Ramsbottom was a positive genius at persuading his daughter that what *he* wanted was what she had most desired all along.

"You must allow Pevewil to call on me here at the house, Marwy!" Belinda came back to the present and looked over at her companion with a sulky expression on her face, marring her perfect features.

"You know that your father will not allow it, until he has met the gentleman for himself," Mary repeated wearily. No matter how many times she attempted to explain to Belinda that Mr. Ramsbottom's very explicit orders made it impossible for the viscount to formally call at the house, Belinda would frown and complain at such an unfair edict. Mary's rational words frequently resulted in a storm of tears, or a bout of name-calling from Belinda, who accused Mary of trying to thwart young love.

"Oh, you're just being mean!" she complained predictably. "You act like an old maid who's never been in love!"

Mary had learned it did no good whatsoever to attempt to argue with her charge when she was out of humor. So she did not point out that it hardly mattered that Lindford did not call at the house. Belinda met him everywhere anyway, and was more in his company of late than in that of any of her approved suitors.

Belinda smiled at herself in the glass. She might complain about Lindford's not being allowed to call on her openly, but in truth she reveled in the air of secrecy surrounding the assignations she made with him to meet her at various places. It was thrilling to meet the so-handsome and so-devoted viscount in this clandestine manner. It was as good as one of the stories in her favorite books, she decided.

"Pevewil says my eyes are like the sea with the sun shining on it and my lips are like wosebuds. He's ever so womantic, you know," she told Mary complacently. "And he can kiss like—well, never mind. I won't tell you *that!*" Belinda put her hand to her mouth and giggled.

Belinda relished the delicious knowledge that she had succeeded in her plan to get the viscount to kiss her. Their first kiss had been a mere touch of the lips. But the second had been a fiery embrace with all the ardor she could have wanted. She shivered as she remembered it, a little frightened of her hot-blooded suitor after that one passionate encounter.

Startled, Mary exclaimed, "You've allowed Lindford to kiss you? Oh, Belinda, you must not. Really, my dear, you must not. Whatever will the viscount think of you, to be granting kisses so freely? And, you know that if you were observed, you will soon be the subject of unpleasant gossip and your reputation will be severely damaged."

"Oh, pooh! Little you know about it. Have you ever been kissed, Marwy?" Belinda asked boldly, sensing that her own experience was greater than her companion's. "I would wager you haven't."

Mary looked at Belinda helplessly. She could not answer. In all her two-and-twenty years, she had never been kissed on the lips by a gentleman. She remembered how the viscount had so impulsively embraced her and kissed her on the cheek at the Claremont ball, and the idea of her young charge experiencing his lovemaking gave her an odd sensation in her midsection, like butterflies let loose and fluttering around madly. She tried to ignore the feeling.

"Really, Belinda, you mustn't let a gentleman kiss you at all, until you are betrothed," she admonished.

"Why not? I like him ever so much."

"But you'll give the gentleman the wrong idea of your morals. He'll consider you fast, and you don't want that, do you?"

"No," Belinda answered doubtfully, wondering why it would be considered fast to engage in such a pleasurable activity.

"Well, the viscount may well think you forward, if you continue to allow him liberties of that nature. And your father would be very displeased, if it should come to his attention, for you might well ruin your chances for a brilliant match in the *ton*."

"Oh," Belinda answered airily with a toss of her gleaming blonde ringlets, "I can handle Papa."

"Well, if you say so, but your papa can be quite formidable on occasion," Mary reminded her.

Belinda looked conscious for a moment, then assumed her airy expression again and dismissed Mary with a wave of her hand.

Oh, lord, Mary thought in alarm, was the foolish girl so set on a match with the viscount, then? She had been sure that Belinda, so predictably fickle, would forget her infatuation in a week.

She wondered how her employer would react to the situation when he returned to London. He had been so hugely satisfied when his daughter attracted the attention of the Duke of Exford. To have a duke for a son-in-law—and the prospect of an heir to a dukedom as his grandson—would have been the crowning climax to Mr. Ramsbottom's lofty ambitions. She could not imagine that he would let go of the dream to settle for a viscountcy, and possibly an impoverished one at that.

It was the end of October already, Mary recollected. Mr. Ramsbottom's return could not be much longer delayed, she thought with some apprehension.

Chapter 8

"Brr! It's deuced cold to be out walking today, Miss Marlowe. Seems old man winter's decided to put in an early appearance this year," Peveril remarked to Mary as they strolled along in Hyde Park just behind Belinda and Peregrine Fowler. The viscount was holding onto his hat with his free hand to keep it from blowing off in the fierce wind. "Hard to believe it's only autumn."

"Yes, it is cold. Unseasonably so. Though I suppose we must expect it. It *is* the end of October, after all," Mary replied, shivering a bit in her serviceable grey woollen cloak. "And I must point out, my lord, that it was your choice to come with us."

"Don't know what possessed me. Must have been all about in my head!" he agreed, looking down at her with an exaggerated expression of frozen stiffness on his face and giving her a wink.

"The wind does have quite a bite, doesn't it?" she asked, her lips curving up in a playful smile.

"Bite? It has dashed foot-long fangs that seem to have lodged right inside my coat!"

They both laughed.

The viscount had turned up at the Ramsbottom residence in Curzon Street just as Peregrine Fowler was handing the ladies into his elegant closed town carriage. Belinda, showing a deplorable lack of good manners, disregarded Mr. Fowler's prior claim on her attentions, and invited Lindford to accompany them.

Lindford had brazenly accepted her impromptu invitation, to Fowler's fury. Fowler had glared at his rival and made one or two rude comments and even issued a cold set down as the viscount prepared to step into the vehicle after the ladies, but Lindford had taken no notice. Instead, he had vaulted inside and seated himself comfortably beside Mary and proceeded to engage both ladies in light conversation to Fowler's furious irritation.

Fowler found there was little he could do to depress the audacious behavior of his rival. But when they had all stepped down from the carriage for their walk in the park, he had taken great satisfaction in taking Belinda on his arm and strolling off with her at a brisk pace, soon outstripping Lindford and Miss Marlowe.

Peveril felt he had scored a minor victory over the obnoxious Fowler and was now content to be strolling along with Mary while he kept the Beauty in his eye.

Mary was not surprised to find herself walking along alone with Lindford once again with her hand resting in the crook of his elbow. It had become his habit to attach himself to her when her charge was with another gentleman. She had been amazed at first to find that the viscount favored her with his attentions whenever Belinda was otherwise engaged, but she had soon grown accustomed to his behavior.

Whenever they were at dancing parties, she knew that she could count on him to ask her to stand up with him for two sets, one of which was usually the supper dance. She didn't flatter herself that it was for the pleasure of her own company that he asked for that particular dance, but realized that he used the simple expedient of claiming her hand so that he could join her and Belinda at their supper table, where Belinda would be with one of her approved suitors. And whenever he joined them when they were at the theatre or standing about in a group, if Belinda were talking to another gentleman, Lindford would talk to Mary instead. But at other times, rather than turning his attention to some other young lady, he seemed to seek her out solely for the pleasure of her company and conversation.

Mary had to confess that she had come to look forward to his attentions. He was always an engaging, light-hearted companion. She suspected that he wanted to ingratiate himself with her so that she would help him in his campaign to win Belinda's hand. But, to be fair, she had to admit that he seemed to feel happy in her presence, and did not constantly prose on about his devotion to Belinda. Instead, he entertained her by relating amusing anecdotes about his boon companion, the Honorable Percival, and his other friends, and in general seemed to have some care for her comfort when they were together. And lately he had taken to teasing her wickedly, twitting her about what a sensible and proper little chaperone she was, just to put her to the blush.

As they walked along in the almost deserted park, Mary noticed that Lindford was using his free hand to adjust the scarf he wore round his neck, pulling it up to cover his chin and the tips of his ears that were exposed to the chill air beneath the brim of the elegant beaver hat he wore.

"No doubt Belinda will beg to return to the carriage in another minute or two, my lord. It is just that she has a new Russian mantle trimmed with chinchilla fur she wishes to show off, and, unfortunately, she could not bear to wait for a day more suited for a walk through the park," Mary told him in a dry tone, noting that there were few people out and about today to admire Belinda's expensive finery.

Peveril did not catch the implicit criticism. "Always dressed in the first stare, is Miss Ramsbottom. Takes the shine out of all the other ladies," he said with his eye on the girl ahead of them who was leaning perceptibly closer to Fowler's shoulder.

Unwittingly imitating the couple ahead, Peveril pulled Mary closer to his side and tucked her hand more snugly into the crook of his elbow. He was quite content to have the sweet little Miss Marlowe on his arm today. He had grown comfortable with her and, all unconsciously, he had begun to look forward to her company as much as to Belinda's. With the Beauty to look at and Mary to talk to, he enjoyed the best of all possible worlds.

A hint of rose just touched Mary's cheeks at his intimate action. She gave him a quizzical look from under the rim of her cloak's hood. She saw that he was still watching Belinda and seemed all unconscious of how tightly he was pressing her to him.

"Yes, Belinda is fortunate. She can afford the best clothes money can buy. But there's no denying that she would look lovely even in rags," Mary agreed with an honest assessment.

"Not to say you don't always look well, Miss Marlowe!" Peveril cried hastily, abashed that he had unthinkingly offered his companion an insult.

She laughed. "Oh, do not think to offer me Spanish coin, Lord Lindford. I have no illusions about my wardrobe or my appearance."

"Burn it! Nothing wrong with your appearance, Miss Marlowe," he asserted, turning his eyes away from Belinda to stare down fully into Mary's gentle eyes. They looked enormous in her glowing face. "Always look a treat, you do," Peveril added, trying to find his way out of the muddle his thoughtless words had created.

"Gammon!" she said, her smile wide. "No need to perjure yourself, my lord."

He saw the disbelieving smile on Mary's face and grinned down at her. "You ain't disparaging my word, by any chance, ma'am?" he queried, still grinning. He lifted his hand and touched his gloved finger to her little nose briefly.

Mary was quite unable to utter a word.

"You're a taking little thing, Mary Marlowe," he said spontaneously, realizing the undeniable truth of his casual words with surprise as they left his mouth.

Mary blushed scarlet. She could feel a pulse beating furiously in her throat at such praise from him.

"Got no business setting up as a companion. Thought you was a sensible chit, but now I come to think on it, must have windmills in your head to do such a thing!" he exclaimed. "You're the granddaughter of an earl, after all."

"Not windmills, my lord, only a stubborn insistence on not being dictated to in the matter of choosing my husband," Mary told him.

"Old man tryin' to force you, eh? Well, I can't blame you for refusin' to knuckle under. Daresay, I'd do the same myself, if I were in your shoes."

"Well, as to that, the less said, the better," Mary replied sensibly, regretting her impulsive words of a moment before. She didn't want to drag him into her affairs. She was doing all she could, using all the resources at her command, to make the best of her present difficulties, and she didn't want Lindford to feel sorry for her, as though she were some timid creature who couldn't stand up for herself.

"Confidences at an end, eh? Well, just remember, I'll stand your champion should any of these dashed highhanded relatives of yours land in on you all unwanted and try to force your hand."

"Th—thank you, my lord," Mary said, embarrassed and touched by his warm offer of friendship. "It is kind of you to offer."

"Make some lucky devil a bang-up wife one day," he continued impulsively. "If it weren't for Miss Ramsbottom, would lay siege to you myself!" he declared in a rallying tone, clearly remembering Percy's words of praise for her, "Got a friendly face and a friendly nature—a man can feel comfortable with her," though he didn't repeat them aloud.

"You, my lord, are a shameless flirt," Mary responded briskly to this outrageous declaration as she tried to overcome her confusion. She was desperately attempting to cover the breathlessness she felt at his touch and hoped he could not tell how deeply his light words had affected her.

"And you're even prettier when you scold! Puts the roses in your cheeks," Peveril teased on, trying to see if he could deepen that attractive blush that was staining her cheeks. "Got a way with you, sweet Mary," he said, boldly using her given name. His very blue eyes twinkled down at her and he squeezed her arm even more tightly against himself.

Mary turned her head away from his interested gaze and tried not to react to the feel of her body pressed all along the length of his. "No need to use your flummery to try to turn me up sweet, Lindford," she said as calmly as she could. "I've not opposed your friendship with Belinda, though perhaps it was my duty to do so."

"That's true. You've been a real trump, ma'am!" he replied gratefully. "With all her other beaux running tame round her the whole time, think I'd be ready to take myself to the devil by now, if I didn't have you to stand my friend!"

Mary's heart twisted painfully at these words and she thought ironically that he had revealed her *true* value to him. It was as she had always known—through her, he was able to enjoy Belinda's company.

All unaware of how he had made Mary's heart ache with his teasing, Peveril was feeling pleased. Really, he thought with a small smile to himself, little Miss Marlowe was the kind of lady he hadn't come across before. Friendly. Dependable. Easy to talk to. A fellow knew where he stood with her, not like her friend there, who recently had run hot and cold when she was in his company. Just lately he was beginning to find the beautiful Miss Ramsbottom's fits and starts just a trifle tedious.

"Look! I do believe Belinda is waving us toward the carriage. It's about time! I'm feeling frozen to the bone, are not you, my lord?" Mary said with relief, gathering up her skirt an inch or two with her free hand, preparing to stride rapidly to the waiting vehicle.

Mary went home with her cheeks burning after Lindford's careless remarks. Really, he had a loose tongue to say such warm things to her. A less level-headed woman might have taken him seriously, she scolded herself. But there was a warmth in her breast toward the charming rascal, that no amount of sensible counsel could overcome. He had but to smile that boy's charming grin of his and look at her with his head a little to one side, his blue eyes twinkling, to set her pulses fluttering madly.

She had learned much about his character, both from her own observations and from the confidences freely bestowed on her by the Honorable Percival and his giddy cousin, Emmy. And nothing she had learned about Lindford diminished her favorable but clear-headed opinion of him.

She had seen for herself that Lindford was friendly and open in his manners, impetuous and a bit thoughtless in his behavior, perhaps, but never mean spirited or spiteful.

She couldn't help remembering how Emmy had repeated Percy's praise for his friend to her only the previous evening. "Pev's purse is always open, though he ain't often above the high water mark, himself. Can always count on him to help a fellow out when he's in a bind."

And she recollected Lady Belfours' comment, "Oh, my dear, there's no real harm in young Lindford, for all his supposedly wild ways. He's an amusing scamp, I'll admit, but for all his quick temper, he's just as quick to admit his fault. And he's generous to his friends, too . . . I'll lay odds he'll make a fascinatin' man when he grows up a trifle!" she had added with a laugh, tapping Mary on the hand with her fan for emphasis. "It'll be a lucky lady who'll net him some day."

Feeling restless the following afternoon, Peveril had Ajax saddled and headed out to Hyde Park, hoping there would be few people about so that he could indulge in a good gallop. He had been unable to winkle Percy out of his comfortable chair in front of the fire at Brooks's, and Jer was nowhere in sight, so he had gone alone.

There was a damp chill in the air on this bleak, overcast afternoon and traffic was not heavy in the park, but several closed carriages were being driven slowly along the carriage track, nonetheless. Peveril recognized Lady Belfours' heavy maroon landau, with its jointed heads snugly closed against the misty air, rumbling along with the other carriage traffic. He wheeled his horse around, and trotted over to ride alongside the landau.

"Well, Lindford, I see a little moisture ain't

enough to keep you sittin' at home," Lady Belfours hailed him. "Where's that lazy nephew of mine?" she asked in a booming voice.

"Catchin' forty winks at the club, if I know Perce, Lady Belfours," Peveril replied with a grin as he tipped his hat to the lady.

"And so would I imagine, too, you young dry boots!" Lady Belfours laughed loudly, then shouted to her coachmen, bidding him to pull up so the girls could say how-do to Lindford.

"Miss Ramsbottom, Miss Belfours," Peveril greeted the two girls who were seated in the landau with their backs to the horses. "Deuced brave of you to risk yourselves in this weather."

"Oh, we're snug enough, Lord Lindford," Emmy said with a wide smile. "It is you who risk taking a chill, as you're riding in this dreadful weather."

"It's worth a wettin' to see so much beauty before me," he said fulsomely, waving his hand to indicate all three ladies. "You ladies brighten up this demmed dull day."

"Oh, Lowd Linfowd," Belinda asked coyly, looking up at him through her lashes, "how did you know where to find me?"

"Just devilish good luck on my part," he replied, glancing at the empty seat next to Lady Belfours and noting the absence of Belinda's companion. "Where's Miss Marlowe?"

"Oh, Marwy's taken it into her head to cosset herself just because she has the tiniest little sniffle," Belinda answered dismissively. She frowned, remembering that she had almost been stuck at home all day with nothing to do. It was lucky that Emmy and her mother had called, otherwise she would not have been able to get out at all, with Mary in her bed, insisting that Belinda could not go out unaccompanied.

"Nonsense, Belinda," Lady Belfours contradicted gruffly, frowning at the girl. "Mary has developed a severe head cold, Lindford. I recommended she stay in bed for the next few days and have the cook brew her a posset. There's no sense in risking an inflammation of the lungs by taking herself out in this weather, just because this minx was feeling bored."

Belinda pouted and tossed her head at Lady Belfours' chastising words.

Lady Belfours was an easy-going woman who had seen no harm in her daughter's friendship with a cit, especially such a wealthy one, but she didn't like Belinda's uncaring tone toward her companion. Mary Marlowe was quality and Lady Belfours wouldn't sit by and hear her belittled by a chit like Belinda Ramsbottom.

"We'll miss her tonight," Peveril began thoughtlessly. He quickly amended what he had been going to say when he spotted the flashing eyes and look of annoyance on the Beauty's face directed at him. "Er, that is, guess you won't be attending the rout tonight, Miss Ramsbottom, without your companion?"

"Oh, but I will, Lindfowd. Emmy and Lady Belfours have asked me to accompany them," Belinda replied sweetly, giving Peveril the full benefit of her beguiling smile.

"That's splendid news! Wouldn't enjoy it above half, if you weren't there. You'll save a set for me, then?" he pleaded hoarsely, undone by her dazzling smile. When Belinda had coyly promised to do so, he tore his eyes from her lovely profile and turned to Emmy. "And beg the honor of a set with you, too, Em—I mean *Miss* Belfours. Er, that is, with your permission, Lady Belfours."

"Humph! About time you asked for someone's permission for something you wish to do, Lindford!" Lady Belfours exclaimed, "instead of careerin' heedlessly along, as you are wont to do."

"Oh, most adored lady, if I'd only known you'd been waitin' for me to ask, would've saved myself a heap of trouble, wastin' my time tryin' to turn these chits here up sweet," Peveril declared melodramatically. There was a gleam of fun in his eyes as he asked, "What do these green girls have to offer a man, that a lady with your maturity—er, mature charms—doesn't have a hundred fold, heh?" He arranged his features into a perfect picture of anxious supplication and with a gleam of wicked humor dancing in his blue eyes, pleaded "Take supper with me tonight, Belle, and make me the happiest of men!"

Lady Belfours shouted with laughter. "Get away with you, you young jackanapes! Save your flummery for gullible peagooses," she advised him with a shake of her finger. "Drive on, Hawkins," she called to her coachman, leaving Peveril gazing after the departing carriage with a large grin on his face.

The viscount and his friends adjourned to Brooks's that same evening after the rout. The three sat in deep leather chairs in front of a blazing fire in the hearth, with their feet comfortably resting on the table in front of them, sipping a rich golden brandy while they played a desultory game of three-handed whist.

Peveril was holding a hand of cards in front of him, but he wasn't concentrating on them. Something had been bothering him all evening. He had had a bit of a dust-up with the Beauty at the recent entertainment. And now he sat wondering how the beautiful girl could have changed from the most glorious angel one minute into an ill-natured crosspatch the next, right before his eyes.

All he had done after he'd said good evening to Belinda, was to ask her how her companion did. He had been taken aback when she narrowed her eyes, made a petulant remark about how Mary exaggerated her illness just to win sympathy, then accused him of being more interested in her dull little chaperone than he was in her.

His ready temper was roused at this unfair accusation. He had clamped his jaw shut on a criticism of her manners, turned on his heel and stomped off. Why the spoiled little ninnyhammer! he had thought with a spurt of anger. To become so pettish just because he had shown a polite interest in Mary's welfare!

He had then spent a decidedly flat evening chatting to and dancing with a lot of giggling schoolgirls while Belinda collected her usual crew of admirers around her and didn't glance once in his direction for the rest of the evening. He had gathered up Percy and Jeremy and taken his leave well before the evening was half over.

Now something else in addition to Belinda's pettish behavior was bothering him, but he couldn't put his finger on just what it was. It didn't occur to him that he had grown accustomed to another lady's company on such occasions and that he had missed her pleasant, soothing presence to a remarkable degree.

Chapter 9

Justin Didsbury-Marsh, a thin, highly-strung young man of a blond beauty to match Belinda's own, had called for Belinda and her companion to take them for a drive in the park this crisp November afternoon. He was tooling them along in his handsome phaeton, explaining some of the finer points of driving, when Belinda grasped his arm and interrupted him with a little squeal.

"Oh look, there's Sir Thomas Nichols and Mr. Wichard Wigley waving at me. Please may we stop for a minute, Didsey?"

At Belinda's prettily-phrased plea, Didsbury-Marsh pressed his lips together in annoyance, but nevertheless pulled the phaeton to a halt at the side of the carriage track as she requested so that she could chat with the gentlemen on horseback. They had been riding dangerously close to the vehicle, trying to have a word with her.

When Mr. Didsbury-Marsh stopped, Mary got down to stretch her legs, asking to be taken up again when they circled round the track. It was uncomfortably crowded in the carriage. Phaetons were never meant to hold three persons, she decided ruefully, supposing that it was just one of those little inconveniences a companion had to endure.

Mary knew from experience that Belinda would not be ready to move on for some time when she had a court of admirers dancing attendance on her, so she felt free to wander away from the phaeton and stroll along a pathway where a particularly fine display of red, yellow, orange, and gold autumnal colors in the hedges and trees had caught her eye.

When she glanced back to the phaeton, she was not at all surprised to see that Lindford had ridden up to join the two or three other horsemen gathered round Didsbury-Marsh's vehicle. She continued her walk.

As soon as her other admirers had ridden away, Peveril took the opportunity to ask Belinda to save him two sets of dances at the Mentmore-Jones' ball that was to be held that evening. Her ill-natured behavior at the rout was all but forgotten. He was preparing to turn his mount and ride off when he heard her teasing young Didsbury-Marsh to allow her to take the ribbons of his phaeton.

"As you've asked so prettily, my dear Miss Ramsbottom, and as you will have me to guide you as you attempt to learn to drive, I believe it will be safe enough for you to take the ribbons for one turn about the park," Didsbury-Marsh capitulated. "I shall keep my hands over yours, you see." He had a puffed-up sense of his own ability to handle the ribbons and thought it would be easy enough to teach her to drive, if she followed his instructions. Besides, he had learned to his discomfiture that the Beauty showed a disturbing inclination to pout if she weren't given her way. He didn't want to chance such a scene today, when it finally seemed he was making some headway with her.

Peveril took a long assessing look at the pair of white-stockinged chestnuts that were harnessed to the phaeton. He recognized them. In fact, he had been at Tatt's when they were sold about a sennight ago. His driving might leave something to be desired, but the viscount knew horseflesh. Showy and willful and not properly broke to the bit, he summed them up in disgust.

"I say, Miss Ramsbottom. Not thinking of trying to drive these showy bits of blood, are you?" Peveril asked disbelievingly, suddenly finding himself in the unusual position of urging caution on someone else.

"Yes, I am, Lindfowd. Why shouldn't I? Other ladies dwive their carwiges in the park," she insisted with a pout when she saw his heavy frown. "Why, look over there. There's Lady Wufus in a high-pewch phaeton!"

"Lady Rufus is not at all the thing," he told her severely, fighting a mad desire to lift her down from the phaeton and shake some sense into her. "These nags ain't docile enough for a beginner. Don't even think of carrying on with such a harebrained idea!" he thundered. "You'll end by breaking your neck!"

"You just want to spoil my fun," she accused pettishly, narrowing her eyes and frowning at him.

Feeling harassed, Peveril turned to Didsbury-Marsh. "Wouldn't let her do it, if I was you. Blast it, she'll likely break her neck, and ruin your horses' mouths into the bargain!"

"I see no harm in it, Lindford. I will have my hands over hers, after all," the young man answered huffily, disliking the viscount's proprietary air toward his fair passenger.

Seeing that Didsbury-Marsh would not refuse the foolish chit, Peveril wanted to shout at the young gudgeon to have more resolution in denying her such a dangerous treat. Feeling unaccountably irritated by the tricks the Beauty had used to get her way, he clamped his lips shut on a hot retort as Belinda and Didsbury-Marsh drove away. Trying to restrain someone else's mad starts was certainly a new come out for him, he thought with a shrug.

He ground his teeth together when he saw Didsbury-Marsh drive the pheaeton round to the other side of the park where there was less traffic along a straight section of the carriage way. "Silly chit," he muttered under his breath when he saw Belinda reach out for the reins, and wondered if it would be best, after all, if he followed them. He sat irresolute for a moment, but then out of the corner of his eye he saw Mary standing some distance away.

He turned his horse and rode over to where she stood near a blaze of red, orange and yellow shrubbery with her hands on her hips, gazing after her charge with a look of helplessness on her face.

"Hello, Mary. Hope you're feeling more the thing today," he addressed her as he came up to her and dismounted.

"Yes, I am, thank you, my lord." Her voice was still a little hoarse from her recent head cold. "But you mustn't encourage her in these mad starts, Lindford," Mary admonished him. "She has no more idea of how to drive than a baby!"

"*Me* encourage her! No such a thing! Used her tricks to cajole that young cawker Didsbury-Marsh into allowin' her to take the ribbons. I told her it was a deuced harebrained thing to do!"

"Oh, I see," Mary said with some chagrin. "I apologize, my lord. My scold is misplaced. I shall save my breath to ring a peal over Mr. Didsbury-Marsh's head."

"Told her it was foolish beyond permission, besides not being at all the thing for a chit to take the ribbons in that bold way. 'Fraid she wouldn't listen to me. Said it was a bang-up idea. All the crack for ladies to drive themselves. Tried to tell her they needed to learn what they were about first, but she took a pet, accused me of tryin' to spoil her fun."

Peveril halted in his animadversions on the subject, seeing that Mary was smiling at him with a twinkle in her grey eyes. He looked twice to make sure he did not mistake the hint of humor he saw there.

"You think *I* encourage her in these mad starts! I ain't such a sapskull, ma'am!" he protested. "Silly chit will break her neck and it's all that young gudgeon's fault for not having the gumption to stop her."

"Yes, but we both know that Belinda is hard to stop when she's got the bit between her teeth, my lord."

"You're in the right of it there, ma'am!" Peveril agreed wholeheartedly. "Unfortunately, it's Didsbury-Marsh's devilish cattle that have the bits between their teeth at the moment."

Mary looked away just then and gave a little cry of alarm. "Oh, my lord! The horses have run away with her!" She turned wide eyes toward the carriage that was racing out of control down the tan, heading their way.

"What the devil—" began Peveril, but then he too saw the runaway carriage.

They could both see Belinda screaming and holding onto her seat for dear life while the reins dragged on the ground under the horses' thundering feet. Didsbury-Marsh was no longer sitting beside her in the carriage.

"Blood and thunder!" Peveril exclaimed. He wasted not a second, but threw the reins over Ajax's head, leapt on his big bay, and galloped after the runaway phaeton. "I told the silly widgeon she would break her neck!" Mary heard him say furiously as he rode off.

"Oh, please take care, my lord!" Mary called after him, knowing his propensity for heedlessly throwing himself into the midst of danger.

Mary saw young Didsbury-Marsh running down the carriage track, a long way behind his runaway carriage, waving his arms frantically and shouting helplessly. She could only guess that Belinda had cajoled him into getting down while she plied her nonexistent skill, seeking to turn admiring eyes her way and create a new sensation. She had created a sensation, all right, but not the kind she had planned.

Not only the viscount, but three or four other brave (or foolhardy, depending on one's perspective) gentlemen galloped after the runaway phaeton as riders, carriages and pedestrians scattered in all directions, trying to get out of the way of the dangerously careering vehicle.

Lindford, riding in his typical neck-or-nothing style, reached the vehicle first. His mad gallop took him up along side the runaway horses. Risking life and limb, he was stretching out over the runaway team trying to grab the bridle of the lead horse.

Mary found that she was holding her breath. Her hands were clasped tightly to her breast and her heart was hammering against her ribs as she saw the viscount lean precariously out of his saddle. She watched with wide-eyed horror as she saw him slip to one side of his horse. It seemed as though he would lose his purchase in the saddle at any moment. She put her hands up to her mouth to stifle a scream. He would surely fall under the pounding hooves of the stampeding horses!

But, no! There! He had his hand on the lead horse's bridle and the phaeton was slowing. Thank God! She let out a shuddering breath, picked up her skirts and began to run toward the vehicle along with a crowd of others. Her head was in a whirl, but she knew she would have to give Belinda a blistering scold for this most foolish, perilous escapade.

"Thunderation! What in hell did you think you were about, you foolish chit?" Peveril shouted. His face was covered with sweat and his heart was pounding fit to burst from his chest as he jumped down from his mount and walked up to where Belinda sat shaking and crying in the now motionless phaeton.

Belinda's eyes were like saucers and her mouth fell open in shock at his words. Tears that had been streaming down her cheeks stopped abruptly. She had expected her gallant savior to lift her down into his arms and comfort her. She had expected him to tell her that she was safe now and that he had been frightened out of his senses for her, afraid that she would be killed or take some dreadful hurt.

Instead, Lindford was raging at her like a madman. He looked as though he would like to give her a good shake rather than comfort her.

"You could have gotten yourself killed, you foolish widgeon! or killed someone else!" he continued. "Don't you have enough sense in that yeller cockloft of yours to know better than to try to drive these devilish pieces of mischief! Or any horseflesh, for that matter!" he shouted at her, then felt like the worse kind of traitor to see crystal tears form in her lovely emerald eyes and begin to trickle down her porcelain cheeks.

Peveril took a deep breath, trying to calm his racing heart and his raging temper. "Deuce take it! Don't cry, for the Lord's sake! All we need is a fit of the vapors to top off this mad start of yours! Frightened me out of my wits, you did, when I saw you careering along like that!" he explained, feeling rather more like an older brother than a suitor, as he tried to excuse his heated words.

Belinda began to sob. "You're horwid and mean, Lindfowd. Leave me alone! I hate you!"

Peregrine Fowler had witnessed the whole episode. He had left his barouche when he had seen what was happening and now came running up to the phaeton on foot. Seeing Belinda sobbing and Lindford staring at her angrily, he reached up to lift her down, saying in a voice full of concern and worry, "Oh, my dearest Miss Ramsbottom, are you unhurt? What a fright you gave me when I saw you in that runaway carriage! That damned Didsbury-Marsh should be horse-whipped!"

"Oh, Pewegwine. How glad I am to see you!" Belinda exclaimed through her tears, reaching her arms out and allowing him to lift her down from the vehicle.

He received her in his arms with the greatest care. "Say the word and I shall issue a challenge to Didsbury-Marsh! Leaving you to manage his demon horses like that was unconscionable! At the very least, I shall give him such a bear-garden jaw, it will be heard all the way to Billingsgate!"

"Lindfowd is so mean!" was all Belinda managed to get out before she began to sob again against his shoulder. Fowler patted her back and murmured soothing words to her, giving the viscount a gloating sneer over the top of her now bonnetless golden head.

Peveril lowered his brows at the man, but, being powerless to mount an attack against this rival with Belinda standing between them, he mounted his horse and rode back to pick up his hat that had fallen off in his mad dash. He then rode away out of the park, frustration and fury flashing in his blue eyes.

Hurrying toward the phaeton, Mary watched in consternation when Belinda turned to Fowler rather than to Lindford for comfort. How could she allow Fowler to hand her down after the viscount's heroic actions in riding to her rescue? Mary wondered. Lindford richly deserved the girl's thanks—and abject apology, too, for being so foolish—for his brave actions in saving her from her own folly. But she had snubbed him, instead.

Mary could not understand it. He had risked his own life, after all! She resolved to have the story from Belinda as soon as she got her home. Then she would ring such a peal over the girl's head, her ears would not stop ringing for a week.

Didsbury-Marsh reached the carriage just as Mary did but was in too sorry a state to do more than mumble incoherent phrases of concern for his horses, his phaeton, and his passenger, in that order. Fowler gave him a rare trimming, but Belinda paid him no heed. She was leaning heavily against Fowler's shoulder and still weeping.

Peregrine Fowler saw them home in his barouche. Belinda did not emerge from behind her handkerchief during the entire journey. Mary sat beside her charge with a supporting arm about her waist. But she felt no sympathy for the foolish girl. None whatsoever. She was still shaken by the danger Belinda had posed to herself and to any number of innocent bystanders, deeply embarrassed at the spectacle the girl had made of herself for everyone in the park to see, and angrier than she had ever been at her charge's thoughtless, dimwitted, actions.

But, oh, how her heart had been in her throat when Lindford had reached to stop the phaeton's runaway horses. For a few heartstopping seconds it had looked as though he was poised in mid-air. It had seemed certain he would fall and be trampled under those thundering hooves! How had he done it? she wondered incredulously. Thank God, he had not been hurt, she thought with heartfelt gratitude and relief.

* * *

"Look just like an angel tonight, Miss Belinda. Don't recall ever seeing a more beautiful vision!" Peveril exclaimed fervently when he came upon Belinda and Mary that evening.

Peveril's breath had caught in his throat when he gazed upon her exquisite beauty once more. All trace of his earlier anger and disgust with her witless behavior evaporated on the instant. She looked utterly enchanting in a shimmering silk gown of deepest emerald green overlaid with an overdress of the most delicate, gossamer thin, spun silver lace. Her hair was dressed *à la Sappho* and the style added to her air of ethereal loveliness.

He carried her hand to his lips with something of his old fervor, remembering the passion he had felt for her when she had first appeared to him out of the mists of the night.

"Lord, chit, but you gave me a fright this afternoon," he said. "I swear, my heart was in my throat, thinking you were bound to crash. But you held on all right and tight, and no harm done. Cry friends, again?" he pleaded with an entreating look in his vivid blue eyes.

Belinda looked at Peveril reproachfully, still not having forgiven him for his roughshod treatment when she had been so frightened and helpless that afternoon. But after Peregrine Fowler had left them in Curzon Street, Mary had taken her to task for her behavior and told her how the viscount had risked his life to save her, recounting Lindford's heroic actions in the most glowing terms. All Belinda's former admiration for him had been rekindled. Still, she decided to mete out some slight punishment for what she deemed his mistreatment of her.

"Oh, hello, Lindfowd," she said with a sniff, turning her lovely profile slightly away from him as he bowed over her hand.

"Sorry if I overset you this afternoon, Miss Ramsbottom, but—devil take it—I was frightened out of my wits for you," Peveril told her with engaging candor.

"Well, I was fwightened, too, my lowd. I'm sorwy I ever twied to dwive those silly horwses, anyway," she said with a shudder, turning to look him in the eye as he still held to her hand. Seeing that he was suitably contrite, she decided to forgive him. "They were not nice, like I thought they would be, but quite beastly instead."

"Knew you'd forgive me!" Peveril exclaimed with a happy grin. "Angels always do, you know." He carried her hand to his lips and planted a fervent kiss there.

Mary stood to Belinda's left, watching the proceedings with a glint of exasperation in her eyes. Belinda ungraciously accepted the viscount's apology to *her,* but would not apologize to *him,* as Mary had told her she must. The girl still would not admit her own fault in the incident, despite Mary's representations of the danger she had stood in. She was too willful by half.

" 'Evenin' Miss Marlowe," Peveril greeted Mary politely as he straightened from his bow. He was having difficulty tearing his eyes away from the radiant vision of Belinda. At last taking in Mary's gown of rose pink satin that made her complexion glow and her dark hair gleam, he exclaimed with a grin and a wink, "Look like a seraphim yourself tonight, ma'am!"

"We minions sometimes bathe in a ray of the reflected glory," she responded wryly.

Peveril gave a crack of laughter. "Comin' it much too strong, ma'am."

"Oh, Lowd Lindfowd, you were so wough with me. I don't know how I can fowgive you," Belinda said with a pretty pout on her rosebud lips, drawing the viscount's attention back to herself.

"Angels are too heavenly to hold grudges, ain't that so, Miss Marlowe?" Peveril again turned to Mary for support, giving her a crooked grin and another wink.

"Oh, indeed, my lord. Angels are too far removed from the mundane to take much notice of the failings of mere mortals. They are creatures so far above us that they overlook our failings with indulgence. They forgive us before we even ask."

"There, you see? Come, agree to dance with me, angelic Miss Ramsbottom, and show that Miss Marlowe is in the right of it," Peveril coaxed her with a boyish grin lighting up his blue eyes.

Belinda was not proof against his charm and granted his request, but she could not quite reach the heights of divine forebearance Mary described, and was determined to exact still more revenge. Therefore, she would promise Lindford only one dance, instead of the customary two.

"Ah, here you, my dear Miss Ramsbottom. Looking as lovely as the most precious flower that ever bloomed," the Duke of Exford boomed effusively as he came up to Belinda to claim a dance.

"Oh, hello, Dukey," Belinda greeted Exford with fluttering lashes and a simpering smile, giving him her hand with a little curtsy.

Mary felt rather than saw Lindford stiffen at her side, but he said nothing.

Eyeing the viscount with open hostility, the duke greeted Mary in a perfunctory manner, possessed himself of Belinda's hand, and guided her to the floor without further ado.

Mary suppressed a smile at the look on the duke's face. He reminded her of nothing so much as a pugnacious little bulldog, ready to fight over a bone.

She turned to Peveril and put her hand lightly on his sleeve. Drawing a deep breath, she said, "Lord Lindford, how can we ever thank you enough for the actions you took this afternoon? Were it not for your bravery, Belinda well might not be standing here this evening. You risked your life to save hers. I—I just want to thank you most sincerely." She looked deep into his blue eyes as she spoke and blushed when she saw a spark of emotion kindle there. "Belinda really is most grateful, too," she finished lamely.

She had been utterly dumbfounded that afternoon when she took Belinda to task over her extremely foolish behavior and learned that her charge had not even thanked the viscount for risking his life to rescue her. Mary was determined to make up for that omission now.

"Think nothing of it, ma'am. Neck-or-nothing—one of my faults, I'm told," Peveril said, smiling right into Mary's eyes, causing her pulse to flutter.

"Must admit was a close run thing, though. Still—couldn't stand by and watch the blasted thing crash with the Beauty in it. Never would've forgiven myself, if she'd come to any harm."

"I was so afraid you would fall. How did you manage to hang onto your horse and still reach out to stop the phaeton, my lord?" Mary asked, marvelling at his courage and athletic ability. "I must admit, my heart was in my throat as I watched you."

"Secret's in the heels, Miss Marlowe. Keep 'em pointed down at all times and you won't lose your seat and fall off."

Mary was disbelieving, prompting Peveril to say he'd give her a lesson one day.

"Thank you, my lord, but I believe we've had enough *lessons* for the time being," she responded with a twinkle in her grey eyes.

"Oh, my lord, I'll get dizzy!" Mary laughed as Peveril twirled her about exuberantly as the dance ended with a musical flourish. She had been dancing the supper dance with him and enjoying every minute of it. It was the second dance they had shared that evening, and Lindford had been all flattering attention, when he wasn't teasing her unmercifully.

Peveril was laughing down at Mary. She was a cuddly little armful. Curves in all the right places, he had discovered when he had daringly and most improperly pulled her against himself on two occasions. He was enjoying his evening prodigiously. He reached forward to tweak one of the dusky curls that framed her pretty little face when he saw her grey eyes widen in alarm, or some other unnamed emotion. She was staring fixedly over his shoulder at someone who had just entered the room.

"What's put you in a quake, Mary?" he asked immediately, turning around to see who she was staring at.

Giving a little gasp of outrage, Mary stared at the gentleman who had just entered the ballroom. It was the one person above all others she least wished to see.

"Noth—not a thing, my lord," she said with a bright smile, trying to damp down the urge to beat her fists against her sides in frustration and stalk from the room.

"Doing it much too brown, m'dear! Ain't like you to lose your composure," Peveril said, looking at her keenly. He saw her brittle smile, too bright to be genuine, but he also saw something burning at the back of her eyes and was glad that he had done nothing to raise her ire. At least he hoped he was not the cause of that fierce look, for he quite counted on her friendship these days. "Something's upset you. Wish you'd tell me what."

Before Mary could answer, a tall young man with silvery-blond hair, cold grey eyes, and a body sculpted like a Greek statue come to life—all wide shoulders and long, muscular legs, and with the same marble-like stillness on his haughty features—approached them and addressed himself to Mary.

"Good evening, Cousin Mary!" the newcomer greeted her with stiff familiarity. His severe black cutaway jacket and black pantaloons were in stark contrast to his light coloring and set off his masculine beauty to perfection. "I hope I find you well," Sir Cedic Ledbetter uttered in a voice almost devoid of inflection as he reached his cousin's side. His urbane greeting was accompanied by a stiff bow.

"Very well, indeed, Cedric."

As Cedric raised his brows and looked inquiringly at the gentleman who stood next to Mary, she made the two gentlemen known to one another. She saw that Cedric looked at the viscount coldly, while Lindford directed a hot glare at her relative.

"What on earth brings you to London at this season, Cedric?" Mary asked sweetly, all the while wishing him at perdition.

All thought of Belinda was completely forgotten while Peveril watched with growing annoyance as this unknown silvery-haired god paid his compliments to Mary with unwonted familiarity.

"Mary," Sir Cedric said reproachfully, giving Mary a stern look from his frosty grey eyes. He stiffened his tall, well-built form as he addressed her. "You cannot be unaware that your precipitous and extremely ill-advised departure has occasioned much concern and disappointment at Wyndham. Indeed, Mary, I find it impossible to understand why you should have left at all. So unlike you to disregard the duty you owe to the earl and disobey him in this distressing, unladylike way. I urged the earl to take steps to see that you were found and returned to Wyndham immediately when he wrote to me that you had gone. It is a tribute to his forebearance that he has not compelled your return before now, though I am not sure I consider it his wisest course under the circumstances. He has finally come to the end of his patience, and when he learned that you were in London, he bade me come here in search of you so that I could rescue you from your misbegotten attempt to earn your own living and restore you to his protection at the earliest possible time."

Mary's anger burned brighter as Cedric's lecture continued, but she controlled herself enough to answer offhandedly, "Oh, Grandpapa need not have worried about me, Cedric. I have written every other week, letting him know that I go on swimmingly."

"Yes, but you haven't let the earl know where you have been staying, Mary," Cedric reminded her, almost wagging an admonitory finger at her in public. "It was most remiss of you, you know. But he received information more than a week ago that you were to be found with a family with the vulgar name of Ramsbottom in Curzon Street. When I called at the house earlier this evening, I was informed that I could find you here. It is lucky that I have some prior acquaintance with the Mentmore-Joneses. However, more to the point, I have come to escort you back to Wyndham Park for Christmas. There is no further point in delay. I think it best if we leave the day after tomorrow."

Peveril, standing at Mary's shoulder, instantly decided he didn't at all care for the priggish, long-winded fellow. The jabbernowl was evidently one of those relatives Mary had run away from, one of those family members who was trying to force her into an unwanted marriage. By Jupiter, Peveril thought, his protective instincts thoroughly aroused, just let the pompous rasher of wind try to force her to return to her grandfather. He would find a glove slapped in his face before he was much older, if he tried to carry sweet, little Mary off against her will.

"I shan't be going back to Wyndham Park in the foreseeable future, Cedric. I've made that clear to Grandpapa. I have made plans for my own future."

"Mary. You cannot continue with this charade. You are embarrassing the family with your ridiculous pose as a companion to a vulgar cit. You will marry me in the spring and take your rightful place in society. The earl has made all the plans. You can't expect to prepare for a wedding from here."

Peveril heard the words with fury. So this pompous ass was the man Mary's family was trying to force her to wed! This was the man she had run away from. Devil take it, any girl with any sense in her cockloft would have done the same thing. The fellow was a curst preachy bore.

Mary's ire increased with every word Cedric uttered. She would not stand for his interference. She felt she would explode if he continued to remonstrate with her. "Of course I shall not prepare for a wedding from here! It seems to have escaped your notice, Cedric, that I have not consented to marry you," she said with as much dignity as she could muster while making a supreme effort not to stamp her foot and create the kind of scene she was forever warning Belinda against. "And I never shall."

At Mary's plain speaking, a bit of color crept into Sir Cedric's cold face and his grey eyes hardened. He looked superciliously at the viscount who stood at Mary's side as though stuck there by glue. "We need not air our dirty linen in public, Mary. Come, let us discuss this somewhere in private," he said ponderously, making to take Mary's elbow and lead her away.

Mary pulled against his commanding hand on her arm and unexpectedly felt the viscount place one of his hands at the small of her back while his other hand took hold of hers. It was a gesture of protectiveness that was as unforeseen as it was welcome. Almost unconsciously, she pressed herself back into the warmth and comfort of his semi-embrace.

" 'Fraid you're too late. Miss Marlowe's already promised to me for supper," she heard Lindford say with smooth assurance, not missing a beat. As hot-headed and daring as he was, she hadn't known he possessed so much cold arrogance.

"Don't know who you are, but I assume you're a gentleman." Peveril's comment was a calculated insult to Cedric's knowledge of polite behavior and good manners.

"Do you think to insult me?" Cedric began frostily, almost audibly grinding his teeth, but the tableau was interrupted before hostilities could progress further when Percy came up to them with his cousin, Emmy on his arm. Mary stepped away from Lindford and presented Cedric to the newcomers before the impetuous viscount could further provoke her relative.

"I say, Percy, why don't you take Mary's cousin here and introduce him to Lord and Lady Mentmore-Jones," Peveril suggested in a commanding tone. He felt a burning desire to consign the man to blazes.

"I am already acquainted with his lordship and her ladyship, my lord," Cedric replied haughtily. "They are neighbors and close friends of my relative, the Earl of Wyndham." Sensing the viscount's animosity toward him, Cedric began to suspect that the gentleman had more than a passing interest in Mary. He was doubly determined to hold his ground.

"Ah. Then you'll certainly want to pay your respects to them," Peveril answered.

Cedric felt the ground shifting from beneath him.

Emmy, being quick-witted, easily divined the viscount's purpose. He wanted Sir Cedric out of the way for some reason. Probably feared Belinda would be taken with him, she guessed. Well, she was not averse to the company of such a handsome gentleman for the next half an hour. She remembered being introduced to him some months earlier, but had never had a chance to converse with him.

"Well, Sir Cedric, you must want some supper," Emmy said. She smiled up at him impishly. "And I know all the best things that Lady Mentmore-Jones has provided. Best come with me," she told him, boldly linking her arm with his before he could answer.

Harassed and outmaneuvered on all sides, Cedric felt that to decline the young lady's offer would be very impolite. He turned and looked down at the irrepressible Emmy, gave a stiff bow, and said ponderously, "I would be honored, Miss Belfours." He gave Mary a stern look. "We shall talk later, Cousin."

Mary smiled to see Cedric walking away stiffly, with Emmy talking to him animatedly as they went. "That was quick thinking on your part, my lord. Thank you. You saved me from an unpleasant half hour," Mary told him with a warm look.

"Think nothing of it, ma'am," Peveril answered

with a grin. "Was worth it to see that deuced prig's face turn purple."

"Hello, Belinda. Your grace," Emmy greeted the couple at the door to the supper room. Straightaway she made Sir Cedric known to them, mentioning his relationship to Mary.

Belinda's eyes widened and her mouth fell open to see so much masculine perfection standing before her. Why, he almost matched her for flawless beauty, she thought in awe. Lindford, Exford, Fowler, Nichols—all her other suitors were forgotten in a second.

"Why, how do you do, Sir Cedwic," she said breathlessly, her eyes wide and interested as she inspected him from head to toe. "I'm sure Marwy's never mentioned you before." She blinked at him, unable to believe her eyes. If she had thought Lindford resembled one of the fanciful illustrations in her picture books, Sir Cedric was the living, breathing embodiment of one of her pictures. He seemed to have stepped right off one of the pages into Lady Mentmore-Jones' ballroom.

"Miss Ramsbottom," Sir Cedric replied arctically, giving her an infinitesimal nod. "A pleasure, ma'am." So this is the little upstart Mary is companion to, he thought coldly.

She continued to gape at him, then recollected herself and gave him a dazzling smile. "Why, if you are Marwy's cousin, then you will be calling on us fwequently, won't you?" she concluded happily. "We live in Curwzon Stweet, you know."

"Indeed, ma'am. I hope to call on Mary tomorrow."

"Oh, good! I'll see you then." Belinda gave him her most flirtatious look, but to her dismay Sir Cedric remained impervious to her charms.

He nodded stiffly and allowed Emmy to lead him away.

For the rest of the evening, Belinda stared and stared at Sir Cedric, unable to believe he wasn't instantly smitten by her charms as all other gentlemen were.

Chapter 10

"Coming Belinda?" Mary inquired as Belinda's footsteps in her new kid boots lagged on the pathway outside Hookam's, the fashionable circulating library where Mary planned to change the book she had recently finished reading for another. It was a cold, overcast day and Mary didn't wish to linger outside, but the Duke of Exford had just crossed the street to greet Belinda and her charge had made no move to follow her inside.

Mary glanced up at the heavy grey sky, thinking it was going to snow soon. The day was so cold she could see her frosty breath heavy in the air.

"Oh, Marwy, you know those old books are always so dusty they make me sneeze. And I wouldn't want to have a wed nose, Dukey," she said to Exford, wrinkling her nose in girlish fashion. Belinda wore her new white swansdown cape and hood trimmed with red ribbons over her heavy dark red wool carriage gown, and was quite happy to stand outside on the pavement where she was drawing admiring glances from the gentlemen who happened to be passing by.

"Shall I get something for you to look at?" Mary asked, phrasing the question precisely, for she knew it was worse than useless to try to get Belinda to *read* a book. On the list of Belinda's accomplishments, reading was nowhere to be found.

"Oh, no, Marwy. You go on. I will be alwight, for Dukey will look after me," Belinda replied smugly, placing her arm in the crook of Exford's elbow, "Won't you, your gwace?" She bestowed one of her bewitching smiles on Exford, who stood gazing at her with appreciation.

"Indeed I will," Exford averred, patting her gloved hand where it rested on his arm.

With a glance back at them, thinking she could safely leave Belinda with the duke for a few minutes, Mary disappeared through the doors to the establishment saying, "I won't be long."

Belinda wished Sir Cedric would come along to see her dressed so becomingly. She was sure he would be enormously impressed. She greatly desired to see that particular gentleman at her feet. She had been bewildered when he had not taken the opportunity to further his acquaintance with her last night after they had been introduced. However, she would see him when he called on Mary.

In the meanwhile, the she would make do with the duke.

"If I may say so, you look a real treat, Miss Ramsbottom," the duke complimented.

"Oh, thank you, Dukey," Belinda simpered, glancing at him from beneath her artfully lowered lashes.

"I'm ever so fond of my wed mittens," she said, lifting her hand from his arm and holding it up for his inspection.

"Indeed, they add a bright touch to your outfit, my dear. You are always dressed in the height of fashion, Miss Ramsbottom. Proud to be seen anywhere with you!" he exclaimed fervently reclaiming her little hand.

"You look vewy handsome today, too, Dukey!" she said with a girlish giggle.

"Thank you, my dear Miss Ramsbottom!" His chest positively swelled with her praise. If things continued in this vein, he would ignore the forceful objections of his formidable mama, and his disapproving sister, and press on with his suit. He was convinced the girl's beauty would overcome all the disadvantages of her birth, and he would like nothing better than to make her his duchess.

"I wonder what's taking Marwy so long. She will come back with an armload of books to wead, I expect. She is always twying to get me to wead some of them, but I'm always too busy, you know."

"I'm glad to hear you aren't planning a retreat from society, Miss Ramsbottom, mewing yourself up in your room, reading a lot of rubbishy novels. We who live for the sunshine of one of your smiles would languish in the darkness of your absence, were you to do so," the duke averred fulsomely, with a blandishing smile.

"Oh, no, Dukey, I would never do that! I vow, weading is so tiwing. I'm afwaid it hurts my eyes to wead. They're vewy sensitive, you know," she said, opening her big green eyes wide and blinking at him.

"Indeed, Miss Ramsbottom," he said, gazing into her eyes with all the admiration she could wish. "I wish you to rest those perfect emerald orbs as much as possible, so that when I see you they will be as sparklingly bright and beautiful as they are at this moment." Exford reached out and chucked her under the chin. Belinda simpered, then looked up at the sky as she felt a drop of moisture on her cold cheek.

Snow flakes had begun to fall from the heavy clouds that hung overhead in the grey November sky. Belinda shivered, realizing that even her new cape couldn't keep out the biting cold. "Oh, Dukey, I'm so cold. Let us wait for Marwy in my carwiage," she said, moving toward the ornate, brightly-gilded Ramsbottom town coach which stood at the curbside.

She was just about to mount the steps into the carriage, where she could rest her dainty little feet shod in her new leather boots on a hot brick and cover herself with the luxurious lap-robe that rested on the seat, when Peveril and Percy arrived on the scene.

Belinda turned to the viscount with a bright smile lighting her lovely countenance and waved her red-gloved hand at him, all memory of the miff she had been in with him over the driving incident forgotten. "Oh, hello, Lowd Lindfowd!" she exclaimed, happy to add another personable gentleman to her court, though she wished it had been Sir Cedric who hailed her. "And Mr. Thwockmowton, too."

"Miss Ramsbottom! You look like a beautiful snow maiden, all decked out in white," Peveril declared, by now knowing her fondness for fairy-tale maidens and choosing to compliment her in a way that would find most favor with her.

"Not all white," she said with a giggle, pointing out her red mittens and the red trim on her cloak.

"Lindford. Throckmorton," the duke ground out gruffly, ill-concealing his belligerence toward the viscount as he greeted them.

Peveril nodded almost imperceptibly to the duke. "Can we accompany you somewhere, Miss Ramsbottom?" Peveril asked. He had twigged to it that Belinda would immediately invite him to accompany her, even if she were with another gentleman.

"Was about to see Miss Ramsbottom home, Lindford. No need to trouble yourselves," the duke said, dismissively.

"No trouble at all, duke. Only out on the toddle. Don't have any specific destination in mind. Ain't that right, Percy?" Peveril looked all around. "She can't go home yet, at any rate. Her companion ain't here. Miss Marlowe must be somewhere about."

The duke clenched his fists at his side and gave Peveril a basilisk stare. "I'll thank you to be a little less busy about Miss Ramsbottom's activities," Exford said in his best ducal manner.

"Hadn't heard you owned her, Duke," Peveril snapped back with a martial gleam in his eyes. His jaw clenched in anger, he took a step closer to the duke, not about to be intimidated by such a posturing mannikin.

Percy stood by twirling his cane in his hand, his eyes on Peveril and the duke, ready to offer his friend assistance should this little contretemps come to blows.

Mary came down out of the library just then, her arms filled with books. She looked up in dismay to see the dramatic tableau set out before her eyes and nearly slipped on the slick pathway now coated with newly fallen snow.

"Whoa there, Miss Marlowe!" Peveril exclaimed, turning from his confrontation with the duke to catch her by the elbow. "You ladies will be wanting to get home before the blasted stuff really starts coming down."

He assisted Mary into the carriage where Belinda was already sitting cozily, her eyes glowing with excitement at the scene she had provoked.

Before the gentlemen could bid the ladies adieu and close the door of the vehicle, Percy remarked to no one in particular, "This snow . . . might ruin the fun at the bonfire set for tomorrow night." He had been standing nearby, gazing up pensively and studying the sky. "Guy Fawkes Day—the fifth of November, you know. Deuced shame to miss all the fun."

"Lord, yes, if I hadn't forgotten that!" Peveril exclaimed. "Givin' out a dashed fortune to every little beggar who comes along asking for a penny for the guy. Used to collect 'em myself, when I was a lad. Remember spending ages stuffing a deuced lifelike guy that was burned to cinders in no time at all when it sat atop a blazing bonfire."

"Humph!" mumbled the duke. "Foolish nonsense, these Guy Fawkes' celebrations. Ought to be enough to go to church and give thanksgiving the traitors were discovered in time. Don't know why a load of maggotty hey-go-mad young rapscallions want to be buildin' enormous woodpiles and playin' with fire. Can easily rage out of control. Sure to burn someone's house down one of these days."

"Hang it all, Duke!" Peveril expostulated. "The thing's held on an open common. No buildings around at all."

"We're going to the one on Chelsea Common," Percy piped up. "Famous celebrations they have there. They'll have all manner of peck and booze—sure to have ale and roast sausages on the bonfire and maybe even have some of that cake—what's it called Pev?"

"Bonfire Parkin. Lord, yes! You're in the right of it there, Percy. Oatmeal cake, flavored with molasses and ginger—very filling. Just what you want on a cold night! Probably have some roast chestnuts, too."

"Oh, it sounds such fun! I want to go, too!" Belinda cried, clapping her mittened hands. "Do say we may go, Marwy! Please? May we, Marwy? Oh, please?" she turned a pleading look on her companion, reminding Mary of nothing so much as a child begging for a longed-for treat.

Embarrassed at Belinda's poor manners in so blatantly inviting herself along, Mary suppressed her own memories of the fun of past bonfire nights in the village near Wyndham Park and said in a soft voice, "Hush, Belinda. You know you always complain of the cold. I'm sure it would be too much for you to be out after dark on one of these freezing November nights."

The duke and Lindford spoke at once.

"Must listen to Miss Marlowe's sensible words, my dear," the duke began to say, but the viscount spoke in a more penetrating voice, or maybe his words were the ones Belinda wanted to hear.

"Be pleased if you and Miss Ramsbottom would

come with us, Miss Marlowe," Peveril invited promptly. "Perce and Emmy will come along, too, and Jeremy Fletcher will probably join us, as well. We'll have a bang-up time, and you'll have me and Perce and Jer to protect you."

"Oh, *yes!*" Belinda cried breathlessly, giving a little bounce on the seat of the coach, all thought of Cedric and the duke forgotten and the viscount back in highest favor for the moment. "I would like it of all things. If dear Emmy is going, then it would be pwoper for me, too. Do let us go, Marwy. Since the gentlemen have been so obliging as to invite us," she said shamelessly. "I shan't complain about the cold, I pwomise, for I shall wear my new Wussian mantle. It's twimmed with chinchilla, you know. Oh, Marwy, I shall be woasting hot in that! And I'll take my chinchilla muff, too."

Much to her consternation, a time was fixed before Mary could marshall her arguments to gainsay Belinda's acceptance. She knew very well her employer would not approve of this expedition, but she found she had no desire to forbid it. It *did* sound like fun. She decided she would just have to take the consequences of Mr. Ramsbottom's disapproval, should he learn of it.

The duke took umbrage at this turn of events. Forgetting his promise to see Belinda home, he stomped away, slipping and sliding on the slick, snowy pathway. Only the adroit use of his cane prevented him from taking an embarrassing fall in the middle of the fashionable street.

* * *

"Ohh! This is sûch fun!" Belinda cried. She squeezed Peveril's arm as they stood watching the sizzling red and orange flames of the bonfire leap higher and higher in the black sky amid the cheers of the noisy bystanders. They stood among a large crowd of shouting, cheering revelers of all stations who had gathered on Chelsea Common to commemorate the safe deliverance of the English Parliament from the conspiracy to blow it up. It was a raucous scene.

"Knew you would like it," Peveril nodded at her shoulder. In the bright light given off by the blaze, he could see her exquisite features clearly. Her beauty never failed to set his heart to pounding in his chest. All his disgust at her recent foolish behavior and pettish whining was forgotten. He thought he would never get tired of looking at her, and vowed to himself that he would steal another kiss before this night was over, as any other red-blooded young buck worth his salt would have done in his boots.

"Oh!" Belinda clapped her hands over her ears as a cannon was set off somewhere over to their left.

"Just part of the celebrations," Peveril told her when the booming echo had died away.

Mary stood a few steps away from the viscount and Belinda with Emmy and Percy. Jeremy Fletcher had cried off at the last moment, recalling some longstanding engagement or other.

Mary was neglecting her duty, she knew. She should be standing at Belinda's shoulder and preventing the viscount from putting his arm around her charge's waist and drawing her into an almost public embrace as he was doing, but she could not bring herself to do so. Feeling just a bit lonely amid all the crowd, she had swallowed hard and moved away from them to stand on the other side of Percy to watch the bonfire.

The pyre had been set alight moments before, and the flames were just now licking at the uppermost reaches of the gigantic pile of discarded wood and old rubbish that had been topped with a whole host of effigies of Guy Fawkes, the Catholic conspirator who had allegedly hidden thirty-six barrels of gunpowder in the cellars under the House of Lords so that he and his friends could blow up Parliament, and King James I along with it.

The Gunpowder Plot had been discovered in the wee hours of the morning of the fifth of November in 1605—only just in time to foil the conspirators. The king had been scheduled to open Parliament later that day. Ever since that time, the narrow escape had been commemorated with thanksgiving services in the churches by day and by night with the lighting of bonfires all over England and the burning of effigies, or guys as they came to be called, of Guy Fawkes. Food and drink had become part of the celebrations and appeared at these jollifications like magic.

Please to remember the fifth of November,
Gunfire treason and plot.
I see no reason why gunpowder treason
Should ever be forgot!

Someone in the crowd took up the familiar chant and others joined in, shouting the rhyme until it could be heard easily above the roar and crackle of the sizzling flames and falling timbers.

"Oh, gracious! Pardon me, sir!" Mary exclaimed as she fell to her knees, grabbing Percy's arm as she did so to prevent herself from falling over completely. She had been standing next to Percy, watching the bonfire, but she stepped back when cinders began to blow against her face and stepped into a gully where cold, wet slush, the remains of the previous day's snowfall, had accumulated. She lost her balance and fell to her knees, soaking the lower half of her cloak and gown.

"You hurt, Miss Marlowe?" Percy asked, wincing at the tight grip she had on his arm, as he helped her right herself.

"No, I don't believe so," Mary answered, standing upright again, feeling inordinately foolish. She stepped out of the puddle quickly, but the frigid water had already seeped into her boots. "I'm sorry, Mr. Throckmorton," she apologized, "but I lost my balance when I stepped back. There seems to be a hollowed-out depression in the ground just here and it's filled with fre–freezing wa–water. It mu–must be the snow that acc–accumula–lated from yesterda–day that's me–melted and tu–turned to slu–slush," she got out. Her teeth were beginning to chatter as the freezing water soaked her feet and the cold spread up her body.

"Oh, dear! Miss Marlowe's boots and cloak are soaking wet with freezing water, Percy!" Emmy exclaimed. She could feel Mary shivering beside her and put her arm around her waist. "I think we should get her back to the carriage, Percy," Emmy declared with concern.

"Oh, no! I shall be alri–right in a mo–moment," Mary protested, trying her best to clamp her chattering teeth shut. How very lowering, she thought, when she couldn't stop her shivers and realized that she would have to request that she be taken home.

"Dash it, Miss Marlowe, think Emmy's in the right of it," Percy said with uncharacteristic decision.

"What's toward, Percy?" Peveril asked, seeing his friend turn toward Mary and take her by the elbow. The noise was fierce now, both from the crackling fire and the slightly bosky crowd.

"Miss Marlowe's stepped in a puddle of freezing water. Her boots and cloak are soaked, Peveril," Emmy told him in a loud voice before Percy could speak up. "I'm sorry we'll miss some of the festivities, but I think we must take her home."

Hearing Emmy's judgment, Belinda protested loudly, "Oh, no, we can't go home, now. I'm having such fun! Marwy will wecover in a minute, you'll see."

Hearing Belinda's selfish remarks, Peveril withdrew his arm from about her waist and walked over to take Percy's place beside Mary. He wanted to see for himself how matters stood. Putting his arm about her and feeling her convulsive shivers, he made an instant decision. "I'm taking you back to the carriage," he told her.

"We've got to get Mary home quickly where she can get warm again. She's chilled through," he shouted to the others.

"Oh, no, Pevewil, don't go! I'm not weady to

leave yet," he could hear Belinda's shrill objection behind him. "Marwy will be alwight. Everyone's feet are a little cold. Don't make me go when I'm having such a good time!"

"Now don't be birdwitted!" Peveril called impatiently over his shoulder to Belinda. "Mary's freezing to death. We've got to get her home."

"Oh, no, my lord. I don't wa–want to sp–spoil everyon–one's f–fun," Mary protested quietly. She feared Belinda would have a tantrum if she were forced to leave before she was ready to do so, but her teeth wouldn't stop chattering and she stopped speaking, too cold for further protests. Involuntarily she leaned against Peveril, seeking some warmth.

"Have sense now, Mary, do! You've only just recovered from a blasted headcold. Don't want a deuced inflammation of the lungs on top of that, now, do you?" he asked, feeling her shivering against him. He tightened his hold and pulled her more securely against his body.

Without further ado, he picked her up in his strong arms. "I'm taking Mary back to the carriage. Bring Emmy and Miss Ramsbottom along, will you, Percy?" he called over his shoulder as he began to make his way through the crowd of revellers standing about watching the bonfire. He could hear Belinda's high-pitched complaints trailing after him as he moved quickly through the crowd.

"Oh, my lo–lord!" Mary objected as he carried her along. "I ca–can wa–walk."

"Oh, you can, can you?" he asked, making a clucking sound with his tongue. "Thought you was a sensible chit, Mary. Your boots are soaked through and you're shivering so hard, you can hardly get your breath. We'll make faster time to the carriage this way and have you warmed up in no time. So I'll have no more arguments from you, my girl. Understood!" Peveril strode on, clutching Mary tightly to his chest.

"Ye–yes m–my l–lord," she got out, in truth glad to have her half-hearted protests overridden. She would like nothing more than to go home and roast herself in front of a blazing fire.

Her head sagged against the viscount's shoulder. She felt almost lightheaded.

"Open my cape and pull it over you, Mary, and open my coat, too," he told her.

"Oh, heavens, I c–can do no s–such thing, my lord! It would be m–most imp–proper."

"Mary . . . do as I tell you, my girl!"

At his stern command, Mary was too cold to protest further and did as he recommended, burrowing right inside the heavy wool evening cape he wore over his outer garments. She managed to pull the folds over herself, then hesitantly, fumbling a bit with the buttons, she opened his coat and tucked her head and shoulder snugly against his muscular chest, where she could hear the reassuring beat of his heart through his shirt. Oh, but he did smell good! she thought, detecting the smell of sandalwood soap mixed with his own lightly musky masculine scent.

She was warmed by his body heat. Her teeth stopped chattering and she began to thaw out, except for her feet. She tried to wiggle her toes, but she couldn't feel them. They were so cold they had gone numb.

They reached the carriage in a matter of minutes

and Peveril lifted her inside, then climbed in himself. Sitting beside her, he helped her remove her heavy, sodden cloak, and wet boots, then pulled a carriage blanket up over her, tucking it in well around her icy-cold little feet.

She did not protest, but allowed him to chafe her hands as she leaned her head back against the soft squabs of the well-appointed carriage and closed her eyes, not wishing to disturb the dreamy feeling of warmth and tenderness and security that had stolen over her in the past few minutes.

"Warmer now, Mary?" Peveril asked, a note of anxiety in his voice.

"Oh, yes. Almost toasty warm. Thank you, my lord!"

"Peveril."

"Thank you, *Lindford,*" she said obstinately, and a bit breathlessly. His face was only inches away from hers.

"Thank you, *Peveril.* Say it."

"Peveril, then. Thank you. I am so sorry to ruin the evening for everyone else. Belinda was so looking forward to it."

"Now don't be a goose!" he said. He let go of her hands and sat back along the seat from her. The tension between them eased somewhat. "We'd already seen the blasted pyre go up in smoke. Wouldn't have stayed much longer, on any account. Crowd was getting too rowdy."

She smiled ruefully. "She'll create a scene when she gets here, you know."

His eyebrows shot up and he grinned. "You don't say! Never would've thought it!"

They laughed together and Mary went home warmed by Peveril's thoughtful care of her and cheered by his teasing words, feeling that perhaps he was beginning to get the measure of her charge after all.

"Been worrin' me," Percy remarked to the viscount the next day as they sat in Brooks's looking over the morning papers and mulling over the events of the previous evening while they enjoyed a haphazard meal of beefsteak and ale.

"What maggot's rattling round in your cockloft now, Percy?" Peveril asked. He noticed that Percy was chewing his food with unusual attention—a sure sign his friend was grappling with some weighty thought.

Percy scratched his head, struggling to find the words to express what was bothering him. "Not the thing, the Beauty wishin' Miss Marlowe to stay out in the freezin' night just 'cause she wasn't ready to leave," he said with a frown wrinkling his youthful features, giving him the appearance of a wizened old man. "Tell you what, Pev. The Beauty's spoiled."

Peveril gave his friend an offended look, then sighed and admitted, " 'Fraid you're in the right of it, Percy. Still, have to admit, she's a rare treat to cast your glims over."

If he were honest in his review of the evening's events, Peveril would have to concede that Belinda's behavior had been deuced unpleasant. She had been decidedly cross and had created a terrible scene when she reached the carriage last night, berating both him, for spoiling her fun, and Mary, for being so silly as to step in a puddle in the first place, as though she'd done it on purpose.

Then, when Emmy had given Belinda a well-deserved set-down, telling her she was behaving like a totty-headed wet goose, she had burst into tears and complained that she was mistreated by one and all.

Peveril didn't openly admit it, but he had begun to find the Beauty's conversation, centering on her self so constantly, a trifle dull and repetitive. He frequently found himself bored to flinders when he was with her. And now that he had had a taste of her petulant behavior, he had a pretty clear idea that she was one of those women who would set up a screech or dissolve in a fit of the vapors every time her will was crossed. It had dawned on him that her temperament was not as sweet as her face.

But, even if Belinda's temperament was not all he could desire, every time he looked at her, his heart beat faster and his temperature rose several degrees. However disillusioned he was about her character, his admiration for her unmatched beauty hadn't dimmed.

Lord, what a coup it would be to possess so much beauty, he mused, ignoring the fact that it was proving to be only skin deep.

"Guess you can't have everything," Peveril said with a sigh.

"Guess not. But Miss Marlowe's a beauty, too, and she ain't spoiled."

"Mary a beauty? Ain't never noticed. Taking little thing. Sweet. But I wouldn't say she's precisely a beauty, Percy."

"Well, she is, Pev. All soft eyes and pretty smile. Figure's good, too."

"Don't you think she's a trifle on the managin' side, though?" Pev asked, with his eyebrows drawn together in concentration, trying to suppress his traitorous thoughts. He was remembering all too well the feel of that curvaceous little body pressed so trustingly against his when he carried her to the carriage last night. He had been reluctant to put her down and had been tempted to keep her on his lap after he had lifted her into the carriage.

"Lord, what's that to say to anything. A man likes to have his household well managed, don't he? Saves a heap of trouble."

Peveril grinned. "You're right, Percy. Mary will make some lucky dog a bang-up little leg-shackle all right and tight!"

Percy had a faraway look on his face as he continued, "Dear little soul. A man can relax with her. She don't put on airs and graces the whole time, as some chits I could name."

"Taken a notion to live under the cat's paw, have you, Percy?" the viscount exclaimed in surprise. The idea of Percy making an offer to Mary was extremely unsettling for some reason Peveril couldn't put his finger on.

"Me?" Percy gaped at his friend. He gave a strangled cough. "Ain't a ladies' man, Pev," he denied with some feeling.

Peveril relaxed. "Sounded positively besotted there, Percy."

Percy appeared to consider this for a moment.

"Well, a man could do worse than cuddle up to a soft little lady like her, Pev."

"Good God! You are serious. Never thought I'd live to see the day that Percival Throckmorton talked of becoming a tenant for life!"

"No. Ain't thinkin' of taking a wife, Pev," Percy denied. "Just pointin' out that Miss Marlowe's got a kind nature. Got a look about her that I like, too."

A sudden memory of Mary smiling sweetly up at him when he had been teasing her about something or other flashed into Peveril's mind. His heart gave an odd little jerk. "Blister it," he muttered under his breath, "either you're courtin' her, or you ain't, Percy. Make up your mind. P'rhaps another gent would want to make her an offer, but if you're seen dilly-dallying around her, it would put him off."

"Who?" Percy asked, greatly puzzled, for he hadn't noticed any gents nosing around Mary.

"Don't know precisely. Anyone."

Percy gave the matter his attention, gnawing on his knuckles. "Maybe Ledbetter—her cousin, don't you know," he said looking up brightly after a few moments of effort.

"The devil he will!" Peveril ejaculated with a belligerent glint in his eye. He was unaccountably irritated by the idea of that bombastic prig ever having a claim on Mary.

"I don't know, Pev. Earl of Wyndham's heir. The old earl wants her to marry him. Would make her a countess some day, you know. Hard to resist a title and the fortune that goes along with it."

"No. Mary don't want to be a countess. And she damned sure wants none of that puffed-up rasher of wind!" Peveril insisted, suddenly feeling hot under the collar. "He'd better not try to force her to go home, if he don't want his damned pretty features re-arranged for him!"

"You would mill Ledbetter down for Miss Mar-lowe's sake, Pev? Thought you was only interested in the Beauty."

"I am," Peveril insisted somewhat crossly. "But Mary's been a bang-up friend, and if Ledbetter both-ers her, he'll have me to answer to," he declared fiercely. His color was heightened and his hands had curled into fists as he thought of how that damned prig Ledbetter had tried to order Mary about. He had been within an aim's ace of calling him to account.

"Oh," Percy said meekly, looking at Peveril with raised brows. A question hovered on the tip of his tongue, but on second thought, he wisely decided to keep his own counsel, not wanting to make a remark that would put his volatile friend in a pucker.

Chapter 11

"Oh, Sir Cedwic, over here!" Belinda squealed when she spotted him in the vestibule of the Drury Lane Theatre where she and Mary were standing with her escort Sir Thomas Nichols, an unprepossessing young baronet. She waved Mary's relative over to join them.

"How lucky to see you here tonight! I quite thought you meant to ignore us, as you haven't called on Marwy yet, as you pwomised you would," she accused. In fact, Sir Cedric had called several times in Curzon Street, but on Mary's instructions, Mr. Ramsbottom's butler had denied him entrance each time.

"I bid you good evening, Miss Ramsbottom," Cedric said stiffly, giving her a small, unsmiling nod before he turned to his cousin. "Good evening, Mary. I was sorry to miss you these past few days. Perhaps you can give me an idea of when it would be *convenient* to call tomorrow," he said with a hard stare at her.

"Your doing so tomorrow or at any time would be fruitless, Cedric, as I've tried to tell you." Mary met his eyes without a blink. She hoped to make him understand that she was not to be moved.

"Are you here all alone, Sir Cedwic?" Belinda asked, making great play with her eyes as she looked up at Mary's tall, handsome cousin.

When he confirmed that such was the case, she immediately said, "Then you must sit in our box tonight." Belinda ignored the claims of Sir Thomas to her company, and completely disregarded the fact that she had no right to issue such an invitation, for her party was to share Lord Belfours' box with Emmy, Percy, and Viscount Lindford at Emmy's invitation.

Emmy herself arrived just then in a flurry of welcoming words and dazzling smiles for her friends. Her cousin Percy and Lindford were with her. Unfortunately for Mary's peace of mind, Emmy seconded Belinda's invitation to Sir Cedric.

Seeing Sir Cedric at Mary's side, Peveril moved forward, took her hand in his in greeting and asked with a grin, "Quite recovered from your wetting last night, Mary?"

"Oh, I'm none the worse, my lord," she assured him, looking up at him with a glad light in her eyes, adding that all of her toes seemed to be in working order, despite their state of numbness the previous evening.

They laughed together and Belinda cast a resentful eye their way. She was put out to see Lindford greet Mary first, solicitously inquiring if she were recovered from her ordeal. Ignore her, would he? Well, he would learn that he did so at his peril. She would pay him back for such casual behavior, and for his treatment of her last night at the bonfire party, too, she thought petulantly.

When he finally did turn to greet her, Belinda turned a cold shoulder on him, giving her attention to her mild-mannered escort, Sir Thomas, and the unresponsive Sir Cedric, trying to get the handsome but starchy man to flirt with her.

"Cousin, allow me to escort you to the box," Cedric said, bowing formally before Mary and extending his elbow.

Mary felt trapped. She cast a speaking glance Lindford's way.

Peveril responded to her unspoken plea. He took her hand and placed it through his arm, saying, "Too late, Ledbetter. Mary's promised to explain the play to me. Much better to do the polite with young Emmy here. She invited you, after all. Must want your company."

"Miss Marlowe is my betrothed, my lord," Cedric said through clenched teeth.

"Oh, *is* she, by gad?" Peveril asked with a lift of his dark brows, his jaw jutting forward threateningly. He covered Mary's hand where it rested along his sleeve with his other hand, curling his fingers around hers possessively.

Fearing that the viscount would create a scene with the least provocation, Mary spoke quickly and firmly. "No, Cedric, we are *not* engaged." Noticing out of the corner of her eye the general exodus from the vestibule up the grand double staircases to the boxes above, she said, "Do let us go up to the box now. I'm sure the performance will be starting in a few moments."

Cedric looked grim, but had enough manners not to continue the argument in the crowded vestibule of the theatre.

"Oh, yes, do let us go up, Sir Cedric," Emmy said, slipping her small hand through his arm and smiling up at him. "I vow, I am greatly looking forward to this performance," she said with a small laugh. "I've never seen *As You Like It* before. Perhaps you know the play and can tell me about it," she said, with just the right amount of flattery to soothe his ruffled feelings.

Belinda wanted to scream. She had fully counted on having Sir Cedric take her upstairs, but now she was left with the earnest, but dull, Sir Thomas, and the silly Mr. Throckmorton as escorts. Inexplicably, it seemed the two more handsome gentlemen of the party had forgotten all about her.

"I shall be pleased to explain the play to you, Lord Lindford," Mary said aloud. She allowed him to lead her up the stairs, ahead of the rest of the party.

"I very much doubt that any *explanation* will be necessary, but I'm grateful to you for delivering me from my cousin," she whispered conspiratorily, leaning her head close to his shoulder. They stood under the impressive Corinthian rotunda at the top of the stairs awaiting the others before proceeding to the box seats.

"Think nothing of it, my dear. A dashed windbag, is your cousin," Peveril replied with a boyish grin. "Enough to make one want to head for the Antipodes, when he starts prosing on. Wonder what Emmy was about to ask him along? Must have a word with that young chit about prosy bores." A recalcitrant lock of his dark hair fell appealingly over his forehead as he leaned toward her.

Mary swallowed. "Well, with your help I'll be able to keep him at a distance and my ears will be spared. At least for tonight." She smiled. She was pleased to find that their thoughts were in accord regarding her stiff-rumped cousin.

Lindford was looking impossibly handsome tonight, she noticed with a tiny shiver. His coat of mulberry velvet, worn over black silk knee-breeches and a waistcoat of patterned silver satin, hugged his broad shoulders tightly while his dazzlingly white neckcloth tied in an intricate knot served to highlight his dark good looks. He looked the most complete man of fashion and Mary was proud to be on his arm.

She was glad she had taken special pains with her own toilette. Her hair was freshly washed and her dark curls brushed until they shone. She wore one of the gowns she had taken with her when she left her grandfather's. It was one that her Aunt Caroline had selected for her season debut, an aquamarine satin, with a square-cut bodice that left a good deal of her neck and shoulders bare. Over the bodice of her gown, she wore a short worked lace overjacket, with a matching square-cut neck, that extended to her waist and whose lace sleeves fell to her wrists. At her neck, she wore a simple necklace of gold filigree, with matching earrings in her ears. It was not an elaborate costume, but it was elegant. Mary knew it suited her well.

Sitting next to the viscount at the front of the

Belfours' box, their arms touching, Mary felt positively giddy. There was a current of electricity between them that sent her pulse racing. Since his care of her at the bonfire party last night, her feelings toward him had been more confused than ever. Despite his faults, she found herself hopelessly attracted to him.

He had virtually ignored Belinda earlier in the vestibule. Was his infatuation for her beautiful charge beginning to weaken? Mary wondered. She sighed. Even if he no longer fancied himself in love with Belinda, that didn't mean that he was ready to turn to her with a regard deeper than friendship. And she was not sure she would welcome his attentions, anyway, should they turn her way. His was by no means a steady character, she conceded, remembering Lady Belfours' opinion that "the boy still has some growin' up to do."

"What in blazes is that hen-witted shepherdess about to be prasin' Rosalind so, Pev?" Percy leaned across Mary to ask the viscount as they sat together in the front row of Lord Belfour's box. There was a happy buzz of conversation all around them. The third act had just ended and people were taking advantage of the interval to move about and stretch their legs, go in search of refreshments, or to visit acquaintances in other boxes until the next act.

Mary had to stifle a laugh at the perplexed look on Percy's face.

"Deuced if I know, Perce! You know, Mary?" Peveril asked. Sitting beside Mary during the play, he had been as caught up in the action on stage as she was. He had almost forgotten the presence of Belinda, who sat in the row behind them with Emmy, Sir Cedric and Sir Thomas.

"Well, you see," Mary explained, her eyes full of laughter, "Rosalind is disguised as Ganymede, a beardless youth, and Phoebe—that's the shepherdess—has formed a tendre for her, er, him." Mary laughed and threw up her hands at the difficulty of clarifying the tangled situation.

"Confound it all! Can't the foolish wench see that dashed Ganymede is a woman?" Peveril asked in some ire at Phoebe's blindness.

"N–no, evidently not," Mary answered, trying to restraint her mirth. "She has no idea *he* is really a *she!*"

"It's all a dashed take-in, Percy!" Peveril decided. As he leaned over to speak to Percy, his face brushed against Mary's shining curls and he caught the faint scent of violets.

"You mean to say that featherheaded Phoebe has fallen in love with a woman? Never heard of such goings on!" Percy exclaimed, greatly scandalized by such a turn of events.

"Beats me how the wench can be so blind. I wouldn't be fooled by such a disguise," Peveril asserted confidently.

Mary slanted him a look from under her lashes. Perhaps a woman in disguise as a man wouldn't fool him, but a beautiful face had certainly rendered him blind to the reality beneath for a time.

"Phoebe thinks Rosalind's not a woman and Orlando thinks Rosalind's a man," Percy said aloud, trying to get it clear in his own mind. He raised his brows and stared at Mary and Peveril with such a look of outraged confusion on his cherubic face that Mary giggled.

"Ye–yes," she sputtered. "Tha–that's the joke, you see!" she managed to gasp out before she went off into peals of laughter.

"Beats me how they'll all come to rights in the end," Percy said, shaking his head as he tried to puzzle out the various disguises and love triangles.

Peveril glanced at Percy, then looked back at Mary with a grin on his face to see her so overcome. Her mirth was infectious. He gave a great guffaw and joined in her merriment. His laughter mingled with Mary's, drawing several pairs of interested eyes to their box. Percy eyed them askance, wondering what the deuce had set them off so.

"Oh, Sir Cedric," Emmy said on a giggle behind them, "do let us ask Lord Lindford and Miss Marlowe what they find so amusing. I dearly love to share a good laugh."

"I cannot say that I care to do that, Miss Belfours. Such excessive levity must be deplored," Sir Cedric replied ponderously. "I fail to see what Mary could possibly find so amusing," he continued plaintively. "I have always found her to be a most sober and sensible young lady. Indeed, I have always commended her sobriety. The influence of such a rackety young gentleman as the viscount cannot be a beneficial one, I fear . . . the earl will not like this."

"Oh, my," Emmy said with a hint of compassion

for him in her tone. "How unfortunate that you feel so. Perhaps you are not to be laughed at, either?" She looked at him and marveled that so much masculine beauty should be wasted on a man so lacking in any *joie de vivre.*

"*I* be laughed at? My dear young lady, whatever can you be thinking?"

Emmy turned away to hide a smile. Sir Cedric was certainly the most gorgeous man she had ever seen, but he was so humorless and staid that she wanted to poke him with a knitting needle to see if he had more than ice water in his veins. Such a shocking waste! What would it take for him to unbend a little? she wondered. Perhaps a rocket set off beneath him would put some life into him, she thought mischievously, and put her hand over her mouth to stifle her giggles at the absurd idea.

Belinda had insisted that Sir Thomas and Sir Cedric sit on either side of her when they reached the Belfours' box, but she was not satisfied with the attention of the two gentlemen. She wished to have all masculine eyes turned her way and was quite miffed to see Lindford, her once ardent suitor, sitting beside Mary, and laughing with her as if they would never stop. She was already peeved that he had ignored her when he had arrived at the theatre. Never before had a gentleman turned to greet another woman first when she was present!

And he had not even turned about in his seat to pay her his compliments during the interval! Well, she had the handsome Sir Cedric at her elbow now. She would show Lindford! She turned to Sir Cedric, put her hand on his arm, smiled sweetly up at him, and bade him take her out in the corridor where they might procure refreshments and a breath of air.

Cedric glanced to Mary, but seeing that her attention was still distracted by Lindford, he pressed his lips together firmly and unsmilingly agreed to Belinda's request.

Belinda glanced over her shoulder as she left with Cedric to see how her departure affected the viscount, hoping to see him jealously watching her. But she was foiled in this attempt to attract his attention. Lindford didn't even notice her departure. He was still laughing with Mary and Percy, too engrossed in his conversation with the others to have an inkling that she was leaving his company. She flounced out, with a frown turning down her rosebud lips.

"Well, Sir Thomas, seems we're to bear one another company," Emmy said to that mild young gentleman as Belinda callously abandoned him. She giggled at the look of astonishment on his face as he watched Belinda leave the box. Her lively sense of humor was tickled at the predicament they found themselves in.

"Oh, sorry, Miss Belfours. Did you wish to take a turn outside?" Sir Thomas asked. He looked a bit pink about the gills, clearly abashed at his impoliteness in ignoring such an attractive young lady.

"Indeed, sir, that would be delightful. And you must tell me what you think of the play thus far," she requested prettily, rising to her feet and accepting his outstretched arm. She smiled up at him impishly, seeking to put him at his ease. Really, he was a pleasant gentleman. Perhaps she should cultivate his regard, Emmaline thought with a twinkle in her eyes.

* * *

Mary and Peveril laughed so hard that tears ran down their cheeks, and Mary's side began to ache.

Percy, still puzzled about what they found so hilarious, scratched his head and rose from his chair, announcing he was going for refreshments.

"Bring us back some lemonade, will you, Perce? There's a good fellow," the viscount said, when he could speak again. At Percy's nod, Peveril looked down at Mary to see that she was wiping her streaming eyes with her finger tips. He proffered his handkerchief.

She smiled at the rueful look on Peveril's face as he passed her the square of linen. He shook his head at her over such nonsense and she laughed again.

"Devilish fellow that Shakespeare. Called him Willie Wobbledagger at school, you know."

"Did you, my lord? And whose clever idea was that?"

"My Uncle Sherbourne's. Brilliant fellow. A dashed genius, in fact. Went up to Oxford, you know. Loved Shakespeare. Would've twigged to it straightaway, all this disguise business."

Peveril's arm rested along the back of her chair as he tilted back in his own seat, raising the front feet of his chair off the ground, and teetering back and forth in a haphazard fashion. As he rocked, his hand carelessly brushed Mary's bare shoulder now and again, sending little shivers of excitement down her spine.

"You'd never seen the play before tonight then, my lord?"

"No. First time. Dashed interesting that wrestling

scene. And, Mary, thought we'd agreed you're to call me Peveril. Feel a hundred years old with you lording me to death all the time," he teased, brushing the back of her neck where her curls ended with a careless finger.

Mary blushed faintly at his touch and the sound of her name on his lips. "Think you could challenge Orlando and best him in a wrestling match, do you, Peveril?"

"I'd have a dashed good go at it! Can you see me in those tights the fellows wear, though?" he asked with a wicked grin.

"Do you know, I believe I could," she answered boldly, then blushed at her own words. They went on teasing one another in this fashion until the others returned to the box and the next act of the play began.

Peveril went home that evening realizing once more what an entertaining little lady Mary was. Why, he thought in surprise, he hadn't spoken to the Beauty above two or three times all evening. And he hadn't even missed her company!

Some six or seven weeks after he had intended to be back in London, Mr. Ramsbottom returned to his house in Curzon Street. He offered no explanation as to why he had been delayed so long, believing it was not his employees' concern where or how he spent his time. But his sojourn in the north had been very lucrative, very lucrative, he reflected with satisfaction.

"Mr. Ramsbottom's come 'ome, ma'am, and 'e's wishful for you to wait on 'im in 'is office straightaway," a frightened-looking housemaid informed Mary soon after the master's return.

"Thank you, Sarah, I shall go down directly," Mary replied with a calmness she was far from feeling. Well, she told herself after the maid had left her bedchamber, she had done the job she had been hired for to the best of her ability and her employer would have no complaint to find with her.

She tidied her hair, ran her hands over her skirt to smooth out the creases, straightened her back and left her room with her head held high. She walked calmly down the stairs and, when she reached Mr. Ramsbottom's office, she raised her chin and rapped sharply upon the door.

In answer to Mr. Ramsbottom's demand for a report on what introductions Mary had secured for his daughter among the *ton* and on how Belinda had spent her time, and with whom, since he had left them in London in early October, Mary gave short, succinct replies, not elaborating on the details or volunteering her own opinion about how matters stood between Belinda and each of her suitors.

She also mentioned the attempted robbery in Green Park and their rescue by Viscount Lindford and Mr. Throckmorton.

"Seen much of the two heroes since then?" Mr. Ramsbottom asked, with a shrewd look.

"Belinda has frequently seen them when we've been out, but, in accordance with your wishes, sir, they have not called upon her here at the house."

Mr. Ramsbottom looked at Mary carefully and asked, "My daughter favors this young daredevil Lindford, does she?"

"She seems to be happy in the company of both gentlemen, Mr. Ramsbottom." Mary evaded the question. Something in her demeanor must have alerted her employer that Belinda favored the viscount, she thought uneasily. Having no wish to give him all the details of the ups and downs of Belinda's relationship with Lindford, she took care to school her features to blandness.

"But she is also happy in the company of the Duke of Exford, Sir Thomas Nichols, Mr. Peregrine Fowler, and several other gentlemen," Mary continued. "She has met also my cousin, Sir Cedric Ledbetter, my grandfather's heir, and has allowed him to dance with her and join us at the theatre. Indeed, sir, Belinda enjoys the admiration of many gentlemen, as you had hoped."

"She does not favor Exford, you say?"

"No, sir, not over any of the other gentlemen. Though she gives his grace a pleased welcome whenever he approaches her."

"I'm surprised. Thought I'd made it plain to her that she would enjoy bein' a duchess. Expected things to be in train for that happy event by now," Mr. Ramsbottom remarked. He looked keenly at Mary with small, piercing dark eyes.

She colored under his scrutiny, but gave him back a firm look, meeting his eyes calmly.

"She'll be very sparin' of her company with these other young rapscallions from now on. Don't want her consortin' with Fowler or Nichols more'n a how-de-do in public calls for. As for the duke, she'll find herself very partial to his company. Very partial. As for this Lindford rascal, she's not to see him, until I say she might. Got to look into matters. Look into matters. Expect you to carry out my wishes in this matter, missy, carry out my wishes," Mr. Ramsbottom directed, his heavy, bushy brows coming down over his eyes as he frowned.

Mary knew her employer favored the Duke of Exford, but she very much disliked being a party to a conspiracy against Belinda. She did not care to see anyone else, not even her silly charge, forced to wed a man not of her own choosing. In that instant she suddenly realized how much Mr. Ramsbottom resembled her grandfather, the Earl of Wyndham. Both were trying to force their female relatives to marry for titles and financial gain.

"I'm sure you will wish to discuss matters with Belinda herself, sir," she replied with a straight look, her chin raised.

"Aye, no doubt I will," he said, staring hard at her. "No doubt I will." He hooked his thumbs in the pockets of his waistcoat and dismissed Mary, turning to look out into the small garden through the French windows on one side of the room.

Mary had no doubt that as soon as the door closed noiselessly behind her on its well-oiled hinges Mr. Ramsbottom would put into motion an investigation of Viscount Lindford and Mr. Throckmorton. She very much feared that the viscount would prove to be as purse-pinched as Emmy and her friends had hinted. If Mr. Ramsbottom forbade his daughter to see the two young gentlemen, she didn't know what to expect from her notoriously flighty charge. She could only hope that Belinda's feelings for the viscount had weakened to such an extent that she wouldn't throw a tantrum.

As for herself, she would be very sorry not to see Lindford any more, especially now, when there seemed to be some hope of his turning his attentions away from Belinda. The more she was in his company, the more Mary felt the tug of friendship—and something else—between them. It would be hard to give up the acquaintance of such a charming—and handsome—young gentleman, she thought sadly, going upstairs to rouse Belinda from her beauty sleep.

Chapter 12

News of Mr. Ramsbottom's return spread rapidly through the ranks of Belinda's suitors, leaving a few smiling in satisfaction, and many more frowning in consternation. Viscount Lindford was one of the first to learn of the financier's return to the metropolis.

"By God! This passes all bounds, so it does, Percy!" Peveril thundered when he read the curt note he had received from Mr. Ramsbottom's legal adviser, informing him that he was to cease his attentions to the heiress forthwith, or beware the consequences. He crushed the paper in his fisted hand and swore vehemently.

"What is it, Pev?" Percy asked apprehensively, seeing that his friend was in a furious temper, pacing about the sitting room and banging his fist against any furniture in sight.

The viscount tossed the crumpled paper to his friend. Percy was astounded to read the boldly-worded letter which said that certain outstanding notes of hand bearing Lindford's signature were in Mr. Ramsbottom's possession and hinted strongly that the gentleman would not hesitate to use them to his advantage, were the viscount to continue his pursuit of Miss Ramsbottom.

"Blood and thunder confound it, I won't stand for this! A damned cit trying to blackmail me!" Peveril was in a towering fury.

"What are you going to do, Pev?"

"By God, I *will* see Belinda! As soon as I can contrive it! By hook or by crook, I *will* see her!" he swore, pounding his fist into his hand.

Percy was not surprised. His intemperate, hotheaded friend, was going to do what any self-respecting young blade would do—he was going to defy the edict.

"And by God, I'll speak with her, too. Not only that, but the very next time I'm alone with her, I'll steal a kiss!" he swore as he paced about the small room. He was determined to persuade Belinda to agree to meet him in public and in private whenever he wanted.

So, although only days before he had been on the point of acknowledging that his affections had cooled remarkably toward the Beauty, now that the association had been forbidden, he experienced all the fierceness of lovesick longing he had felt on first glimpsing her exquisite features. The fire to possess drove him to reckless measures.

Percy saw his friend move purposefully to his cluttered desk where he swept all the assorted papers, letters, bills, and whatnot on top of the desk to the floor with his arm. Then he wrenched open the drawer, drew out a sheet of paper, picked up a feathered quill, and began to write furiously.

Forgetting all about what a vain, empty-headed little peagoose she was, and about how he had been finding her tantrums and conversation a dead bore of late, Peveril scrawled a hasty note to Belinda, telling her he was devastated by her father's decree and begging her to grant him at least two dances at the Belfours' holiday ball to be held in less than a week's time. As an afterthought, he hastily scribbled some suitably mawkish protestations of his everlasting devotion.

"You writin' to the Beauty, Pev?" Percy asked uneasily, wondering if he could escape the awful fix his impetuous friend was about to land in.

"You can be devilish sure I am, Percy!" Peveril answered, not looking up from his task.

When he had finished the letter, the viscount sat pondering for a moment, quickly deciding that he must redouble his efforts to mend his fortunes. And in the fastest way possible, too.

So it was that he repaired to an exclusive establishment notorious for its high-stakes gambling games, located just off St. James Street, that very evening. There he threw what little caution he possessed to the wind and played piquet for one-hundred pounds a point with a certain Captain Jonas Swinton, an adventurer of dubious background.

Lindford jumped up from the small deal table where he had been playing piquet in a dimly-lit corner of the elegant gaming establishment, oversetting a bottle of claret. It spilled over the cards spread out over the green baize covered table.

"You're a damned cheat, Swinton!" Peveril swore violently as he leaned over the table and grabbed his opponent by the neckcloth. "You've marked the cards and gulled me out of a thousand guineas. I'll see you in hell before I'll let you get away with it!"

Percy leapt forward from his position behind the table where he had been watching the play and grabbed the viscount by the tails of his jacket to pull him away from Captain Swinton.

"Don't do it, Pev!" Jeremy Fletcher joined Percy, hoping to prevent the viscount from issuing the challenge that seemed to be hovering in the smoky air.

"You dare to impunge my honesty, Lindford? By God, you'll meet me on the field of honor, if that's what you're implying!" the balding Swinton exploded savagely. Almost foaming in his anger, his long, bushy black mustaches reaching over the top of his cruel mouth and across his sunken cheeks to meet his long black side whiskers, the captain was the picture of dissipated malevolence.

"No, no, Swinton! He don't mean any such thing," Fletcher told the man who was glaring at them suspiciously out of narrowed, red-rimmed eyes. "Thing is, Pev's taken on a deal of liquor. Don't know what he's saying."

"Duellin'. Not at all the thing. Law against it," interjected a much discomposed Percy.

A hush had fallen over the noisy, smoky room and all necks were craned their way.

The viscount tried to break free from his friends' hands. "Let me go, Jer! I ain't foxed enough not to know when I've been cheated," he objected passionately. "Fellow's a damned snake. He's fleeced me, as sure as check. A curst card sharp, if ever I saw one!"

" 'Fraid you're in the wrong, Lindford," interrupted Peregrine Fowler who had been lurking nearby, observing the game. "The game was fair. Seems you can't hold your liquor, my boy. Time to go home." Still smarting from his unsuccessful interview with Stanley Ramsbottom just that morning, where he had requested the hand of the divine Belinda and been sent away with a flea in his ear, Peregrine was in a foul mood. He was determined to even a whole host of scores against the viscount.

"Why, you jackass!" Peveril thundered, his fists flailing in Fowler's direction as he tried to break free from Jeremy's hold. "I'll give you a taste of the home-brewed, if you don't take your damned interfering nose out of this."

"Keep out of this, Fowler," Jeremy warned the viscount's antagonist. "Ain't none of your concern."

"Take him away, Fletcher, or I'll have you all thrown out of here. If you don't leave peaceably, I'll see to it that you're barred from all respectable establishments in future!" Fowler threatened menacingly.

"No need to resort to that, Fowler. We're leaving," Jeremy said as he struggled to help Percy hold on the savagely swearing, struggling viscount.

"Fellow's mad! Should be locked up!" Swinton grumbled as he carefully folded the viscount's note of hand and stowed it in his pocket.

"Jer, Jer! Blister it, don't let that curst villain get away with it!" Peveril begged in a passion as his friends each took one of his arms and began to drag him toward the door.

* * *

"Should have let me challenge that damned loose screw of a swine, Jer," Peveril complained as he sat back with his eyes closed in one of the dilipadated chairs in the sitting room of Jeremy's lodgings in the Albany. His head was throbbing abominably and he hadn't yet touched the cup of coffee resting on the table at his elbow. He felt so miserable, he began to suspect the claret he had been drinking was doctored with some sleeping potion or other to deaden his senses.

"You're foxed, Pev. 'Sides, Swinton had Fowler to back him up. The captain's accounted a deadly shot, you know. Don't fancy seein' you with a hole blown through you," Jeremy said.

"No, by Jove. Not at all the thing. Ladies wouldn't like it," interjected a bleary-eyed Percy.

"No way to prove he's a cheat. Best to just let it go this time. Spread the word quietly that's he's a deuced gull catcher and try to keep other young gudgeons out of his clutches," Jeremy counselled.

"Guess I behaved like a dashed greenhead, didn't I, allowing myself to be plucked by a captain sharp that way?" Peveril said bitterly.

"You'll have to pay up. Only thing to do."

The viscount looked at his friend bleakly.

"Chalk it up to experience, Pev," Jeremy advised him.

"I'm all to pieces, now," groaned the viscount, his hand clutching his aching head. "Have to sell off all my cattle to pay the bastard. But not Ajax. No way will I ever sell him."

"How much did you lose?" Jeremy asked quietly.

"Just over a thousand guineas."

There was silence in the room as the other two digested this enormous sum. Percy whistled between his teeth.

"Was trying to make a recoup. Already owe twice that much. First part of the evening, I was winning, you know. Had about five-hundred guineas to my credit. Should have quit then. But Swinton wanted to double the stakes. I was a fool to accept," the viscount admitted dejectedly.

"What'll you do, now, Pev?" Percy asked, waiting in some trepidation for his friend's answer.

"Don't go near the cent-per-centers, Pev!" Jeremy interjected quickly. "Probably better to mortgage your property to pay off the most pressing of your debts. Have to rusticate for a time, too."

"Been planning to go home to High Acres soon anyway, but to leave now would mean leaving the Beauty, and letting her old goat of a father win!" Peveril protested.

"Old Ramsbottom will never give his consent to let you court her," Jeremy said in a sympathetic voice, hoping his friend would see the truth of the situation. "You might as well face it."

Peveril heaved a sigh and admitted, "You're right, Jer. Time to give over my pretentions to her hand, I suppose . . . was never the prospect of her dowry, you know."

"We know, Pev," Jeremy assured him. "The Incomparable's an uncommon beauty, and no mistake. Still and all, a beautiful face has been the ruination of many a man."

"Just like Helen of Troy," Percy interjected.

The other two looked at him with raised brows.

"Leave it to Percy to come up with such a corkbrained notion, eh, Jer," Peveril said with the suggestion of a grin on his tired young face.

"I don't know, Pev. Seems to me, there's something in his nonsense this time," Jeremy said with a laugh. "Helen led all of Troy and many of the mightiest Greek heroes to their destruction and sent the others wandering the world for years. Just shows you what havoc a beautiful face can wreak."

Mary was not privy to the various reports that reached Mr. Ramsbottom, but they were all in agreement. Young Viscount Lindford was a wastrel, in the manner of his spendthrift father and gaily frivolous mother. His estates brought in no profit, and he seemed to be living on a very meagre income that he frittered away in the most careless fashion imaginable.

Four days after his return, Mr. Ramsbottom summoned Belinda and Mary to his office, for such he called the grand room on the first floor that held his wide mahogany desk and several locked cabinets. He had not use for the frivolous room the upper classes called a library. In his bluff, no-nonsense way, he called the room what it was in plain English.

Mary went downstairs with a sinking heart, afraid she knew what was to come.

It was worse than she had imagined.

Mr. Ramsbottom had found that not only were the

viscount's pockets to let, but that he was in the habit of attending gaming hells, usually with disastrous results.

"I've learned the young rascal has got the gamblin' fever. Thinks nothing of wagerin' money he ain't got in gamin' hells, riskin' everything on the turn of a card. The young fool! He ain't sound. Ain't sound, I tell you!" Mr. Ramsbottom pronounced, pounding his fist heavily on his solid desk. "The young gudgeon's all to pieces! Can't understand it—fritterin' away his time and money like that. Must have maggots for brains. Allowed himself to be plucked like a chicken more than once, from what I've heard. Plucked like a chicken!"

Mary heard his words with dismay.

"Now, missy, I've given orders this young fool Lindford is not to attempt to so much as speak to you. You'll cut him dead when you see him in public. Cut him dead, do you hear," he roared at his daughter.

"Oh, Papa," Belinda wailed, tears trembling on the ends of his exquisite eyelashes, "how can you be so cwuel! My heart will bweak."

"What's that you say? I'll have no talk of broken hearts, missy. No talk, do you hear! Thought you didn't like the fellow above half, anyway," he said, rolling an inquiring eye Mary's way.

She looked stoically back at him; she did not so much as blink her eyes at his look of accusation. She had stood up to far worse from her imperious grandfather.

Belinda dabbed at her eyes with her ever-present handkerchief. "But, Papa, he wescued us, just like a handsome knight in my book," she argued, recollecting now the romantic scene that had begun to fade from her memory.

"I'm grateful to him for that and from what I've gathered, you've showed him enough courtesy over these past weeks to repay him handsomely. You've repaid him handsomely, I say."

He dismissed Mary, then tried to cajole his daughter into looking upon the match with the Duke of Exford more favorably, for he had found during his travels that although the duke was not overly burdened with ready cash, his richly-appointed country estate, Exford Court, held untold treasures. And, too, the duke had an adequate income from his tenant farms and other investments to provide for himself and a wife and family.

Mr. Ramsbottom used all his considerable persuasive powers to entice his daughter to encourage Exford's suit. He pointed out that as a duchess she would be living out her dreams. Were not most of her picturebook heroines really high-born ladies in disguise? And did not most of them wear tiny crowns of diamonds on their heads? he asked cunningly, appealing to her love of the dramatic, as well as to her penchant for costly jewels and other finery.

Belinda was swayed by her father's description of the life she would lead among the upper echelons of society as a duchess. She was especially taken with the image of herself wearing a diamond tiara and an ermine cape and being addressed as your grace. Almost she was persuaded. Almost.

But Mr. Ramsbottom's lecture had had another

effect, an effect that would have annoyed him greatly. It had served to reignite her interest in the viscount.

Although her father had always been able to talk her round to his point of view before, she was not to be cozened this time. This time, seeing herself as a real maiden in distress, she had taken it into her head to act out her fantasies. Of course, the fact that Lindford was so much younger and more handsome than the duke, and so much more physically desirable, had something to do with her decision, as did her rememberance of the stolen kisses she had shared with him, deliciously spine-tingling and somewhat frightening as they had been.

So, although her feelings for the viscount were not profound and had even begun to cool under his occasional flashes of temper and his outright criticism, as well as his stubborn insistence on having his own way sometimes even when it was directly contrary to hers, and lately his blatant disinterest, she determined to see him again, not so much to spite her papa as for the excitement of a clandestine meeting. The fact that her association with him was forbidden made it irresistibly romantic.

When his secret note arrived, she was thrilled. But with her limited skills in reading, she had no luck in puzzling it out. She consulted Bessie, but her maid was of no help, for the young abigail could not read a lick.

Mary was surprised and relieved at how docilely Belinda had accepted her father's commands, but she had no suspicion that her charge had received a secret communication from the viscount until she came upon her unexpectedly.

"What have you there, Belinda?" she asked, walking into Belinda's bedchamber through the door that had been left ajar.

Belinda gave a little gasp. "Ohh!" and whisked the paper under her skirts spread out over her chair. She had not heard Mary come into the room. She was too busy once again trying to decipher what the viscount had written to her.

Mary regarded her charge's trembling lips and the high flush on her cheeks with dismay. Oh no, she thought, with foreboding. She was not surprised when Belinda burst into tears.

Incoherently through her sobs, Belinda accused Mary of being a traitor who had no romance in her soul and who would act as her jailor again now that her papa was home.

Clasping her hands loosely before her, Mary took a deep breath. "Now calm yourself, Belinda. Your note is from the viscount, is it not? Never fear. I shan't report it to your father. I cannot approve his treatment of you."

"You can't?" Belinda blinked away her tears as she stared up at Mary round-eyed.

"No. It is just such as I have been subjected to by my grandfather," Mary said with a martial light in her eyes. "Mr. Ramsbottom thinks to marry you to the Duke of Exford. But if that is not what you wish, also, you do not have to agree. You must choose your own husband, Belinda. A man who will make *you* happy, not one who will make your papa happy."

After Mr. Ramsbottom's words that morning, Mary had decided that she could no longer remain in his employ. She could no more approve his actions toward his daughter, than she could her grandfather's toward her, and the idea of earning her wages by helping Mr. Ramsbottom coerce Belinda into a marriage that perhaps the girl did not want was repugnant to her.

She had gone directly to her room and penned a note to the school in Oxford, asking if she could return to her teaching post there. She had written to her Cousin Caroline, as well, thinking that perhaps she would visit her for a week or two in the new year before returning to the young ladies' seminary, if they should agree to have her back. In the meantime, she saw no way she could avoid accompanying Mr. Ramsbottom and Belinda to Sidmouth in a few days time where her employer planned to spend the Christmas holidays.

"Oh, you are wight!" Belinda exclaimed. "Yes, I will choose my own husband, for how can Papa know who will suit me best?"

"But you would be wise to take much care when you choose. I—I am not at all sure Viscount Lindford is the right husband for you, Belinda. He is very young and volatile, you know. Sometimes it has seemed to me that he is not always as considerate of your feelings as you would like." Mary hoped to remove some of the glow of romantic adventure attendant on secret letters and meetings with the viscount by reminding Belinda of his shortcomings.

"You have time. Why not enjoy the Season next spring before you make up your mind? Think of the many more admirers you will have when all the *ton* returns to London."

In her opinion, Belinda would be more content with an older man who would humor her and take care of her and give in to her every whim, not a wild young man who was as stubborn as she was and who would argue with her as soon as not. "You will want a husband who always puts your wishes and desires first, and who will adore you and always think you the most beautiful woman in the world, will you not?" Mary tried to state her case fairly, and not let her own feelings in the matter influence her argument.

Belinda darted Mary a look, then said, "That is twue." She put her little finger on her chin as she considered the matter. "But it would be too cwuel not even to answer Pevewil's letter," she added with more cunning than Mary realized. "He loves me so!"

Mary spirits sank. Her heart did not break precisely, but she thought she felt a distinct crack at the words.

"Will you wead it to me, Marwy?" Belinda asked cajolingly, pulling the note from under her skirts and holding it out.

Mary hesitated. Seeing that Belinda's curiosity was too strong to be denied, as was only to be expected under the circumstances, she agreed. "Of—of course," she said, overcoming her reluctance.

With difficulty, she deciphered the hastily scrawled note, then summed up its contents for Belinda. "Lord Lindford has been devastated by your father's orders forbidding him to see you. He begs you to save two dances for him at the Belfours' ball. He has something peculiar—no, that can't be it—ah, *particular,* he wishes to say to you there."

"Oh, yes, I will. Indeed, I will!"

"And he expresses his undying devotion to you and begs that you will not be so cruel as to dash his hopes," Mary repeated dully, letting the paper drop from her hand onto Belinda's dressing table.

Belinda clapped her hands and then hugged herself with joy when the note was read to her.

Well, Mary thought to herself after perusing the contents of the viscount's letter, she had to give Lindford credit. He certainly knew how to pique Belinda's interest and gratify her vanity. Not many young ladies would be able to resist such a romantic communication. The girl had a positively beatific smile on her lovely face as she gazed off into space.

It was distressing to find that Lindford had not given up his pursuit of her charge, as she had hoped. He seemed determined to act foolishly, spurred on, no doubt, by Mr. Ramsbottom's opposition to his suit. Her own heart dropped to her shoes.

Ah well, she thought with an wry little smile, she knew she had been air dreaming. He was a careless and unreliable young gentleman and it would be altogether better for her if she forgot what a charming companion he could be. Her mind didn't touch on the other matter—how his slightest touch made her pulse leap and sent shivers tingling down her spine.

Belinda's brilliant smile faded quickly and she said

in a small voice, "Oh, but Papa will never allow me to go if he knows Lindford will be there." Then she brightened and exclaimed, "But he will let me go if Dukey is my escort! Oh, Marwy, you must help me wite to Pevewil stwaight away." She laughed delightedly, her spirits swinging from dejection to giddiness in a moment. "It is a good thing Papa cannot accompany me, for he would spoil all my plans," she exclaimed unfeelingly. The *beau monde* might grudgingly bend a bit to accept the beautiful, well-dowered Miss Ramsbottom, but it would never accept her bluff tradesman of a father.

Much against her better judgment, but afraid it would be a show of jealousy unworthy of her to refuse, Mary reluctantly agreed to answer the viscount's note in Belinda's name. When she had finished penning the letter Belinda dictated, her charge took it from her and insisted on sealing it in private.

After Mary had left the room, Belinda dabbed the paper with her own special perfume and snipped a tiny lock of her hair, pressing it carefully between the folded page before sealing the letter with a wafer.

Without telling Mary of her intentions, Belinda conceived the notion that the escapade would be considerably enhanced if she sent a secret message to Lindford. She was determined to squeeze every ounce of romance from the adventure she could. Therefore when she sent Bessie with the missive, she instructed the abigail to tell the viscount that her mistress was in floods of tears, that her love for him was undying, and that she was relying on him to rescue her from her cruel father and the terrible fate he had in store for her that was worse than death.

Chapter 13

"Don't Emmy look up to all the rigs tonight, Miss Marlowe?" Percy asked proudly. He stood beside Mary, watching his cousin Emmaline and her parents, his Aunt Belle and Uncle Simon Belfours, greet their guests for their Christmas entertainment. Emmy's sparkling vivacity and Lady Belfours' good humor ensured that the family's circle of friends was quite extensive and despite their best intentions, their small entertainment had mushroomed into a full-blown ball.

"Yes, indeed, she looks very lovely, Mr. Throckmorton," Mary agreed, watching the animated young girl greet each arriving guest with equal enthusiasm before she turned and smiled glowingly at Sir Thomas Nichols who had come to claim her hand for the first set. "And she looks as though she's enjoying every minute of this ball."

The elegant gold and white ballroom was festooned with evergreen boughs swathed in wide red ribbons, and the fresh scent of the greenery filled the room. Bunches of mistletoe tied with gaily-colored, trailing ribbons hung overhead and the glow from a hundred candles lit the room with soft, dancing light. The orchestra was playing seasonal music and Mary observed that high spirits and laughter bubbled everywhere around her.

Mary glanced over at Belinda who stood across the room from her with the Duke of Exford. One of her little gloved hands rested against the duke's lapel and she was looking up at him adoringly. Mary was surprised that she was showing so much attention to her middle-aged suitor, but as the viscount had not yet put in an appearance, she supposed that Belinda was making do with the duke's attention until Lindford arrived.

Belinda had been in a fever of suppressed excitement all that afternoon about her assignation with the viscount. She had taken the duke by surprise when he came to collect them. Instead of making her usual grand entrance by sweeping down the curved staircase of her father's house, she had been impatiently pacing about in the entrance hallway, awaiting his arrival.

"All Emmy's idea—this party, you know," Percy recalled Mary's attention with a beaming smile. "Wanted to celebrate in town before Aunt Belle and Uncle Simon retired to Wiltshire for the holidays. Chit's made a splash during the little season. Think she's testing her wings tonight, hoping to fly high next spring."

"Oh, I'm sure Emmy will be one of the toasts of the season next year with her infectious high spirits and kind nature," Mary complimented him on his relative. "All the other girls like her. There's no jealousy there, and I've noticed that the young men already seem to flock around her." If Belinda had been more like Emmy Belfours her job would have been a great deal more pleasant, Mary thought with a suppressed sigh.

Percy's chest swelled with justifiable pride at her words. "Yes, Emmy's a taking little thing, all right and tight!"

"The chit looks as fine as fivepence tonight," Peveril remarked as he joined them, but his eyes were not on Emmy but on her, Mary saw with a blush. "Look dashed fetching this evening, Mary," he told her with a gleam of appreciation in his blue eyes, noticing that her wide eyes appeared enormous in the sparkling candlelight of the ballroom.

Mary's smile was warm as she met his eyes. She was gratified by his compliment, for she had dressed with special care. As she would soon be leaving Mr. Ramsbottom's employ, this would likely be the last time she would be appearing amongst the *ton.* She had chosen to wear one of her favorite gowns, a dark red velvet, cut low over the bosom and trimmed with pale cream ribbon threaded through the hem, and along the sleeves and neckline. It had been a Christmas present from her grandfather last year. She wore her pearl choker at her throat and tiny luminescent pearl earrings in her ears.

Peveril continued to look at her, his head a little on one side as Percy chattered on. "Aunt Belle has done a bang-up job to arrange all this in such short order, you know."

"Daresay your uncle came up trumps with the blunt," Pev interjected with a quirk of one eyebrow.

"Oh, yes, Uncle Simon can never resist Aunt Belle. M'father's the same with Mama. Sisters. Guess that accounts for it."

Mary, unable to follow Mr. Throckmorton's disjointed remarks, turned inquiring eyes to the viscount for elucidation.

"Lady Belfours—sister to Percy's mama. Same kind of women. Easy to get along with. Don't cut up stiff with their offspring. Wind their husbands round their thumbs. Only difference is, Lady Belfours don't have cats," the viscount said with a darkling glance at Percy.

"Cats?" Mary asked, once more at a loss.

But Peveril didn't enlighten her. He had spotted Belinda who was taking the floor to dance with the Duke of Exford.

"Come and dance with me, Mary," he said without preamble, stretching his hand out for hers.

"Here! I say, Pev. Was just about to ask Miss Marlowe to dance m'self," Percy protested.

"Well, you're too late, Percy. Go find some other lady to pester," the viscount called over his shoulder as he led Mary into the dance.

" 'Fraid I've got myself in the devil of a fix, Mary," he confessed as they took their places for the country dance.

"Oh? What sort of a fix, my lord?" she asked anxiously.

"Would feel much better if you'd call me Peveril, Mary," he said.

"What sort of a fix, Peveril?"

He sighed and said remorsefully, "Daresay you know about the dashed note I wrote to Belinda." At

Mary's nod, he continued, "Should never have written it. Silly thing to do when I know—when I know I have nothing to offer her, or—or to any woman . . . 'fraid I'm badly dipped. Must leave town and return home for a time, and try to mend my fortunes."

"Are you in serious trouble, Peveril?" Mary asked with a lurch of her stomach, fear for him causing her insides to churn.

He didn't answer for a time, but gazed down at her, his troubled blue eyes filled with regret. "It don't redound to my credit but—I've been every kind of a fool, Mary," he cried. "Gambling with money I didn't have, like the veriest greenhorn." His jaw worked as he swallowed the oaths aimed at his own unmitigated foolishness. "Blister it! I've learned my lesson now, when it's too late. Going home to rusticate. Tonight will have to be goodbye." He looked at her with tender sadness in his eyes.

Mary swallowed over the lump in her throat. "I—I don't know what Belinda will do. She's been so looking forward to this evening. You—you will tell her gently."

He looked at her uncomprehendingly for a moment. "Belinda? Oh, aye. I'll let her down easy," he promised. "Lord!" he said with a lopsided grin, "She's enough to turn any man's head when he first casts his eyes over her. But it was never on the cards from the start, was it? I just wish—" he broke off, sighing, gazing soulfully down into her eyes.

"What?" Mary whispered, not looking away from his intense blue gaze.

"Never mind, sweet Mary. That idea's as nonsensical as the other."

When the dance ended, they stood looking at one another for a few moments before Mary began to say shyly, "I will miss your company, Peveril, but I wish you well, and if you're determined to turn things around, I think you'll come about before—"

She was cut off when Belinda abruptly left the duke's side and hurried up to them saying, "Oh, Pevewil, here you are at last! I had quite given up hope, you know. You are vewy naughty to keep me waiting. But you are just in time for our dance, after all," Belinda said in a rush, almost casting herself against his chest as she looked up at him with her eyes sparkling feverishly and her cheeks becomingly heated.

Unhappily, Mary watched them go off to join the next set. She saw Belinda stop and whisper something to the viscount. He bent his dark head down to her golden one and when he straightened up again, Mary was surprised to see them circle the floor and then walk out of the ballroom through the double doors that led to the refreshment room.

He undoubtedly wished to bid her farewell in private, she thought, then shuddered, imagining the scene Belinda was capable of creating. She was preparing to follow them so that she could quiet Belinda's stormy reaction, when Lord Belfours appeared before her, bowed, and gallantly requested her hand for the set just forming. She did not feel that the sudden complaint of a sprained ankle or torn flounce would be quite polite to her courtly host, so with one anxious look over her shoulder at the doors through which the couple had disappeared, she went off to dance with Emmy's father.

When Belinda and the viscount had not reappeared in the ballroom by the end of the set, Mary was seriously alarmed and resolved to go in search of them.

"Oh, Pevewil, my papa is so cwuel," Belinda cried, casting herself against the viscount's chest when he had closed the door of the unoccupied room she had led him into. His arms came round her immediately.

"He says I mustn't see you anymore. And he wants me to marwy Exfowd."

Belinda had by now convinced herself that she loved Lindford quite desperately. The anticipated thrill of this meeting had been building in her for days. All her excitement crested at this auspicious moment and she was determined to play the scene for all it was worth.

"Oh, does he, by Jove? And what have you to say to that?"

She looked up at him through a haze of tears. "Well, I would like to be a duchess, and wear a tiara, but Dukey is so old!" she exclaimed innocently. She rested her head on his shoulder and gave a little hiccup of a sob.

"Yes, yes, he is," Peveril agreed distractedly, patting her back as he would a child's. A modicum of sense began to seep back into his brain. He already regretted his over-hasty note filled with overblown pledges of undying devotion, and now he was beginning to see that he had been most unwise in allowing the foolish chit talk him into leading her into this deserted room.

Then she looked up at him pleadingly.

"You must wescue me again, Pevewil, like you did that night in Gween Pawk.—Only it was wonderful, weally, because I met you.—But you must take me away from London before Papa bweaks my heart," she pleaded, raising her breathtaking tear-drenched emerald eyes to his. "After all, we are going to be marwied."

"What!" he exclaimed, startled. "Going to be married?" He squinted down at her, trying to recall if he had ever been foxed in her company and done such a dashed silly thing as propose marriage to her.

"Well, of course we are."

"Daresay you're in the right of it, my dear girl, but deuced if I can remember popping the question."

"Oh, silly! You didn't *say* anything exactly, but I knew when you kissed me that you wanted to marwy me. I wouldn't let someone kiss me, if we weren't going to be marwied, you know," she said on a trill of laughter. "You surwely wemember kissing me, don't you?"

"By Jupiter, don't I just!" he exclaimed. He found he was not as indifferent to her ravishing beauty as he'd thought. He looked down at those full, pink lips, trembling for him as he fancied, and couldn't resist just one more taste.

As he tasted those delicious lips, covering them briefly with his own, he remembered that this was goodbye. It made his blood boil to think that when he left town he would leave the field clear for her other moonstruck suitors, the assorted tulips, beaux, and fribbles who hung around her, making cakes of themselves.

"Dashed if I won't do it again!" He lowered his head and kissed her once again, more thoroughly this time. The lingering kiss set his blood to pounding through his veins. He promptly lost his head and whatever good intentions he had formed as he deepened the kiss and crushed her to his chest. Hearing her little moan of protest and feeling her hands pushing against his chest, he released her, keeping his arms gently about her as her head dropped to his shoulder. She sniffed delicately.

And before he knew it, he had promised that he would rescue her from her tyrant of a papa in the only way that occurred to him.

"How would you like to be my viscountess, eh? I'll get us a special license and we'll go to Hampshire and be married all right and tight before your papa even knows we've gone . . . daresay we'll be the talk of the town for a week or two, but, Lord, what's a little gossip among the old cats to stop us."

Peveril heard his own words with dismay. It was not in the least what he had meant to say. He grimaced.

Belinda gazed up into his eyes, looking radiantly beautiful and taking his breath away. All his reservations were forgotten in an instant. "Oh, Pevewil! Oh, yes! I should like it of all things! It will be so dawing and wisky. You are so bwave to take me away. Will you carwy me on your saddle in fwont of you on your horse?"

She was in a fever of excitement, wanting to run back to the ballroom and tell everyone in sight about their secret, romantic plans. It even occurred to her that the duke would propose on the spot, if he knew her on the verge of running away with the viscount. Her heart beat faster at the very thought.

"On a horse? Egad, no! We'll go in a carriage like civilized folk."

Her face fell ludicrously at this sensible statement. "Oh," she said with an air of disappointment.

Peveril immediately saw his mistake. "Er, that is, sure to be much more comfortable in a carriage. Only a week till Christmas. Dead of winter, you know. Don't want my new bride to catch a chill on our honeymoon. Can't risk a delicate lady like you in the dashed chilly winter air."

"Oh, well, if we're to go in a carwiage, we might as well take Marwy with us." Taking her arms from about his neck, Belinda turned to gaze at herself in the carved, gilt-framed mirror that hung over the intricately-carved marble mantlepiece while she patted her curls back into place.

"Take Mary with us?" Peveril was stunned to think Belinda wanted to take her companion along on an elopement, and chagrined when he remembered the disturbing new feelings for that lively lady he had been experiencing lately.

"Oh, yes. I will be so fwightened to go with you on my own. I want her to come with me."

"I suppose we can take her along with us," he agreed reluctantly. "Sure to help the scandal die down sooner, if you have your chaperone along." Somewhere in the mists of his confused thoughts, he knew he would be wise to have someone with a little sense along to help him control Belinda's tantrums and vapors.

"Oh, yes. And I shall be ever so much more happy with Marwy along."

Neither of them stopped to consider what they would do with Mary once the knot was tied.

"Eh, yes . . . now you mustn't go blabbing this out to anyone, you know," he cautioned her. "Not even to Mary."

"Oh! Oh, no!" she agreed breathlessly, her green eyes wide. "It will be a gweat secwet." She put her hand over her mouth and giggled with delight.

"We'll tell Mary we're going for a drive, but we won't tell her where we're bound. And, by Jove, now I come to think of it, we must have a plan to get you safely away from London."

Belinda agreed with this idea, thinking it would be such fun to fool her papa and Mary and everyone else. They put their heads together, and with two such incautious brains working as one, soon devised a suitably imprudent scheme.

Mary was on her way out the door in search of the missing couple when she saw Belinda and the viscount returning to the ballroom. They were gazing at each other in a besotted fashion, unmistakeable stars in their eyes. It was a painful sight. Could Belinda be looking at him like that, if he'd just bid her farewell? she wondered uneasily.

Before she could intercept them and find out how matters stood, she saw her cousin Cedric, walking stiff-legged and with a disapproving frown on his chiseled face, bearing down on her.

She turned to make a speedy get-away, looking

around to make sure she kept well clear of the mistletoe hanging in various parts of the room. But she was not quick enough to avoid him.

"Mary," Cedric said unsmilingly when he reached her side, "You are looking particularly elegant tonight. I make you my compliments. You will do me the honor of dancing with me?"

"Cedric, you must excuse me. I can't believe that standing up together would afford much pleasure to either of us."

"On the contrary. It would afford me great pleasure to partner you, Mary, in this dance and in the future. As your husband."

"Please! We're been through this every morning for the past week when you've called at Mr. Ramsbottom's house and I've received you. I will not change my mind . . . not ever, Cedric." Mary looked at him in utter exasperation. "What can I say to convince you?"

"I am convinced that you will come to your senses and obey your grandfather. You cannot continue upon this rash, unwise course you have chosen."

"Oh, Cedric. Do you not hear what I have been saying to you over and over again this past week and more? Are you deaf or just monumentally stubborn, believing in your male arrogance that I, a mere woman, do not know my own mind?" Even Mary's sweet nature could not stand more of his incessant importunities.

Mary's resolute words seemed to make some impression on him at last. Cedric's haughty features were overcast by a tide of red, rising from his neck to his forehead. He drew breath to speak, but before he could launch into a lengthy diatribe, Emmy appeared beside them to interrupt their tiff.

"Oh, Mary and Sir Cedric," she bubbled, dancing up to them. "I don't believe you've had supper yet. Mama asked me to see that the very best tidbits are pointed out to you. And, Sir Cedric—why do you not join us?" she asked, linking her arm through his with girlish impetuosity before he could answer, and giving Mary a perfect chance to make her escape.

"Oh, Marwy," Belinda said breathlessly two mornings after the Belfours' ball, "I wish to do some shopping on Bond Stweet after luncheon. You must come with me." She spoke in a rather tense, high-pitched voice.

Mary looked up startled from the list she was checking over of the items she would need for the journey on the morrow. "But Belinda! We leave for Sidmouth in the morning where we are to spend the Christmas holidays. I have a hundred and one things still to do."

Mary had spent all morning preparing for the journey to the south Devon watering place where the Duke of Exford promised to spend Christmas with Mr. Ramsbottom and his daughter in four days. Mr. Ramsbottom was greatly put out that they had not been invited to the ducal mansion at Exford, but Sidmouth was near enough that he did not despair of getting Belinda installed in Exford Court before the Christmas holidays came to an end.

"Well, I would ask Papa, but he has gone to his office in the City and won't weturn for ages."

"Can you be all packed and ready to go to Sidmouth tomorrow?" Mary asked, not believing this to be possible, for she had seen clothing, bonnets, shoes, Christmas gifts and all manner of things strewn over Belinda's bedchamber not an hour since.

"I am almost weady, but it is such a puzzle knowing what I will need, and he said I'm allowed to take only a bandbox." Belinda gave a conscious start and blushed bright red as she realized what she had revealed.

"Your father said you were only to take a single bandbox? Surely he was teasing you," Mary replied, puzzled by this statement. She knew Mr. Ramsbottom would want Belinda to take as many trunks of clothing as she liked. He would arrange for any number of baggage coaches to convey all Belinda's trunks to Sidmouth, for he certainly wouldn't want his daughter to stint herself on clothes on such an important visit. He would want her to impress the Duke of Exford in every way she could.

"Oh! Oh, yes," Belinda said, putting her hand up to cover her mouth briefly. "He must have been funning me. Papa can be a gweat tease, sometimes."

Mary gave her a searching look. "Can you not send your maid to purchase what you need?"

Belinda pouted. "No, no, I must go myself. It is only four more days till Chwistmas and I want to buy some more pwesents, and I want you to come with me to help me choose something for Dukey," she said with sudden inspiration.

"You are not proposing to *walk* to Bond Street?" Mary asked, astounded. It was most unlike Belinda to actively seek such strenuous exercise, particularly when there was no prospect of a gentleman escort to flirt with and admire her. "It is quite cold and dreary out, you know, and you could make the journey much more quickly, if you were to call for one of your papa's carriages."

"Oh, but I weally would like to get some air," Belinda improvised, fanning herself vigorously with her little hand. "I declare, it's so stuffy in Papa's house, I'm sure I shall faint if I can't go out in the fwesh air for a time. Oh, but I forgot," she added cunningly. "Ceddie is coming to call. You won't want to miss him, I suppose."

"Oh, is he indeed!" Mary replied with a martial light in her grey eyes. "I shall come with you, then, but we must bundle up, because it looks like it will begin to snow soon."

"Oh, famous!" Belinda exclaimed in relief at Mary's agreement and not hearing her comment about the weather. "I will be weady in one hour," she promised, tripping out of the room with a high flush on her cheeks.

Mary looked after her, perplexed. She supposed Belinda really did need some fresh air for she had been in a fever of impatience the past two days, having Bessie pack and unpack her trunks for the journey, trying to cram all her favorite gowns and geegaws into one particular trunk. Indeed, she had been all atwitter since the Belfours' ball.

After she had seen them together at the ball, Mary had fully expected her charge to receive another clandestine communication from the viscount. But, as far as she knew, Belinda had not done so. And despite careful questioning, Belinda would not admit that anything significant had happened when she left the ballroom for a few moments with the viscount. Indeed, the girl had not mentioned Lindford's name, or that any other gentleman, since the ball, which was most unusual behavior for her.

It would be as well to humor the girl's odd whims, Mary decided with a sigh, and she would welcome a breath of air, too. As it was sure to be a fairly brief shopping trip, she could always finish her packing later that afternoon.

Mary shook her head and went back to her list. She was planning to take everything she had with her on this journey. She had had the forethought to give the seminary in Oxford her address in Sidmouth and hoped a letter would be awaiting her there. With any luck, she would not be returning to the city with the Ramsbottoms. She could not wait to be away from London and Sir Cedric's insistent demands. Despite her strong words to him at the Belfours, she fully expected that he would continue to insist that she accompany him back to Wyndham Park.

As she passed the open door to Belinda's dressing room on the way to her own room to dress for their outing, Mary saw a bulging trunk standing in the cluttered room, strapped and ready to be tied onto the baggage coach the next morning. A goodly number of bandboxes lay about, half packed with items falling out over the edges. The wardrobe doors were open and clothing, hats, shoes, ribbons and other feminine apparel lay everywhere in an untidy tangle.

Mary walked on to her own room wondering what

Belinda's usually competent maid Bessie was about to leave the room in such a mess. It would take hours to sort things out. However would Belinda be ready to leave by morning?

Deciding she had best wrap up warmly against the cold, Mary donned her heavy grey woolen cloak over her woolen carriage dress and chose to wear her fur hat, kid gloves, and a pair of sturdy boots, as well. Although it was only early afternoon, the day was already overcast and grey. There was snow in the heavy dark clouds hanging over the city, she was sure of it, and she was afraid they would be caught out in it, if Belinda did not complete her shopping within the hour.

She tapped her hand on the stair bannister as she waited in the hallway below. Where was Belinda? Finally she appeared at the top of the stairs wrapped in furs. She was surely overdressed for a brief shopping expedition in her elaborate Russian mantle, chinchilla muff and hat, Mary thought.

"Come along, Belinda. We must have our walk now before it starts to snow," Mary said. Belinda was standing on the landing hesitantly, looking like a fledgling sparrow about to take its first flight from the nest.

"Snow? You don't mean it?" Belinda cried in a shrill voice, turning pale and pulling a gloved hand from her muff and raising it to her face. Her nerves were stretched taut.

"The clouds look distinctly threatening. Come along, my dear. If you haven't changed your mind about going abroad this afternoon, that is?" Mary queried, noting that Belinda's eyes were dilated with some strong emotion.

"Oh, no, no! We weally must go," she cried, running halfway down the staircase. She stopped suddenly and looked back distractedly at her maid who stood on the top landing.

"Bessie, wemember to give those boxes I showed you to the man who will come to the back door in a little while," she called to the abigail, then turned and ran down the remaining steps and out the front door being held open for her by one of the footmen, leaving Mary to follow in her wake.

What mischief was Belinda up to? Mary wondered, seeing the girl dash down the path in front of her father's house. If this jittery excitement continued, Belinda would be a most trying companion on the journey to Sidmouth tomorrow, she thought on a sigh.

Chapter 14

"Hurwy, Marwy!" Belinda called. "We mustn't be late!" She was a bundle of nerves as she rushed Mary along to the appointed meeting place with the viscount around the corner from Curzon Street, just at the entrance to the Carrington Mews.

A closed black traveling chaise stood to one side of the street. The four strong horses attached to it stood pawing the ground, their breath steaming in the frosty grey air.

Mary glanced at it, then was taken completely off guard as Belinda ran across the street toward the waiting vehicle.

The door of the coach opened and Viscount Lindford stepped out. "Bless my soul! Miss Ramsbottom and Miss Marlowe!"

"Lord Lindford!" Mary exclaimed in dismay.

"Afternoon, ladies. It's a dashed cold day to be running about on foot. Glad to give you a lift somewhere." He tried to smile but his face felt frozen and the smile went awry. For the past day and a half, he had been cursing himself for being every kind of fool for allowing himself to be cozened into this ill-advised elopement by a beautiful little peagoose. But he could see no way out, after he'd been rash enough to give his promise.

"Oh, Pevewil," Belinda exclaimed almost throwing herself into his arms. Her acting skills had been strained to the limit. "I've had such twouble getting away."

"Hush, for the Lord's sake, Belinda! Don't want to give the game away just yet!" he muttered in an undertone as he helped her mount into the vehicle.

He turned and looked shamefacedly at Mary as he held his hand out to help her inside the coach. "Mary . . . care to take a turn about the park with us?"

When Mary made no move to accept his hand, he let it drop to his side, where he clenched and unclenched it nervously.

Making a little recovery, Belinda took her cue from the viscount, "Yes, Marwy, I—I want to wish Pevewil a happy Chwistmas." She had already seated herself comfortably in the coach and addressed Mary through the open door.

"You may do so now, Belinda, and we'll be on our way," Mary replied firmly. This was clearly an arranged meeting. She was quite angry that she had been fooled in this way, but knowing her charge as she did, she faulted herself for not suspecting something like this was behind all Belinda's fidgets.

And she was shocked—and hurt, too. Lindford had lied to her at the Belfours, telling her he meant to say goodbye to Belinda there.

She had been trying so hard not to think of him

and their bittersweet parting at the Christmas ball. She had caught herself up short several times in the past two days when she realized she was dreaming of him, imagining that his tender looks and warm words meant that he had come to feel some affection for her. It had been hard, but she had resolutely put him and the unsettling emotions he had stirred up in her breast from her mind. And now here he was, chasing after her foolish charge once again, conspiring to meet her secretly.

"Oh, but you don't undewstand—I want to go for a dwive wound the Pawk with Pevewil," Belinda whined, remembering her lines. She took her trembling lower lip between her little white teeth while ready tears formed in her eyes and she looked beseechingly at Mary from beneath her wet lashes. "You know Papa's orders . . . perhaps I'll never see Pevewil again," she whispered, her chin trembling, before her tears began to flow in earnest. "Please, Marwy."

"This is most unwise," Mary began to remonstrate, but Belinda's tears turned to loud sobs and Mary saw she would gain nothing by persisting.

She stood irresolute for a moment, then sighed and gave her hand to Peveril. "As you wish then." Well, it would be a final goodbye and she would not argue further. Indeed, she hadn't the heart for it, for she herself would probably never see him again after the short journey.

"But it must be a very brief trip for the weather is quite dreadful and we have much still to prepare before we leave for the West Country tomorrow."

Peveril's eyes slid away from hers as he handed her in.

This was a traveling coach with all the comforts of hot bricks, warm blankets and horses built for speed, Mary thought uneasily when she found herself seated inside the well-equipped vehicle. Could it be that the viscount was leaving town immediately after he bid farewell to Belinda?

Peveril vaulted in after Mary to take his seat beside Belinda. Overwrought, she was still weeping silently.

"Nothing to cry about, Belinda, specially when you're looking all the crack today. That's a very fetching hat and fur mantle you're wearing!" he exclaimed, hoping to soothe her fraught nerves. His praise worked wonders. She straightened up on the seat, blew her little nose, and managed a wavering smile.

"Looks to be a dreary day," Peveril said warily to Mary, hoping to allay any suspicions that might have arisen in her mind from Belinda's indiscreet remarks. She would have to know the truth all too soon, as it was.

"Oh, Lord Lindford, this drive is not at all a prudent idea. Can you not bid Belinda farewell and Happy Christmas now?" Mary asked in her most sensible voice. She put aside her own hurt and began to think of the consequences to the viscount. She feared that Mr. Ramsbottom would take strong action against him, if he learned of this meeting.

"Oh, no, Marwy!" Belinda cried, looking not one whit less the beautiful for being all teary-eyed and disheveled. "We must go for a dwive. It's part of my pwesent, isn't it, Pevewil?" she turned to the viscount, screwing up her face and trying to signal him with her eyes that he should confirm her statement.

"Er, yes," he faltered, with a guilty look at Mary. "That's the ticket, a drive round the park. Christmas present. Knew you'd like it of all things," he said with a desperate lack of inventiveness.

"What?" Mary gave a start when she felt the coach rock as something heavy was lifted into the boot. It felt heavy enough to be one of Belinda's trunks, she thought with an ominous premonition, remembering Belinda's whispered conversation with her abigail before they left the house.

Then she heard a squeaky male voice say, "Ta very much, lads. 'Ere's 'alf a crown for yer trouble. Be orf wit ye now."

She looked out the window on her side of the coach and got a glimpse of a little man as he made a hand signal to the viscount who waved back at him from inside the coach. She recognized him as the fellow she had often seen standing in Curzon Street, seemingly watching Mr. Ramsbottom's house.

She could not know that the man was the viscount's servant, Small, who had instructions to ride Ajax to Hampshire and there join Mr. Throckmorton as soon as his master had Miss Ramsbottom safe.

Percy, who had been let in on the viscount's plans, had ridden ahead to the inn in a small village outside Basingstoke where they were all to spend the night. He was to make sure all was well in train for their visit. The viscount had congratulated himself for his forethought in employing his friend's services when he was making the arrangements.

With a whistle to the team from the hired driver,

the coach lurched off, throwing all three occupants back against the squabs.

"Lord Lindford, just what is happening here?" Mary asked suspiciously. Her dark brows were lowered over her eyes, making her gentle little face look uncommonly grave.

Peveril gave Mary a harassed look and Belinda began to wail again. The viscount put his arms awkwardly around the girl and tried to soothe her sobs, but it was clear to Mary he was far from composed himself.

"Don't put yourself in a taking, for the Lord's sake, Belinda!" he remonstrated with the weeping girl. "We've got enough on our plate without the vapors."

"Papa is so cwuel. I can't bear'w it," Belinda sobbed.

"There, there, m'dear. Got you all right and tight now. We'll be wed before old Rams— er, before your papa gets wind of our whereabouts. He'll never catch us, you'll see." Peveril, his own voice strained, tried to assure his distraught companion.

"An elopement!" Mary uttered in a hushed voice. "I might have known she would be easily persuaded to do something so scandalous." She groaned, putting her gloved hand to her forehead in dazed disbelief. "How can even you think to do such a thing, Lindford?" she asked.

Her eyes were sad as she looked at him in disappointment, and Peveril felt doubly guilty for deceiving her and letting her down.

He cleared his throat and swallowed awkwardly as he tried to excuse himself. "Dash it, Mary. I had no other choice," he got out with an edge to his voice. "Promised her I wouldn't let the old moneybags, er, her papa, ruin her life. What else could I do, when she begged me to take her away?" A muscle twitched in his lean cheek as he looked at her.

"Shown a particle of sense, in the first place. And it is not too late to turn back now, you know," she urged, trying to persuade him.

"No! No!" Belinda cried petulantly. "You said you wouldn't let Papa make me marwy someone, if I didn't want to. You know you did, Marwy. But now you just want to wuin everything!"

Mary sat back in defeat and Peveril looked away, not caring to meet her eyes just then. His heart thumped uncomfortably at the look of hurt he saw in her eyes. He drummed his fingers on his knee tensely.

Not only had he had second thoughts about the wisdom of an elopement with the Beauty, but third and even fourth thoughts, too, no matter how much of a monster Belinda had said her father was. But he could not go back on his word as a gentleman.

And then, too, there had been a certain excitement surrounding the adventure of an elopement that had appealed to him. He had not been able to resist Belinda's pleas that he run away with her. She had seemed genuinely to fear her father. What sort of a father would frighten his daughter so? Old Ramsbottom must be an unfeeling monster to make her so desperate, he had thought. And, he admitted reluctantly, his good resolutions had been overcome by her divine beauty. He had lost his head. As for sense, he'd never had much of that commodity to boast of.

But he felt a real cad for thrusting Mary into such a compromising situation. Now, seeing her distress, he cursed the devil—and his own impulsive nature—that had prompted him to agree to this foolish elopement.

He had had the devil of a time securing this carriage and cadging the funds necessary for the journey to Hampshire. He had sold his horses to pay off his gaming debt to Swinton and pawned practically everything he owned to pay off his other pressing debts. Only after he had done that did he give any consideration to what he and his new bride would live on for the rest of their lives. It had belatedly dawned on him that old Ramsbottom would likely cut off all funds to his daughter for serving him such a trick. They would have to slum it together at his ramshackle estate in Hertfordshire, he supposed glumly.

Deciding he owed Mary something of an explanation of their plans, Peveril looked up at her. He pressed the thumb and forefinger of one hand to his forehead for a moment before he drew a sighing breath and said, "Percy will be meeting us at the Green Man this evening. It's an inn just outside the village of Mapledurwell, near Basingstoke. Have a special license. We'll be married tomorrow, then Percy can take you back to London. Or, by jingo, he could take you along to Lady Bramble's Christmas party in Wiltshire!" he exclaimed, much cheered by this sudden idea. "Sure to give you a warm welcome. Lady Bramble—Percy's mama—is a bang-up, er, comfortable lady. Easy-going. Sure to enjoy yourself there!"

"Oh, Pev—Lord Lindford, I mean, you can't have

considered! I can't travel to either place alone with Mr. Throckmorton," Mary pointed out. "Your friend is a most kind and pleasant gentleman, but he is not my choice for a husband, I fear."

"Oh, Lord! Guess you would be compromised," Peveril muttered, crestfallen.

"Not if you stop this foolhardy escapade now and turn back to London," Mary pointed out, again trying to convince him. A fear had begun to grow in her for his safety. "You have no idea of my employer's power, my lord," she whispered. Mr. Ramsbottom was a hard man. "He will certainly seek some sort of revenge against you when he learns you have eloped with his daughter."

She feared that Mr. Ramsbottom might have the capacity to harm the viscount for this mad action. It might even be in his power to have Peveril clapped up in irons for the attempted abduction of his daughter, she thought with a tremor.

Belinda cast herself on Peveril's chest and began to wail afresh at Mary's words.

"Sorry, Mary, but we can't go back. Promised Belinda. She's got her heart set on it, you see," he said, desperately wanting Mary to understand that he could not go back now that he had pledged his word.

Peveril gave Mary a harassed look, as he attempted to calm his prospective bride. When she proved inconsolable, his own frayed nerves got the better of him. "For the Lord's sake, Belinda, don't be such a wet goose! Have some sense for a change!" he exclaimed, his temper flaring.

At the viscount's exasperated words, Belinda

wrenched herself from his side and subsided behind her handkerchief in the far corner of the coach.

Mary heaved a great sigh. She *was* moved. Not by her spoiled charge's hysterics, but by the pleading look in Peveril's blue eyes. "At least I must be grateful you are not contemplating going all the way to Scotland with the weather so threatening. Such a journey would have been difficult in the extreme."

"Lord, no! You have the right of it there, m'dear!" Peveril exclaimed with a shudder. "Don't see the sense of a dash to the border. Can do the thing up all right and tight with a special license right here in England!" He tapped the pocket of his jacket significantly.

Belinda looked up and listened to their conversation wide-eyed, dabbing at the corners of her beautiful eyes with the edge of her ever-present square of linen and giving a few delicate sniffles from time to time.

"Marwy will come with us on our honeymoon, Pevewil," Belinda said in a small voice, her lips still trembling with emotion.

"What? No such a thing, my dear!"

"Why not?" Belinda asked, wide-eyed.

"Not the thing. To take a single lady along on a honeymoon. Wouldn't be proper. Why, it's unheard of!"

"But I don't have my maid with me, Pevewil. Who will help me dwess and take carwe of me, if Marwy doesn't come with us?" she asked ingenuously.

Peveril stared at Belinda, wondering what the chit had for brains. He glanced at Mary who merely looked resigned and slightly amused by the girl's odd notions. Peveril shook his head at Mary and rolled his eyes. She shrugged her shoulders and returned her gaze to the window.

At least Percy would be meeting them at the inn in Mapledurwell for the night, Peveril recollected with relief. Perhaps between them they could contrive some solution to Mary's dilemma.

They had been traveling for a good two hours in near silence. Belinda was dozing in one corner of the coach, exhausted from her repeated emotional outbursts. Her cheek was resting on the viscount's bunched up greatcoat and her own fur muff. Peveril and Mary were each lost in their own thoughts.

Mary became aware that the interior of the coach had grown gloomier. It was almost too dark to see the faces of her companions. She looked over at the viscount who sat with folded arms, staring at one booted foot that was crossed over his knee. His crooked nose was prominent in his shadowed face, and he looked far older than his four-and-twenty years, she thought, her heart turning over with reluctant sympathy.

She turned her eyes away from him and looked out into the darkening afternoon. She was not surprised to see a light drift of snow flakes sifting past her misted-over window. Shivering in her woolen cloak, she wondered worriedly if they would reach their destination before the snow became treacherous.

Peveril looked up from the contemplation of his riding boots and followed the direction of Mary's gaze. Seeing that it was snowing more heavily now, he uttered a low imprecation, "Blister it! Wish this blasted snow would hold off till we're all snug in this dashed inn of Percy's!"

As ill fortune would have it, the coach skidded to the side of the slick roadway just at that moment. Peveril was thrown against Belinda, and Mary against her side of the coach.

Coming awake with a start, Belinda squealed, "Help! The coach is tuwning over! I'm so fwightened! Oh, we'll be killed!"

"For the Lord's sake, take a damper will you!" Peveril barked at Belinda. He shook her slightly as he pulled them both upright again, then put her aside from him.

Belinda looked at him as if he had slapped her. Her mouth was hanging open in shock and her companions both knew it was only a matter of seconds before she went off into hysterics again.

Peveril gave Mary an imploring look. Taking pity on the bedeviled viscount, she responded to his silent plea. Pushing herself to a vertical position on her tilting seat, she changed places with him so that she could try to quiet the distraught girl.

"Now, don't be so poor spirited, Belinda. This is just another romantic adventure, you know. A fairy-tale princess would see this as a test of her mettle and would show herself a heroine."

When she heard these words, Belinda made an effort to control herself, sitting up a little against Mary's shoulder and drying her eyes.

Watching them, the viscount thought exasperatedly that he had eloped with the wrong woman. He was strongly tempted to leave Belinda behind at the first decent inn they came to and continue on with Mary.

Peveril lowered the window to ask the coachman, "What's the trouble?"

"Left-side leader 'as strained 'is leg, me lord," the coachman answered in a gloomy voice. "Coach is too 'eavy for the beasts on this demmed icy road, wit that there gentry mort's trunk weighin' twenty stone nor more," the man grumbled.

"Take 'em along slowly, then, Jarvey," Peveril called to the hired coachman. He was regretting the recent sale of his own cattle and beginning to think the seeming bargain he thought he had made when he hired the team, coach and coachman, was no such thing. "Knew it was a mistake to rely on hired nags," he muttered, stifling a frustrated oath. His nerves were frayed to the breaking point.

Despite Mary's efforts, Belinda had gone off again in sympathy for the poor horse. She was keening in a high, piercing voice.

"For the Lord's sake, will you cease that infernal racket, or I'll come over there and box your ears!" the sorely-tried viscount shouted at her. He clenched his teeth and his hands to prevent himself from doing just that. Blast it, he thought, he could not bear much more of the tedious chit's everlasting megrims.

"Oh, oh! Did you hear what he said to me, Marwy? Take me back! I want to go home! I won't marwy such a monster as you Pevewil Standish for anything. I don't care how handsome Emmy and her fwiends say you are!"

Thus easily did Belinda relinquish her undying love for her romantic cavalier. She wanted nothing so much as to return to the safety and comfort of her papa's home where her every whim was someone's command.

"That's devilish fine with me! Matter of fact, I couldn't be happier," Peveril declared with a ferocious frown on his tired young face. "Wouldn't be tied to such a watering pot of a peagoose for all the tea in China!"

It was bound to come to this between the two of them, Mary decided as she sat with her arm around Belinda's trembling shoulders, biting back a desire to say, "I told you so."

She had given them two weeks before the glow of their mutual infatuation wore off and they were at one another's throats, but she saw that she had been overly generous. Two hours seemed to be the limit of their tolerance for one another.

The pair of them were most assuredly *not* meant for each other. Despite the disasters they had experienced today, perhaps things would all work out for the best, she thought optimistically, for at least the ill-matched couple had found they wouldn't suit before the knot was tied.

"I want to go home!" Belinda wept pathetically into her soaking handkerchief. The adventure had lost all its romantic charm.

Her perfect features were reddened and splotchy and she looked more unattractive than he would have thought possible, Peveril observed dispassionately.

"Confound it all, I'm going to take you home! Might as well turn around right this infernal minute and return to bloody London!" Peveril swore vehemently, putting down the glass again so that he could give orders to the coachman, but Mary stopped him.

She reached a hand across to lay on his arm, "I wish we could do so, Peveril, but I'm very much afraid we cannot. It would be too dangerous in this weather. You can see for yourself that it is almost dark already and the snow has begun to accumulate. I'm afraid we would find ourselves stranded before we reached London. We must not risk it, and you will not wish to risk these horses, either, with one of them injured already. I think we must try to reach the inn where Mr. Throckmorton awaits you and put up there for the night," she said with eminent practicality.

"I will be there to chaperone Belinda, after all, so perhaps we may brush through this escapade with not too much harm done."

"Lord, if I hadn't forgotten about Percy!" Peveril exclaimed. "He'll likely go off in an apoplexy if we don't turn up."

"How far is the inn you speak of?" Mary asked calmly.

"Shouldn't be above five miles now, for we passed the turning to Up Nately some time ago," Peveril answered optimistically, not exactly sure of the inn's location. He had only chosen the place because his friend favored it. Percy had told him that when he had put up at the Green Man, he had found it comfortable and the landlord friendly. Peveril had decided that its location recommended it. Even if they were traced along the road to Basingstoke, no one would think to look for them in such an off the beaten track village as Mapledurwell.

The coach continued on at a slow but steady pace along the slippery roadway as the snow began to fall harder and the light became weaker. Peveril was feeling anxious and glum. He looked to Mary as the only refuge of sanity in the whole mad affair. He felt tremendous guilt for having thrust her into such a damnable muddle.

Belinda refused to speak to the viscount or even to look at him. She sat with her face averted, partially covered by her large muff, and gave a low watery sniff every now and again.

"We can't be far from the inn now," Mary said after they had traveled in this fashion for some half-hour. She was anxious, too, but she tried not to show it, feeling that her two mercurial companions looked to her to impose some order and calm on the unhappy situation.

Suddenly they all heard a rumble of hoofbeats approaching on the snow-covered road behind them. The coachman obediently moved his plodding horses as far to the other side of the treacherous roadway as he could, to let the approaching horsemen overtake them.

But as soon as the riders were level with them, the occupants inside the coach heard a hoarse-voiced shout directed at their coachman.

"Halt yer cattle right there me good man, else I'll put a bullet through yer arm!"

Chapter 15

The vehicle came to a complete stop as the coachman obeyed the hoarse command and pulled up his team.

Belinda screamed. "A wobbery!"

Mary clamped a hand over the girl's mouth before she could go off into hysterics again, and Peveril reached for the longhandled horse pistol he had brought along for emergencies almost as an afterthought. But before he could reach it, the coach door was wrenched open and a woosh of frigid air and snowflakes swirled inside the coach.

Not a footpad appeared, but someone infinitely more terrifying to the three occupants.

Mr. Ramsbottom's livid red face radiated furious anger as he looked in at the three horrified occupants. One of his servants was just behind him, holding a pistol leveled at the viscount's head.

"Papa!" Belinda screamed as her father leaned in the door and reached for her.

"Hell and the devil confound it!" Peveril ejaculated. He moved forward swiftly with some idea of protecting the screaming Belinda from her father. He shoved Mr. Ramsbottom aside and vaulted down from the coach.

Mr. Ramsbottom's servant lifted the handle of his pistol and cracked the viscount over the head, knocking him to the ground where he fell against a stone that gashed the side of his temple and cheek.

"Tryin' to run off with me daughter, was ye, ye young scoundrel! I'll see ye clapped up in irons—or worse!—if ye ever have the effront'ry to come nigh her again, ye miserable wastrel!" Mr. Ramsbottom exclaimed, standing beside the fallen viscount and regarding him without mercy.

Peveril groaned and clutched his cracked head. He got to his feet and staggered to the side of the road where he sat on a large stone that was only lightly dusted with snow. He unwound his neckcloth and pressed it to his bleeding head.

"Oh, Papa, Papa! How glad I am to see you! I've been so fwightened! I want to go home!" Belinda exclaimed as she leaned out the coach door, staring in horrified fascination at the proceedings.

Mr. Ramsbottom turned and thrust Belinda back inside the vehicle, saying, "Sit yerself back, daughter. Sit yerself back. I'll speak to ye in a moment about this foolish behavior of yourn."

Seated on the other side of the coach, Mary was speechless, unable for the moment to react to the fast-unfolding events. She did not know what to say or do for the best. As one in a bad dream, she moved past Belinda to climb out the open door of the coach.

It had stopped snowing now, and the moon was visible through the break in the clouds, giving some light to the scene. She could see Peveril sitting stunned beside the road. His face appeared deathly white in the moonlight and he moaned as he held his head in his hands and pressed his neckcloth to his wounded face.

She ran over to kneel in the snow beside him. "Oh, Peveril, are you dreadfully hurt?" she asked. She pulled his neckcloth away from his face and was horrified to see the stain of red blood seeping through the stark white material. She pressed her own clean handkerchief against his wound.

"Hired ye to chaperone my girl. Show her how the nobs go on. If this is yer idea of proper behavior, missy, then I'm done with ye," Mr. Ramsbottom shouted at her gruffly. "Sadly disappointed in ye, I am. And an earl's granddaughter and all." He shook his head grimly. "Sadly disappointed, I am."

Mary lifted her chin proudly, knowing that he had nothing with which to reproach her, and looked back at her employer. "What do you intend to do now?" She was surprised to hear her voice sounding completely calm and controlled.

"Ain't got me money's worth from yer services, missy. Old Stanley Ramsbottom likes to get value for money. Value for money. 'Fraid I'll have to let ye go."

She stared at him coldly.

"Will take ye to the next inn. Ye can make yer own arrangements from there." He took a leather pouch from one of his pockets and threw it down to land near where Mary knelt on the snowy ground. "Here's yer wages. Twenty pounds should cover your services. And over generous it is too, considering the circumstances. Over generous. Ye've betrayed me, ye have, missy."

"And Viscount Lindford?"

" 'Fraid I'm not inclined to take the young scoundrel up. Might be difficult to keep this temper of mine in check. Might be inclined to take a horsewhip to the rogue. Tried to run off with me daughter. Not a thing to be taken lightly, now is it? Not to be taken lightly."

"Won't you leave us the horses, at least?" Mary was distressed to hear a pleading note in her voice as she requested this boon.

"Can't do that, missy. These are me own nags. Not inclined to let the likes of that scoundrel have the use of 'em," Mr. Ramsbottom returned, unmoved by their plight.

Mary disdained to argue with him. He did have a right to feel aggrieved, she had to admit, but it was inhuman to leave a wounded man stranded in such weather.

Mr. Ramsbottom turned to direct his servant to tie their horses to the back of the coach, then he commanded the coachman in no uncertain terms to turn the vehicle about. When he heard that one of the coach horses had a strained leg, he said they would hire new nags at the next inn. He made it plain to the man that they were to return to London immediately and that he had the blunt to pay for a change of horses and a good hot meal at the first decent coaching inn they came to.

To sweeten the pot, Mr. Ramsbottom promised that if they reached London in under three hours, there would be a generous reward in store. Though red-nosed, stiff-fingered, and half-frozen, the coachman was not averse to such an offer.

"Not coming with us, missy?" Mr. Ramsbottom asked Mary as he settled himself inside the coach with his weeping daughter beside him. He tossed Peveril's greatcoat out the door to land in the snow beside them.

Mary had no intention of accepting his offer. She could not leave an injured man lying in the roadway, no matter that he had committed such a heinous crime as trying to run off with the woman he loved. She would not leave *any* wounded gentleman, she was certain—but that it was Peveril Standish, the charming, impulsive, foolish boy who had won her heart, made it utterly unthinkable.

"Nothing to say for yerself, eh, missy?"

Mary turned her attention to the viscount and did not look at her former employer.

"Oh, Papa, I'm vewy welieved you've come, for Lindfowd and Marwy were quite horwid to me! Lindfowd said I was a goosecap and Marwy said I was not high-spiwited enough to be a hewoine! Oh, I want to go home!" Belinda wailed just before the coach door closed and the coachman began to turn the team.

Mary was shocked that the girl could show so little sympathy for Lindford. He was after all the man she had proclaimed herself to be dying with love for only a short while ago. How poor spirited she was, indeed, Mary thought with a cluck of her tongue.

Mr. Ramsbottom leaned out the coach window to deliver himself up of a few choice last words. "Well, missy, ye've chosen to involve yerself in an elopement. Since that young scoundrel there's so set on a runaway match, ye'll just have to oblige him!" he recommended with a hearty laugh.

As the coach rumbled off back down the road they had just traveled, Mary saw the coachman turn around and stare at her as she knelt beside the viscount. He shrugged his shoulders, whether in apology or resignation, she could not tell.

She turned back to Peveril when she heard him groan and moved to cradle his poor, bleeding head against her soft bosom.

"Oh, you've broke your poor head, my dear!" Mary uttered softly in distress, pulling the handkerchief away from the cut and seeing with relief that it was not as deep as she had feared. It had already stopped bleeding.

Peveril lifted his head a little higher against her breast. "That's not all that's broke," he replied with a grimace at the pain the movement caused.

"Oh dear, I suppose your heart is broken, too, Lord Lindford," Mary said in sympathy.

"Devil a bit of it, Mary, my dear. It's my watch—the lucky Lindford charm." He reached inside his pocket and produced the broken timepiece. Pieces of glass fell off, tinkling against the rock Peveril sat on.

Mary picked up the damaged watch. She saw that the glass covering had shattered, but when she held the timepiece to her ear she could hear that it was still ticking.

"No, I don't think it's completely ruined, Lord Lindford. It's only the covering that's broken, you see. You can have this glass replaced," she said practically.

A grin lurked at the corners of his mouth. "And who is this Lord Lindford you're addressing, Mary? Call me, Pev, m'dear. We're like to be intimately connected after this escapade."

"What do you mean?" she asked, watching Peveril reach up and gingerly touch the side of his head.

"Ouch!" he exclaimed, feeling the extremely tender bump on the side of his forehead. "Least the blasted thing's stopped bleeding," he said with relief, seeing his hand come away clean.

He didn't answer her question but only winced and observed, "I deserved that. Mayhap it's cleared my brain for me."

He made a move to get to his feet and Mary assisted him. When he was standing, she helped him brush off the snow covering his clothes, then worked at her own cloak, as they stood considering their options.

He glanced over to see her regarding him with a worried look on her piquant little face. A few snow flakes had started to fall again and drifted down about her, catching on the hood of her cloak, and on her face. Her eyelashes were wet with them and she licked one of them from her lips.

Peveril put his head to one side and looked at her. He grinned suddenly, crinkling up his blue eyes. "Ouch!" he said, relaxing his face again. "Lord, Mary! We're in a devil of a fix, my dear!"

She smiled back at him ruefully.

He sobered. "It's all my fault. Can you ever forgive me?" he asked, his eyes full of contrition as he reached for her hands.

Mary took a deep breath and looked right into his beautiful eyes. "I forgive you, Pev."

"You're a generous soul, Mary . . . got too kind a heart."

They gazed at one another for a long moment, then Peveril bent his head and kissed her very briefly on the lips.

Mary stopped breathing as a jolt shot through her, leaving her too shaken for words.

Peveril released her hands and went to retrieve his greatcoat. He shook it out and put it on, relieved to find his gloves in one pocket. He tugged them on and returned to Mary's side. "You should have gone with them, you know. I would've found my way to this confounded inn without endangering you."

"I could not possibly have gone with them with you hurt and stranded out here in the middle of nowhere!" she exclaimed indignantly. How could he think for a minute she would have left him in such a state?

"No, I don't suppose you could," he murmured with a lopsided grin and a flick of his finger against her wet cheek. "We'd best begin walking, my dear. Unless I miss my guess, it's above two miles to that inn where Percy should be awaiting us." He took her hand and placed it through his arm, for all the world as though they were setting off for a leisurely stroll.

"Oh! Oh, yes. We cannot risk being benighted here. Perhaps some chance traveler will come along and offer us a lift."

"Deuced unlikely in this weather, but we can hope. Good thing you're so full of pluck, Mary, and don't plan to treat me to a fit of the vapors. Don't think my poor head could stand any more screechin' today. Snow's starting to come down again. We must make it to the inn, Mary, and get you warm and comfortable."

"And you, too, Lord Lind—" He stopped her with a look. "Peveril—Pev, then. We must see to your wounded head."

He waved away her concern with his free hand, then laid it over hers where it rested on the sleeve of his greatcoat. "This has all been my devilish folly," he muttered, disgusted with himself. "Was bowled over by a pretty face and made a dashed ass of myself!"

"I suppose we all behave foolishly from time to time, Pev. We just have to contrive to learn from our mistakes and try to do better in future," Mary said with a slight smile as they trudged along the snowy roadway. The snow was no more than an inch deep but the flakes were coming faster and heavier now so that she feared they might well freeze to death before they reached the inn.

Biting her lips to keep them from going numb, she sighed. "We *are* in a pickle now." She was fearful that they might be stranded for the night with no shelter in sight.

Peveril took her words in a different way. "The solution to our dilemma is simple, my dear. Never fear your reputation will be ruined. You're my responsibility now. I'll marry you, never doubt it!"

Mary's heart bumped uncomfortably against her ribs. How could she let her charming rascal sacrifice his chance for happiness by being forced into an unwanted marriage? He could not really desire to wed her. After all, he had been convinced he loved Belinda and had been planning to marry *her* until only an hour ago.

"Oh, indeed, I thank you, Pev. It's so like you to offer such a generous thing," she said earnestly. "But such a drastic step is not at all necessary!" she declared vehemently. She hoped to assure him that she would not force him to such an irrevocable step, one which might ruin his life forever.

He almost stopped in his tracks at her fervent refusal. It caught him on the raw. "Damme! Why not?" he demanded, his blue eyes blazing at her.

Mary looked back at him helplessly.

"Ain't good enough for *you* either, I suppose," he said bitterly and turned his eyes to the road ahead. "Granddaughter of an earl can't be expected to come down so far as to accept an impoverished viscount."

"Oh, my lord—Pev, it's never that! Don't think it for a minute!"

"Well, what then?" He turned puzzled eyes toward her. "What will become of you, else? You've sworn you won't marry that prosy bore of a cousin of yours, and you're not cut out to be some chit's companion, or some old biddy's either."

"Really, you mustn't concern yourself. I shall come about," she said, keeping her profile averted and not meeting his eyes.

"You think we won't suit? I say we shall deal *famously* together!"

Mary's brain was in a whirl of confused thoughts and feelings. She could not answer him.

When she didn't respond, Peveril said in a rallying tone, "Need some persuasion, eh?" He stopped and pulled her against his side. "Guess there's nothing else for it—I'll have to kiss you until you agree!"

Even though he was teasing his companion to try to lighten her solemn little face, his blood stirred uncomfortably at the very thought. He peered down at her up-turned face, now suffused with color, with its sweet mouth and wide eyes, staring right into his. His heated gaze fell to her lips.

They both quickly looked away. They had been cold before, but now both were so warm as to be uncomfortable.

Peveril cleared his suddenly constricted throat and said quietly, "You still must marry me, you know, Mary."

"No, I cannot," Mary returned in a suffocated voice. There was nothing she wanted more in the world than to be his wife—but not if he were forced to ask her. She did not want him to marry her in haste, then repent his impulsive action for the rest of his days.

"Will you tell me why not?" he asked, serious for once.

"I—I dislike having my hand forced and you feeling compelled, *honor-bound,* to marry me."

"Honor-bound, heh? Devil a bit of it!"

Mary looked at him inquiringly, her lips slightly parted in surprise.

"Never took you for a brainless widgeon like Belinda," Peveril said with a grin lighting up his bruised and battered face.

"So you *did* notice?" she asked in surprise, then clapped a gloved hand to her mouth.

"Ain't as much of a fool as I act sometimes," he

admitted candidly. " 'Fraid I was honor-bound to wed *her,* after some of the silly promises I made when I first knew her and again at Emmy's ball."

"You weren't in love with her?"

He shook his head. "Just blinded by her beauty—just at first, you know. Lord, what a harridan she is, though, and what a lucky escape I've had!" he declared with a wide grin. Mary could hear the genuine relief in his voice.

He released her shoulders and they set off again. Peveril explained to Mary that he had impulsively agreed to the elopement when Belinda pleaded and wept, swearing undying love and devotion to him, telling him her life would be unbearable without him. It was only later he felt qualms.

"Too impetuous by half," he confessed shamefacedly. "I'll be a reformed character after this scrape, and make you a model husband, you'll see," he promised. "It's been enough to age me twenty years," he said with a self-mocking grin. "Wouldn't be surprised to look in the mirror tomorrow morning and see my hair has turned completely grey," he joked, making Mary laugh at the comical look on his face.

"Let us not be too hasty now, my lord," Mary said a bit hesitantly. "There may be an honorable solution to our dilemma that would leave us both free to marry for love, not from necessity."

Peveril gave her a hurt look, but did not press further. A new sense of his responsibility to her had descended on his shoulders and he felt the weight like a lodestone. He would convince her. He must, otherwise he doubted he could live with himself. He suddenly felt as though he had indeed aged a decade in the last few hours. Perhaps he had finally grown up, he thought with a twisted grin on his weary, sore face.

Chapter 16

"At last! Thank the Lord!" Peveril exclaimed. "Never thought we'd make it up that dashed hill."

He and Mary had just crested a small treacherous slope, slipping and sliding as they pulled one another up. As they reached the top and rounded a slight bend in the road, they saw the Green Man.

"Oh, are we there?" Mary asked, making her numb lips move with difficulty. Her chin and face were frozen from the cold and snow.

"Yes. Look." Peveril clapped his arm about her shoulders and pointed to the welcoming lights of the small half-timbered inn that were visible through the snow flakes drifting before their eyes. The lamplight seemed to twinkle merrily in the each and every window.

"Pev! Miss Marlowe! Thought you was never going to get here!" Percy exclaimed as Peveril and Mary dragged themselves, half-frozen, wet and weary, over the threshold of the well-lit, cheerful-looking inn. He had been awaiting them in the hallway where he had been pacing for some time.

"Deuced glad to see you! Been worried sick. Small arrived over four hours ago with your baggage, Pev. Said you was right behind him in the chaise. Talked to Parsnip—he's the landlord here, y'know—about ridin' out to meet you, but here you are all right and tight at last!" Percy peered behind them, then all around. "Where's Miss Ramsbottom? Still out in the chaise?"

The viscount shook his head and waved away his friend's question.

"It's a long story, Percy. Have you hired a private parlor yet?" Peveril asked wearily.

" 'Course I have. And reserved rooms and ordered up dinner, too," Percy confirmed with a satisfied nod. "And you'll be glad to know we're the only guests."

"Good!" Peveril replied in heartfelt relief. "I'm more than middlin' peckish. Hope they serve a decent dinner here."

"They do. Assure you. Mrs. Parsnip's a bang-up cook. What happened to keep you so long, Pev? And where is— you know who?" Percy asked in a whisper.

"For the Lord's sake, let us go into the parlor and get warm," Peveril interrupted his friend before he could ask any more awkward questions. "We are out on our feet, Percy. Tell you what happened later."

A small, burly man with thinning grey hair, a jolly round face and very red cheeks, came bustling up the stairs that led to the cellars. The friendly man came forward and introduced himself as Sam Parsnip, the proprietor of the establishment. He bid the newcomers welcome and asked them all to accept his hospitality and make themselves right at home.

Mr. Parsnip led the way down the hall where he opened the door to the small private parlor Percy had hired. A welcoming fire blazed brightly in the rough stone hearth, immediately cheering Mary and Peveril's spirits. A bowl of steaming punch was prepared and waiting on a scarred oaken table in the center of the rough-beamed room.

Percy busied himself at the table, ladling a large portion of punch into three of the glasses that stood ready while Mary and the viscount divested themselves of their wet garments.

Peveril had quickly ushered Mary over to the fireplace and had helped her remove her sodden cloak, before casting off his own snow-encrusted greatcoat. When she tried to untie the strings of her bonnet, she was chagrined to find that her fingers were so frozen with cold they wouldn't work.

"I'll do that for you, Mary," Peveril offered, seeing her difficulty.

"Thank you," she said, blushing fierily at his intimate touch while she watched him attempt to unravel the wet strings. His long fingers brushed under her frozen chin as he worked at the knotted strings. She saw that the bruise on the side of his face was swollen and purple now. Involuntarily, she raised her hand and touched his face gently with two cold fingers, wanting to soothe the ugly wound.

"Does it hurt much, Pev?"

"No. I think I'm still too frozen with cold to feel any pain." He grinned wearily and his blue eyes gazed right into hers. Mary caught her breath.

He finished the job with dispatch, lifted the ruined bonnet away from her head and cast it aside.

"Here. Come and sit here, Mary," he said, pulling the old oaken settle up before the fire and inviting Mary to sit down. "You'll want to remove those wet boots and your stockings as well so they can dry out in front of the fire," he recommended, pulling off his riding boots and setting them on the hearth.

Mary blushed as she smiled up at him. "You're right, Peveril," she said, bending to remove her boots. She decided her stockings would dry out just as fast if she rested her small feet on the hearth without removing them. She was moved and bemused by having someone show such care for her.

Percy carried over the glasses of punch and offered them to Mary and Peveril. Peveril gratefully accepted his and took a healthy swig.

"What's this grog, Percy?"

Percy scratched his head. "Don't rightly know. Think Parsnip said it was rum and lemon-juice and spices of some sort."

"By Jupiter, rum punch! So it is. Hope old Parsnip's done it up properly—you have to squeeze the lemon over the sugar and press it in well with a spoon before you pour the boiling water and rum over it—to bring out the flavor, you know," Peveril commented with some interest. He rather fancied himself an expert on the proper concoction of rum punch.

"Umm. Think he's softened it by adding some porter. It's devilishly tasty, anyway. Drink up, Mary, it'll do you good," Peveril recommended, even as he drained his own glass.

She looked at him doubtfully, but complied with his suggestion.

"Oh, my!" she choked out after the first fiery swallow. "I don't think this is quite my cup of tea, so to speak," she joked as she wiped the tears from her eyes. But in a moment she felt the potent liquid warm her all the way down to her toes. She took another experimental sip, and found that it didn't burn her mouth so badly this time. She could detect the underlying fruity taste of lemon and licked the sweetness from her lips with relish to Peveril's satisfied laughter. "Knew you'd like it, Mary."

When she'd finished her own glass, she rested her head back against the tall settle and let relaxation and drowsiness drift over her. The warmth from the fire felt good. She no longer felt frozen to the bone. She could hear the murmur of Peveril's voice behind her as he explained their adventure to Percy. And she could hear Percy's muffled cries of surprise as well. Their voices became fainter. She closed her eyes.

"Shh. Mary's almost asleep. For the Lord's sake, don't wake her, Percy," were the last whispered words she heard the viscount say before she drifted off into a deep sleep.

When Mary woke, it was to find herself lying fully clothed on a large bed with a finely-sewn checked quilt carefully arranged over her. Light and heat from the welcome fire burned brightly in the small, iron grate. She had no idea how she had come to be in this cozy, little room. She blushed when she realized that someone must have carried her. She did not have to think too hard to imagine who it must have been. She smiled tenderly, warmed all through by Peveril's care of her. Her stomach rumbled, disturbing her delicious thoughts, and she realized she was very hungry. She had had nothing to eat since a light luncheon before she had set out on the spurious shopping expedition with Belinda.

She had no idea of the time, but she thought it could not be so very late. The fire in her grate still burned red-hot—it could not have been made up for long. She rose and walked on stockinged feet to the window where she peered out into a blizzard. In the semi-darkness, she could see nothing but thick, heavy snow falling.

She found her heavy boots where they'd been carefully placed by the fire, slipped them on, thankfully finding them warm if not yet dried, then made her way along the hallway, down the stairs and through the quiet little inn to the parlor, where she found the viscount and Percy enjoying a hearty meal, fortified with yet another bowl of the steaming rum punch.

"Mary!" Peveril exclaimed when he saw her. "Thought you would sleep the night through."

"Well, I would have liked nothing better, but I was awakened by hunger pangs. Is there anything to eat?"

"Should say so, Miss Marlowe," Percy piped up, waving his hand over the bounty set out over the oaken table. "Lucky for us, Mrs. Parsnip's been cookin' all day."

"There's a veritable feast for you here, Mary," Peveril said and she could see that he did not exaggerate for there was on offer cutlets of pork, fricassed veal, pigeon pie, buttered turnips, a syllabub and several cakes as well as a good hearty beef broth. Mary sat down and eagerly filled her plate. She even agreed to try another cup or two of the punch when she had finished her meal. She was soon as merry as her companions.

Peveril carried her upstairs to bed again, this time because she was too giddy to walk by herself. He was feeling none too sober himself.

"Umm. You smell good, Mary," he murmured, resting his face against her soft curls and nuzzling her neck just before he lay her down on the bed.

Her arms came up to clasp him around the neck. "You, too, Pev'ril," she said woozily.

"Seems I'm making it a habit to put you to bed, Mary," he said with a teasing gleam in his own rather bleary eyes. He leaned down and touched her lips lightly with his own. "Think I could get to like it," he whispered. "Good night, sweet Mary."

Mary smiled dreamily up at him, reached up her arms and brought his head down to hers for a more satisfying kiss. "Goo' night, Pev'ril, m'dear," she slurred as she released him.

"By Jove, Mary, best take care, m'girl, or at this rate you'll find me spendin' the night in *your* bed rather than my own."

"Hmm. Not sussh a bad idea. Would be warmer," she said as she turned over onto her side, tucked her hands against her cheek and promptly fell asleep. Peveril grinned as he removed her boots for her, brought the quilt and other bedclothes up over her and tucked her in, still fully dressed as she was.

He stood swaying slightly as he looked down at her with a tender smile on his face. "G'night, Mary, mine. You'll be my viscountess soon, then I'll stay with you," he promised.

* * *

Mary awoke the next morning to a white world. She had no recollection of the viscount putting her to bed, or their good-night kiss.

She gazed out her window over the endless vista of pure white snow and decided there was absolutely no use at all in repining about the unfortunate events of the previous day. Indeed, she thought, if she were accepted back at the young ladies' seminary in Oxford, no one ever need be the wiser about this escapade. If her grandfather ever learned of the incident, she thought, her head bent as she absently drew patterns on the frosty window pane, well, she would just have to take the consequences of his censure.

She brightened suddenly, realizing it was but three days until Christmas and they would surely be stranded here at the Green Man for the holiday. She decided then and there that she would somehow contrive to make it a happy Christmas for all of them, no matter what happened later.

She ran her hands down her creased gown, trying to press out some of the wrinkles. She was regretting that she had had to sleep in her clothes when she saw a faded red woollen gown laid out over the chair near the fireplace. Oh, it did look warm and clean, she thought gratefully as she picked it up and noticed some practical cotton underthings lying next to it.

She put on the clean garments, thinking that the kind Mrs. Parsnip must have remarked her lack of luggage and provided the clothing. She would thank the generous landlady most sincerely for her thoughtfulness. The dress was several sizes too big, but she belted it as best she could with the twisted cord provided for the purpose, stepped into the too-large slippers left for her, and began humming a seasonal air as she went downstairs.

Despite his exhaustion, his sore face, and the quantity of rum punch he had drunk the previous evening, Peveril awoke from a long, undisturbed sleep feeling refreshed. The side of his head and face were still sore and tender, but no longer ached so fiercely. It took him but a few moments to clear his head and remember where he was, and why he was there.

The room seemed unnaturally bright, as though a brilliant sun were shining outdoors in the midst of winter. Curious to discover the source of the light, he threw back the covers and padded over to the window to look out and see that the snow of the previous day had settled in a fleecy white blanket spread out over the landscape. As he leaned against the casement, he looked out onto an unsullied white world, interrupted only by a few trees and the tops of the tallest hedges. There were still a few snowflakes in the air, stirred up by a light breeze, sparkling like so many diamonds in the bright light.

Despite all the difficulties of his situation, a wide smile escaped hm, splitting his battered face. He felt suddenly carefree and happy. "Lord, if I don't challenge Percy to a snowball fight before this day's over," he said aloud. Laughing at the notion, he donned the clothing laid out for him by Small and went in search of his companions.

Finding Percy still lying in a large tester bed under

a mountainous eiderdown coverlet, the viscount showed no mercy to his lazy friend. "Hang it, Percy, ain't you ever going to get up?" he called loudly from the doorway to his friend's bedchamber.

Percy was aroused suddenly from his pleasant dream of capons roasted to a turn and gooseberry tarts covered with lashings of fresh cream. Sitting up with a start, he muttered, "Confound it all, who's there?" He was still more than half asleep.

"It's only me. What the devil's that deuced odd concoction you're wearin' on your head, Percy?"

Having forgotten all about his headgear, the drowsy Percy put a hand up to his head to investigate. "Called a nightcap, Pev. Don't take too many brains to recognize such a thing," he protested quarrelsomely.

"Don't look like one, with all those dashed ribbons and bows hanging all over it. Makes you look touched in your upper works." Peveril sat on the edge of Percy's bed, but jumped up immediately when he found he'd sat on the now cold stone water bottle so thoughtfully provided by Mrs. Parsnip last evening so that Percy could warm his sheets and his toes.

Percy dashed off the large white nightcap decorated with pink and white bows and ribbons and regarded it sheepishly. "Oh! Forgot to pack mine. Borrowed this one from Mrs. Parsnip," he admitted shamefacedly, tossing it aside. "Only spare one she had about the place. Didn't notice all these dashed furbelows last night. Was too sleepy."

"Beats me why you'd need such a thing anyway. Ain't manly."

"To keep out the chill. Can't stand for my head to

be cold. 'Sides, let's the nightmares in, y'know, if you don't keep your head covered while you sleep."

Peveril regarded him with astonishment. "Ain't never heard such a farrago of nonsense in my life, Percy! Tell you what. The thing's too tight. It's damaged your brain—made you go all queer in your attic. Best leave your head uncovered for the rest of the day and give it a chance to recover."

Percy shot him a wounded look.

Peveril grinned at him and made for the door.

Peveril eventually ran Mary to earth in the warm, cozy kitchen at the back of the quaint little inn. She was sitting on a tall wooden stool in front of the inglenook fireplace stirring up a rich, spicy fruitcake for Mrs. Parsnip. Mary had had to overcome Mrs. Parsnip's reluctance to let her perform such a mundane task.

"What's quality like 'ee, dear, to do in me kitchen?" the good lady had asked when Mary came down to thank her for the clean garments and to ask if she might be of help with the cooking. Though her arrival at the inn might have been a trifle irregular, to Mrs. Parsnip's experienced eyes Miss Marlowe was clearly quality.

Mary had laughed and overcome the landlady's scruples. "Why, ma'am, do you think I'm such a poor, weak creature that I would be incapable of lending you any assistance?"

"Och. Get away with 'ee, miss!" Mrs. Parsnip laughed. "Sit yerself on that stool, and I'll give 'ee the Christmas cake to stir. It takes a strong arm, mind."

" 'Morning, Mary," Peveril greeted her cheerfully. "You're looking slap up to the echo this morning in your new gear, my dear," he teased, running an eye over her too-large, faded dress.

"And a good morning to you, my lord viscount," Mary replied with a gleam in her eyes at his taunt, but, taking his teasing in good part, she smiled radiantly up at him. "Did you sleep well? You look a little better."

"Devilish well, actually. But if you think I look better, you must like your men colorful. This dashed mug of mine must resemble a blasted peacock's tail today," he quipped, gesturing to the red, yellow, and purple discoloration of his bruised face.

Mary laughed and agreed that he did add a bit of color to the unrelieved white covering of snow that enveloped them.

"We look to be snowbound, don't we? Guess we'll be here for Christmas, at the least. Still, this place is snug enough. Percy was right for once."

"It is lovely here, isn't it?" Mary agreed smilingly and went on with her stirring.

"Umm," Peveril murmured sniffing the air. "What smells so good?"

Mrs. Parsnip had already started her Christmas baking and a combination of tantalizing smells coming from the brick oven in one side of the vast fireplace was wafting through the inn.

"Mrs. Parsnip is doing some baking for our Christmas feast. I believe you smell the minced pies." Mary sniffed the air, too. "Or perhaps it's the jam tarts . . . or maybe it's the gooseberry and apple pie."

Peveril laughed. "I can hardly wait to taste all these mouth-watering morsels. Mrs. P. is seeing to it we don't starve, at least."

"Well, as we're like to be stranded here through Christmas, she wants to make it a special holiday for all of us. And lots of good food is her idea of a jolly celebration."

"Mine, too! A woman after my own heart," Peveril declared with one of his patented boyish grins. "You look to be gainfully employed. Can I lend a hand?"

Mrs. Parsnip bustled in just then and overheard the viscount's offer, she immediately cried, "Lord, bless 'ee, yer lordship! As soon as I've given 'ee yer breakfast, I would set 'ee to helpin' my Samuel clear a path to the stables, if 'ee wasn't quality, and hurt into the bargain. But, as it be, I'll have 'ee sort through the box of decorations I've set out in the parlor, if ye've a mind to, that is," she concluded with a girlish blush, her merry blue eyes twinkling in her soft, kindly face.

Mrs. Parsnip was no taller than Mary and almost as round as Mr. Parsnip. In contrast to his thinning hair, she had an abundance of graying blond curls that escaped from her large white mobcap and spilled every which way over her forehead and cheeks.

"I ain't so high in the instep that I have to be treated like some namby-pamby, stiff-rumped nob. Matter of fact, won't stand for it!" Peveril declared stoutly, working his charm on the cheery little landlady.

Mary bit back a grin, thinking he could turn the

sourest of dames up sweet, if he put his mind, and his charming rascal's tongue, to it.

The viscount insisted he was game to help Mr. Parsnip clear the path as soon as he had some of the delicious-smelling vittles cooking in the hearth, adding that he would like nothing better than to sort through the Christmas decorations when he had recovered from his morning's exertions. He recommended that they send Percy to aid him as soon as that slugabed gentleman should make his appearance and be given his breakfast.

Mary gave him a dazzling smile and told him he was very right. Peveril felt his chest swell with pride at her approval and resolved to work like a demon to clear that path.

That afternoon Peveril gave in to his urge to recapture some of his boyhood and challenged Percy to a snowball fight. As the two young gentlemen ran out the kitchen door in great high spirits, Mrs. Parsnip said they reminded her of her two sons when they were young and were given the unexpected treat of a deep snowfall. The two young Parsnips were now farmers over to Chineham way, she told Mary proudly.

At first resolved to stand on her dignity, Mary resisted the urge to peer at Peveril and Percy through the curtains, but finally, irresistibly, she was drawn outside by the mingled whoops, shouts and laughter of her companions. Wrapping up warmly, she went out, unable to resist joining in the fun.

"I say, Pev, there's Mary! Think we should let a lady join in?" Percy called to his friend who had his back turned to the house when Mary came out.

"Oh, ho! So you've decided to show us your skills, have you, Mary?" Peveril teased when he spied her.

"I used to ward off several cousins at a time at my grandfather's house, so you stand warned, Peveril Standish, I have a deadly aim." And she proved it by throwing the large fistfull of snow she had concealed behind her back at his hat. Her aim was dead on. The snowball landed with a splat on Peveril's forehead, sending his hat flying off.

"Why, you dashed little hoyden! All fair's in love and snowball fights, you know, Mary," he said, laughing as he wiped the wet snow from his face with his gloved hand and stooped to scoop up his own weapon.

"We'll see if you can catch me first!" she challenged. Giggling, she turned her back on him and ran down the path to the stables that the men had worked hard to clear that morning. She could hear Peveril coming up behind her and she veered off the path, only to find herself standing almost knee deep in the soft snow.

"Oh, a deuced unfortunate miscalculation, Mary. You'll be made to see the error of your ways now—shattering my dignity like that, sweet Mary, mine!" Peveril declared, wading toward her with a devilish grin on his face and a fistful of snow in his hand.

She backed away, trying to flick snow at him with her fingers and maintain her balance at the same time, but his longer legs gave him a distinct advantage. She could hear Percy in the background whistling and shouting, urging his friends on.

"You wouldn't be so unchivalrous would you, my lord?"

"Oh, ho. Realize you can't escape me, so you think to toad eat me, do you, saucy puss? I've got you now!" And before Mary knew what was happening Peveril scooped her up in his arms, gave her a smacking kiss on her cold lips, then dropped her again into the snowbank. His crow of laughter followed her down.

After a great deal of laughter and fun the pleasantly weary trio of stranded travelers subsided in front of the large fire in their homey parlor that was now festooned with colorful bows and lengths of red ribbon, as well as one or two of Mrs. Parsnip's handmade lace angels. Packages and parcels of homemade wines and cordials, preserved fruits and other foods, as well as items of clothing that had been specially sewn by the busy landlady, lay in gaily-colored piles about the room. Most of the gifts were for the Parsnip sons and their growing families. The other things the Parsnips had intended to take to church with them for distribution to the vicar and their friends and neighbors, but there was little chance they would get to church now, with the snow still too deep for travel and no sign of a thaw.

Mary, Peveril and Percy sat comfortably digesting their large, satisfying dinner that had included an unexpected treat of oysters from the barrel Mr. Parsnip had purchased in Basingstoke when he had gone into town for supplies at the beginning of the week. They had cracked a bottle of their host's homemade currant wine to have with their meal, too, and all had agreed it was surprisingly good.

Mr. Parsnip interrupted them after a time and carried the gentlemen away with him to show them how to prepare, light and smoke tobacco in a clay pipe, as he had promised earlier.

Mary watched them go with an affectionate smile, then sat herself down in the large wing chair Mr. Parsnip had thoughtfully placed in the little parlor specially for her. She picked up the book she had found in her bedchamber and sat holding it on her lap, staring into the fire and musing over the events of the day.

She was conscious that she had enjoyed the viscount's company far more than was good for her, if indeed she meant what she had told him about not holding him to his promise to wed her after this escapade. However, he had not said another word on the subject and she supposed he felt relieved that she had let him off the hook so easily.

"Oh, Mary, you can't have it both ways, my girl," she said angrily to herself. She looked down to her book and determinedly tried to concentrate on it before her wayward longings overcame her sense.

"What are you reading there, Mary?" Peveril asked from just behind her chair, taking her by surprise and causing her to jump. Remembering that he wasn't all that fond of tobacco smoke, the viscount had left the other gentlemen and returned to the parlor. He hung over Mary's chair, trying to see what held her attention so fiercely.

"Sir Walter Scott's *Marmion,*" she answered a bit breathlessly at his nearness in the small, candlelit room. "Have you read it, Pev?"

"No. Scott ain't in my line . . . Had a notion you'd

be bookish, though. Do you mind if I'm not?" He watched the play of firelight and candlelight over her little features and shining hair and felt a strange protectiveness steal over him. She was a lovely young woman, warm and intelligent—the kind of woman who would be a helpmate to a man through thick and thin. He would be proud to call her his wife.

Wishing to soothe away the uncertainty she heard in his voice, Mary put her hand over Peveril's where it rested on the chair back and gripped it tightly. She turned her head to smile up at him. "Of course not, Peveril. I know you prefer outdoor pursuits. You must do what you enjoy. You have many talents and I like you very well as you are."

He turned his hand over under hers and laced his fingers with hers. "Oh, Mary, you're a generous little soul, willing to overlook all my shortcomings like that. Always knew we'd deal famously together," he declared with a fervent light in his eyes.

She smiled briefly, then dropped her eyes and changed the subject. She so badly wanted to believe his impulsive words, but she was afraid to trust that so much happiness was within her grasp. She pulled her hand from his warm, comfortable hold and said, "Listen to this, Pev.

The damsel donned her kirtle sheen
The hall was decked with holly green
Forth to the woods did merry men go
To gather in the mistletoe.

This has given me an idea. Tomorrow is Christmas Eve. We will want to have some decorations for

Christmas Day. Why do we not try to make our way through the snow tomorrow to that stand of trees across the road and gather some greenery to intertwine with the ribbons and loop about the room?"

"That's a prodigious famous notion, Mary!" he responded with enthusiasm. "Never fear that you'll be lost in a snowbank, my dear! Percy and I will clear a path for you, or failing that, we'll carry you on our shoulders and hoist you up so you can reach the mistletoe in the highest branches. Must have some of that. I'll put it to tolerable good use, I swear," he said, tweaking one of her curls and laughing at the way she blushed so becomingly at his teasing touch.

Chapter 17

"Evergreens?—Ain't it unlucky to bring this stuff indoors, Pev?" Percy asked in a worried voice as they waded through the snow in the field across from the inn.

"Lord, no, Percy! Don't know where you come by such deuced corkbrained notions." Peveril was trudging ahead, forging a path through the snow with his long legs for the others to follow.

"Well, actually, Pev, Percy probably remembers the old tale that it is unlucky to bring such greenery as holly, ivy, and mistletoe inside one's house," Mary stated.

"Sounds a nonsensical notion to me. Why should it be unlucky?" Peveril wondered.

"Well, in pagan times people believed that evergreen plants were magical."

"Magical?"

"Yes. Because, you see, they live, and even bear fruit, in the dead of winter. One of my great aunts, who was very superstitious, used to say that holly berries are very powerful against witches."

"Witches, you say!" Percy exclaimed, his eyes almost starting from his head as he looked all round, expecting to see an old crone pop out at him from behind the nearest tree. "Wonder if there are any of those old hags round here?"

Peveril caught Mary's eye and they both laughed at Percy's foolish notions.

"Don't worry, Percy," Mary reassured him, "the prohibition against bringing such plants indoors doesn't apply on Christmas Eve, or at any time during the holiday celebrations. Evil spirits are powerless during this holy time of year. Any witches or other malevolent spirits lurking about are warded off and pagan magic is overcome by the sacredness of the Christmas season. Remember the old saying? 'No witch hath power to charm, so hallowed and so gracious is the time.' "

"Well, if that don't beat all!" Percy exclaimed, his mouth agape in awe, much struck by Mary's explanation. "You hear that, Pev?"

"Of course I heard it, Percy. I'm here, ain't I? As today is the twenty-fourth of December, I guess we're safe in taking armloads of this stuff back with us."

"Yes, we are quite safe today, Percy," Mary assured him as they set out to gather as much of the greenery as they could carry back to the inn on the rickety old sled they had dragged along with them for the purpose.

Peveril spotted some mistletoe growing high up in a gnarled old oak tree. With Percy's help, he managed to set his boot into a crevice between two branches and boost himself up into the tree. He reached higher, trying to capture a sprig of the purportedly magical plant.

He was determined to reach it, hoping it would soon work some magic for him. He would catch Mary under it and kiss her good and proper as soon as may be. Their enforced intimacy these last few days was having a most unsettling effect on him. He hadn't realized before how strongly she affected him. He was deeply attracted to her. And he didn't know how to show it without frightening her. But he felt that if he didn't have some outlet soon, he would commit mayhem.

Mary watched Peveril climb the tree with some misgiving. She put her hand to her throat. He would fall. She was sure he would fall. He had shed his greatcoat and now he set his boot against the branch and reached for the limb above his head, his jacket riding up over his slim hips and well-muscled thighs as he tried to climb higher.

There! He had used the strength of his arms to pull himself up high enough to reach the sprig of mistletoe and was smiling down at her in triumph. She had known that he spent a great amount of his time in athletic pursuits, but she hadn't realized the latent strength in his lean body. She smiled back, her breath coming fast in her throat. From her fear. Yes, she felt so out of breath because she had been afraid, she assured herself, abashed at her reaction.

When they returned to the house, Mary danced into the parlor with the gentleman close behind her, bringing a whoosh of crisp air and the fragrant scent of freshly-cut evergreens into the room with them. She set the gentlemen to decking the room with the evergreen branches they had collected and they proceeded to transform the rough parlor where they took their meals into a colorful, festive haven.

Mary sat on the worn rug in front of the hearth, weaving some of the boughs into a garland, trying not to dwell on this disturbing, physical awareness of the viscount that had taken hold of her imagination. Again and again she had relived that brief touch of his lips against hers when they were making their way to this inn. It had set her to wondering what a lingering kiss would feel like, his mouth covering hers, her body pressed tightly to his.

She blushed at the direction of her wayward thoughts. Bending over her work, she managed to recover her countenance while she adorned her kissing bough with bits and pieces of ribbon and fabric and some small berries and fruits that Mrs. Parsnip had given her, saving until last the prized sprig of mistletoe Peveril had provided. Finally, she attached the sprig with a length of red ribbon, placing it in the center of her garland.

She looked at it critically this way and that, remembering with a pang the elaborately bedizened mistletoe boughs they had at Wyndham Park that always had small packages dangling over the edge for the guests to open Christmas morning. She wished she had some small gifts of some sort for her companions.

An idea came to her. She did have something! Not much, it was true. But, yes, she thought, the little mince pies she had made yesterday would do. She would use some of the colorful left-over fabric and ribbon to wrap them and place them among the greenery on the mantlepiece before she went to bed tonight so that her companions would find them early Christmas morning.

She was no cook, but with Mrs. Parsnip's expert guidance, she had managed to make about half a dozen mince pies from that good lady's richly prepared mincemeat of fat mutton, apples, dried fruits, and spices.

"Make enough for all of us, dearie. Every minced pie ye eat at Christmastime made by a different cook will bring ye a lucky month in the comin' year, so it be said."

The innkeeper's wife had also given Mary some lucky charms and coins to place in her pies to represent good fortune in the new year. She had shown Mary how to form the pie dough into little boxes representing the Christ child's manger. Mary had never heard of this quaint practice.

"Aye, that's a'cause those that be of a Puritan persuasion frowns and looks down their long noses 'pon it. Too idolatrous for 'em, so it be said. They've tried to put it down, and succeeded in most places, I do believe. But me mum taught me and it's happy I am to pass it along to 'ee, dearie."

"What are you dreaming about, Mary?" Peveril asked, wondering what had provoked that mischievous little half smile on her lips and that faraway look in her wide eyes.

"Oh, just Christmases past," she replied evasively, lifting her creation to show the gentlemen. "I think the mistletoe adds the crowning touch to my kissing bough, don't you?"

Percy admired her handiwork and Peveril said,

"Oh, ho! You've finished it already, have you, Mary. The speed with which you worked must show your eagerness to put it to use," he teased, feeling inordinately eager to put it to use himself. "Hope you'll allow me to hang it for you, then Percy and I can claim our reward for all this hard work you've set us to!" Sitting there on the floor all flushed and bright-eyed and happy, she looked good enough to eat, he thought with a growing hunger.

Mary flushed even more deeply as she looked up and met the warm glow in Peveril's eyes. She saw that he had shed his jacket and neckcloth and now stood before her with his sleeves rolled up to the elbow and his shirt open at the neck. He gave her a wink and a lopsided grin before he turned back to help Percy attach a final bough of evergreen over the parlor mantlepiece. She watched the play of muscles across his back under his thin shirt as he stretched his arms over his head to tack the bough in place. She swallowed awkwardly.

"Hard work, my lord? This is mere child's play," she managed a playful reply after clearing her unaccountably constricted throat.

"You're right, my dear. Most fun I've had at Christmastime in years! Right, Percy?"

"Right, Pev. Dashed good thing we're stuck here. It's homey. I like it."

"Anyone know what Mrs. P.'s planning to give us for Christmas dinner?" Peveril asked. "Or for today's dinner, for that matter. I'm beginning to feel devilish sharp set after this morning's hard work." And for more than just food, he added to himself.

"Oh, she had Mr. Parsnip kill a fat green goose

this morning for Christmas dinner," Mary replied. "It was a good thing her flock of geese survived the snowfall, she said, otherwise she hinted that the two of you would have had to join Mr. Parsnip in shooting some pigeons for our dinner."

Peveril shot her a baleful glance, then a slow grin spread across his face. "A roasted goose, with sage and onion stuffing! My idea of heaven, Percy!"

"Can taste it already!" Percy declared with a beatific smile on his cherubic face. "Lord, we've landed on our feet here, Pev, and no mistake. Mrs. Parsnip's a bang-up cook, as I told you."

"You certainly did, Percy, and you were in the right of it for once. Lord! What luck to be snowbound in such a paradise! Even think I've seen an angel lurking about the place," Peveril quipped with a wink for Mary.

Mary smiled back at the viscount, feeling a warm glow of happiness all the way down to her toes. She was cheered by the thought that she would celebrate at least this one Christmas with him, and her resolve to make it a joyful one, despite the circumstances, seemed to be working well. If she never saw Peveril again after the next few days, she would look back on this special time, remembering his affectionate behavior toward her with a glow of tender emotion, even if his words and actions sprang from nothing more than feelings of friendship.

"Angels don't *lurk*, my Lord Lindford. It is those with devilment on their minds who are given to that suspicious activity."

Peveril laughed.

"You seen an angel, Pev?" Percy asked in confusion. "Here? Dashed if you ain't gettin' in the habit of seein' such creatures everywhere."

"The one I saw before vanished though, Percy."

"Vanished?"

"Into thin air. Her wings fell off and her halo cracked, and she vanished. Dashed if she wasn't just *disguised* as an angel."

"Maybe this other one is in disguise, too," Percy said.

"No. The one I've seen hereabouts is a *real* angel."

"How do you know that, Pev?" Percy asked, faint but pursuing.

"She's an inside-out angel . . . her inside shines as brightly as her outside, 'cause she's got an angel's heart as well as an angel's face."

"You don't say, Pev!" Percy exclaimed, looking completely flummoxed. "Ain't never heard of such a thing m'self."

Peveril laughed at his friend and regarded Mary with a warm teasing gleam in his eyes.

Mary held the kissing bough in front of her face to hide her confusion. Oh, he did say the most heart-stopping things sometimes. But she knew he was only teasing her.

"Are you planning to wear that dashed thing on your head, Mary?" Peveril quipped.

"Mm, I was just wondering where I should place it for best effect," she answered, holding her creation away from her face and looking about the room.

"Oh, I think about here would be exactly the right place," he said decisively, taking the kissing bough from her hand and holding it over her head. Patience was not one of his virtues. He couldn't wait any longer to claim that kiss he had promised himself.

Mary rose to her feet and skipped away, but Peveril advanced on her relentlessly. He reached out with his other arm and scooped her against his chest, then claimed a kiss that he had meant to be brief and teasing, but that quickly turned into something else.

As soon as his lips met hers, his body seemed to catch fire. He could feel her soft little body pressed to his, warming him from chest to thighs. Her hands moved from his chest to his back, her arms twined tightly about his waist. When her lips softened against his fiery kiss, Peveril forgot where he was and what he had meant to do. His lips opened and moved gently over hers. He tasted a sweet fire he had never known before and a fierce ache invaded his body and his heart.

He was in danger of dropping Mary's elaborately constructed bough on her head as he tried to bring his other arm around her so that he could deepen the kiss still more.

"I say, Pev. You two gonna be kissin' all day?" Percy asked plaintively, interrupting them and breaking the spell that held them fast. "Might give me a turn."

Mary pulled away, quite breathless and her cheeks a fiery red as she allowed Percy to claim a quick peck on her hot cheek before she made her escape.

That night, Peveril gazed out through his bedroom window up at the stars shining in the midnight clear sky, wondering which was the bright star that had guided the three wise men to the stable at Bethlehem, and thinking about Mary.

Dashed, if he wasn't in love with her, he realized in wonder. Passionately in love. And what in the world did he, a spendthrift and a wastrel, a hot-tempered, heedless, ne'er-do-well, have to offer Mary Marlowe, the most generous little soul in the world, granddaughter of an earl, and quality as sure as check from the top of her shining, dark head to the tips of her small feet, he asked himself helplessly.

He had gone through life carelessly, throwing his money away with never a thought for the morrow, though some of those who knew him best would have called him open-handed and warm-hearted, always ready to give any spare funds to a friend who came begging a loan.

He resolved to reform his spendthrift ways, take responsibility for his past actions and accept the consequences of his foolishness. And whether he married Mary or not, he had to give up his life as a town fribble and start to put his estate right. This time he had managed by the skin of his teeth to avoid mortgaging his property and house. But there was no denying that it would take him a long time to turn a profit from his land after the years of neglect it had suffered. He would have to make sacrifices. And although, with the sale of all his goods in London, he had made a good start on paying off his debts, there were still some outstanding, weighing him down.

But Mary had to marry him! She was now his responsibility, as well as his love.

God! He sighed, then groaned, leaning his face on his arms folded over the casement.

Filled with the glorious and terrible knowledge that he was deep in love with his sweet Mary, he wondered what he was to do. If he did the honorable thing, as the world would deem it, and married her because of the compromising situation he had placed her in, might he not ruin her chance to find true love and happiness, not to mention a more comfortable future with another man, and so blight her life forever? But if he did not marry her, leaving her free to choose the man who could win her heart, would she have such a chance, if her reputation was in tatters?

It was a puzzle that was too much for his tired brain to sort out this night.

Christmas morning dawned overcast and cold. All the household, the Parsnips, Mary, Peveril, Percy, the inn's few servants and the viscount's man, Small, gathered in the innkeeper's private quarters to say a prayer and sing a few carols to take the place of the church service they could not attend.

Mr. Parsnip's voice rang out as he read the uplifting words of Luke's Christmas gospel in a deep, resonate voice, rich with the accents of his native Hampshire. He concluded with: 'And this shall be a sign to you: you will find an infant wrapped in swaddling clothes and lying in a manger.' And suddenly there was with the angel a multitude of the heavenly hosts praising God and saying, 'Glory to God in the highest, and on earth peace among men of good will.'

Mary was moved. Her thoughts turned to her grandfather on this Christmas morning, this the first

Christmas she had spent away from Wyndham Park. She longed to see him again. She knew she must make her peace with him; stubborn though he was, he was her family and she loved him. Surely, surely, he would not force her to marry Cedric, if she went home. She bit back tears of emotion that had welled in her eyes.

With his head bowed as he listened to the innkeeper read the Christmas gospel, Peveril was thinking of Mary and the gift she had given him that morning. It was a little thing, but he had been moved and quite ridiculously pleased that she had cared enough to make the gesture. He was feeling upset that he had nothing to give her in return, for he wished her to remember this Christmas when they had been together always.

When Mary glanced over at Peveril to see his head bowed in prayer as he stood beside her, she felt such a stirring of love for him, that she thought she would burst with it. She reached over to clasp his hand with hers and hold it tightly. He returned the pressure, lifting his head and smiling warmly down at her. It was a loving, intimate smile and his blue eyes were full of dark lights and mysterious promises that set Mary's blood to pounding through her veins.

She blushed and looked down, withdrawing her hand from his warm hold with some embarrassment and some regret. She had been attracted to his handsome, charming person from the first, although she was bemused by his sometimes wild, impetuous behavior, and thought him too volatile a boy on whom to fix her affections. But he had changed in the last few days. Changed into a man she would be happy to share her life with. A man she could share her passion with.

But if she held him to his promise to marry her to save her reputation, she was afraid it would not be fair to him. Would he not come to regret their forced marriage? She loved him too much ever to wish to see him unhappy.

When Mr. Parsnip finished reading, they all lifted their heads and joined in some of the traditional old English carols, "The First Nowell," "God Rest You Merry Gentlemen," "the Sussex Carol," concluding with "I Saw Three Ships."

Peveril's eyes sought and held Mary's as their voices blended in joyous song.

"As we ain't got our family with us this yur, we'd like to bid you, Miss Marlowe, your lordship, and Mr. Throckmorton, welcome to our Christmas Day table. Eat hearty and prosper in the new yur!" Mr. Parsnip toasted his three guests when they all sat down together that afternoon to a scrumptious Christmas feast. The table fairly groaned under the assortment of traditional seasonal foods that attested to Mrs. Parsnip's prowess, and tireless labors, in the kitchens.

"Now, Parsnip, go on, do. Let us have the rhyme!" Mrs. Parsnip laughingly urged her congenial spouse.

The innkeeper hemmed and hawed, then rose to his feet once more, cleared his throat and said with some embarrassment, "It's been a tradition in our family for donkey's yurs to have this here rhyme afore Christmas Day dinner." He took a much creased piece of paper from the pocket of his best jacket, smoothed it out with his large hand, and began to read:

Now thrice welcome, Christmas,
Which brings us good cheer,
Minc'd pies and plum porridge,
Good ale and strong beer;
With pig, goose and capon,
The best that can be,
So well doth the weather
And our stomachs agree.

"Welcome, welcome, one and all!" he cried and they all raised their glasses in a festive toast.

Holding the freshly honed, razor sharp carving knife poised over the golden brown goose that looked to be roasted to a turn, he said with a wink for his wife, "Hope neither of ye gentlemen be partial to the parson's nose. Always save that delicacy for Martha here."

The others laughed. Mrs. Parsnip blushed and said, "If'n 'ee ain't a one, to be puttin' me to the blush so, Parsnip! I'll not give 'ee any Christmas pud, if 'ee don't watch that saucy tongue of yern!"

The viscount said he was sure he spoke for Percy, too, when he declined the honor, assuring their host that they would gladly forego the treat in favor of their hostess.

"Oh, yer lordship, it be too kind in 'ee to say so!" Mrs. Parsnip exclaimed, clearly a bit overwhelmed to be dining with the gentry in this casual way.

And so went the meal, with jokes and good cheer

and many appreciative noises from the gentlemen, and Mary, too, over the excellence of Mrs. Parsnip's cooking.

They were all still in a merry mood as the last piece of Christmas pudding covered with buttered rum sauce disappeared from their plates. Spirits of more than one kind flowed freely as they all enjoyed Mr. Parsnip's special homemade cherry wine with the meal.

"Damme, if this ain't the best Christmas meal I've ever had!" Peveril exclaimed again as he polished off his helping of the rich Christmas pudding. "Bless the master of this house! And the mistress, too!" he sang out gaily.

"Hear, hear!" seconded Percy.

Mrs. Parsnip blushed rosily at this tribute and would have thrown her apron over her head, if she hadn't removed it specially for the grand occasion.

It was late in the afternoon when they finally retired from the table to take a turn outdoors. Percy and Mary and Peveril walked arm and arm down the path that had been cleared to the stables, going to and fro several times, trying to walk down their enormous dinner without giving in to the urge to sleep it off, as the Parsnips had done. The snow had turned to slush and they couldn't fail to note that a thaw had set in.

Our Christmas idyll's at an end, Mary thought, glancing at Peveril to see a preoccupied frown on his face.

Eventually the trio retired to their little parlor where Mary sat reading and Peveril and Percy spent their time playing backgammon and draughts with the old boards and playing pieces their host had unearthed for them, arguing lightheartedly over one another's tactics.

Mary's eyes strayed from her book to watch Peveril as he bent over the board. It had been a lovely day. She bit her lip, thinking that their time together was almost finished.

At nine o'clock, Mrs. Parsnip tapped on the door and came in with a tray loaded with a selection of all the delicacies left over from the massive Christmas feast and insisted they must want some supper. In all politeness, they could not refuse, though Mary could not bring herself to touch a bite, and the two gentlemen ate sparingly.

"I'm so full, I think I'm going to pop!" Peveril told them after raising his glass in another toast to their hostess.

"Me, too, Pev!" Percy nodded in complete agreement.

The three companions, feeling warm and cozy and well fed, let the candles burn down until they guttered out. They sat quietly in front of the hearth, gazing into the flicking firelight. Peveril's eyes were fixed on Mary. He was watching the play of firelight over her delicate features.

The fire in the grate eventually died down, and the glowing embers popped and sizzled on the hearth.

When Peveril moved to put another log or two on the fire, Percy stood up, stretched and yawned, then announced, "I'm for bed. Good night, Mary. Coming, Pev?"

At last! Peveril thought, Percy was taking himself

off to bed and he could speak privately with Mary. " 'Night, Perce. Won't be too late myself."

To Peveril's dismay, Mary rose also and made for the door in Percy's wake.

"I must go, too, Pev. It is late and I am tired. Happy, but tired. Again, I bid you a Happy Christmas," she uttered in a low voice.

"No, don't go for a moment, Mary," he begged, putting out his hand to stay her. "Want to speak to you."

She looked back at him questioningly and a little hopefully, not wanting the day to end. "Yes. What is it, Peveril?"

Their eyes locked across the room and her heart began to hammer against her ribs when he came toward her to stand quite near and look down into her eyes with an expression of tenderness on his face.

He wanted more than anything to tell her what was in his heart, but he could not find the words. "Want to give you my Christmas present, my dear—only it ain't a thing—it's a promise."

"Oh, you don't have to give me anything, Peveril—" she began, but he hushed her with a finger to her lips.

"You gave me a present this morning—"

"But it was nothing!" she protested against his finger.

"Well, it was *something*, and you took the time to make it for me. I was— dash it, I was *touched* by your thinking of me, Mary."

"Oh," she said on a breath of air, gazing up at him, her eyes full of love.

He took a deep breath and began. "I want to promise you that I'm going to reform, Mary. No more gaming. I'm going home to High Acres, that's my estate in Hertfordshire. It isn't much at the moment. My father neglected it, and I'm afraid I've followed in his footsteps. I've put no money into the land and it hasn't been profitable, but at least neither the house nor the land is mortgaged. And I'm going to learn how to make it profitable. Confound it, I'm going to become a model landlord, managing his acres and learning all about tilling and crop rotation and livestock, and I'm going to get to know all my tenant farmers, too, so that I can call them by their names when I see them. Lord knows how long it will take to put things in order, but I promise you, Mary—I swear I'm going to do it!"

Somehow his hands had come to rest on her waist and hers against his chest while he spoke. He held her lightly and looked down at her with determination in his eyes.

"Oh, Peveril! How splendid! I— I don't know what to say. I cannot think of a more wonderful gift than to know that you have decided to take charge of your life, to build a secure, happy future."

Peveril blinked at her, thinking he was uncommonly fortunate to have met such an understanding lady as his sweet Mary. He looked up briefly, trying to swallow his emotion, only to see that they were standing under Mary's kissing bough. A broad grin suddenly lit his face. "Look where we're standing, Mary."

As she looked up, he bent his head and set his lips tenderly against hers, breathing in the violet scent of her, the sweetness of her.

Her hands went up behind his neck. She set the tips of her fingers against his sensitive skin there as she allowed him to pull her tightly to his chest. Her fingers feathered through the edges of his hair touching his collar, then moved down over the muscles of his back, before linking around his slim waist.

A log fell in the hearth, hissing and breaking the stillness in the room lit only by the glow of the dying fire.

"I love you, Mary Marlowe," he said a little unsteadily, raising his head slightly from her mouth. He was moved more than he could ever have imagined by the sweetness of her lips and the feel of her arms about his waist, her little body tucked snugly and trustingly against his.

"And I love you, Peveril Standish."

"You do?" he asked in disbelief. "Oh, Mary! My God, I don't deserve you!" he exclaimed before crushing her body against his and kissing her the way he had dreamed of doing. His mouth moved over hers until Mary's lips opened, giving him the sweet entry he sought. There was no need to hold back now, Peveril thought, taking her mouth in a searing kiss. She was his, he knew, moving his hands down over her soft breasts around to her back and down to her waist, pressing her to him, fitting her little body to his.

After a few long minutes, or an eternity, Peveril didn't know which, he raised his head and said humbly. "God! I want nothing in this world so much as for you to agree to marry me, Mary. But the Lord knows, I've been a fool and a wastrel. I've been careless. I have debts. But I will put things right! I don't have the *right* to ask you to marry me now, but—will you wait for me, Mary?" he pleaded. "Please?"

"No," she said gently, looking deeply into his anxious blue eyes.

"I thought not," he said with a catch in his voice, dropping his arms from around her and making to pull away before he made even more of a fool of himself.

She held him tightly about the waist and wouldn't allow him to pull away. "I won't wait. I want—I wish to marry you now, Pev. More than I can say. I want to help you turn your estate into a model of prosperity. But you must return me to my grandfather first. I see now that I was wrong to leave, but not wrong to oppose his wishes. I am of age. He cannot forbid the match, but I want to ask his blessing on our union. He raised me, you see, and though he's as stubborn as they come, I love him. I want to explain to him that even though I oppose his wishes, I love him. Will you take me to him at Wyndham Park when the weather clears?"

"If you think it best, then of course I will," Peveril promised, but his heart was racing madly with fear. He didn't want to lose his love after he had only just found her. He already loved her to distraction. "And if you cannot overcome his opposition?" he asked anxiously, with more roughness than he intended.

Mary put up her hands to caress his face, wanting to ease his worry. "Then we will be married without his approval, my love. But I must see him first and try to mend matters with him. If he won't accept my olive branch, then so be it. I will happily marry you without his blessing . . . but I must try."

Chapter 18

The household was late abed the following morning and not a one of them realized how much the snow had diminished overnight. The freeze that had held them all captive in a white winter wonderland had broken during Christmas Day and the melting was far advanced by the time the three snowbound visitors at the Green Man arose.

Mary was up and about before the two gentlemen. She made her way downstairs in a happy daze, hugging to herself the delicious knowledge that Peveril loved her to distraction. As she loved him. Her feet hardly touched the ground as she danced along to the little parlor. In this state of euphoria, she opened the door of the room and was immediately taken aback to discover a gentleman standing in front of the fire removing his greatcoat.

"Cedric! However did you get here?" she cried in dismay.

"Mary! I've found you at last. I trust you are unharmed?" Cedric addressed her in a voice of doom.

He lay his coat carefully aside and walked stiffly toward her.

"Of— of course. I am perfectly fine, thank you. You came in search of me, Cedric?" She lifted her chin and looked him straight in the eye.

"Indeed, I did! Knowing you planned to go to Sidmouth with the Ramsbottoms, I called in at Curzon Street five days ago to try again to convince you to come to your senses and allow me to escort you home to Wyndham. I was informed that you and Miss Ramsbottom were out doing some last-minute Christmas shopping. I waited, but when you did not return after an hour, I was forced to take my leave.

"You may imagine my chagrin when I received a communication from Mr. Ramsbottom the following morning, apprising me that you had eloped with the Viscount Lindford! By some means or other, Ramsbottom knew you were to be found in this vicinity. I shall never understand how you could have accepted employment from that vulgar upstart. Of course, I set out from London immediately, but only got as far as Reading the first night, when the snow made it impossible for me to continue. I was forced to spend a thoroughly miserable Christmas in a most inferior establishment, worrying about how I was to inform the earl of what had occurred.

"I was able to ride on early this morning and have been making inquiries at all the inns in the surrounding villages. I discovered you were here through the good information of the innkeeper of this establishment, who seems to be a decent enough fellow.

"I felt it my duty, Mary, to seek you out and impress upon you the shocking impropriety of your actions and urge you to beg the earl's forgiveness immediately. I trust that he and I can manage to overset this shocking mésalliance and scotch the scandal before it gets abroad."

"Well, you have got it entirely wrong, Cedric, and I cannot say that I am at all surprised that you would believe such a thing of me," Mary replied angrily, arms akimbo. "That is why we should never suit, you see. You do not have the least understanding of me."

"You are saying that you did not elope with Lindford?"

"No, of course I did not. But Belinda did. I was duped into accompanying her, but her father found us before she and Lindford could be married. Mr. Ramsbottom's servant attacked Lindford, and when I went to his assistance, my former employer drove off with his daughter, leaving me and the viscount to fend for ourselves in a snowstorm. Luckily for us, we were not far from this inn where we found shelter."

"You are not married to Lindford, then?"

"No."

"I see. But you have been most thoroughly compromised, staying alone here with that dissolute young scoundrel these four or five days. I see I shall have to demean myself and rescue you from this most improper situation you are in, cousin, to avert any scandal attaching to our name. The earl would expect it of me. I shall marry you as soon as we return to Wyndham."

Peveril, coming down the stairs jauntily, whistling a cheerful tune, was about to step into the parlor when he overheard these words through the partially open door. He stopped in his tracks and his hands curled into fists at his side when he recognized the pompous tones of Mary's kinsman, Sir Cedric Ledbetter.

"Indeed, you shall be forced to do no such thing!" Mary objected strenuously, the light of battle in her eyes. "I am engaged to Viscount Lindford and *he* will escort me to Wyndham where we shall ask Grandfather's blessing on our forthcoming marriage."

Sir Cedric scoffed. "Engaged to that reckless wastrel! You just informed me that you were not!"

"No. I informed you that I did not elope with Viscount Lindford and that we were not married."

Cedric lifted his chin and looked down at Mary through narrowed eyes. "The earl will never permit you to marry him," he declared loftily. "Why, the young scamp hasn't a feather to fly with, not to mention having earned a most scandalous reputation during his short time on the town.

"I beg leave to tell you, Mary, you would be foolish beyond permission to throw yourself away on a penniless libertine like Lindford, when you could take your rightful place as my countess and heir to your grandfather's wealth. Come, let us cease this unseemly brangling and prepare to take our leave. I have procured a traveling chaise for your comfort. If we leave now, I daresay we will be at Wyndham in less than four hours."

Peveril was livid with rage. He was about to charge into the room to plant that interfering, pompous ass of a Ledbetter a facer, but Mary's next words stayed him.

"Lindford has changed. He has been the soul of courtesy and propriety since we were stranded here and has taken the greatest care of me and my reputation. He conducts himself with the utmost dignity now, Cedric, and I will not tolerate your disparagement of him."

In his new guise of responsible, level-headed fiancé, Peveril unclenched his fists, straightened his shirtcuffs, and sauntered into the room, resolved to live up to Mary's flattering description of him.

"Ah, Ledbetter. What a surprise! Has Mary given you our news?" he asked in a cool, but not unpleasant voice as he walked into the room.

Cedric's head snapped around and he regarded his rival coldly. "Lindford. I hope that what Mary has been telling me is true and that you have acted toward her with the utmost propriety. Though, of course, the situation itself of your being stranded here together will occasion talk of the most unpleasant kind. I must take her word that you have not presumed upon the situation and taken advantage of an innocent lady?"

All his new-found dignity fell away in an instant at these provocative words and the Peveril of old rose to face his adversary. "Just what the devil do you mean by that, Ledbetter?" he demanded hotly, frowning ferociously and raising his clenched fists in front of him as he assumed a menacing stance.

Cedric backed away from the advancing viscount, raising his brows and looking significantly at Mary, as though to say so this is the courteous, proper gentleman you plan to marry. "I think you should calm yourself, my lord, and consider Mary's feelings in this manner. If she has in any way been *forced* to give her consent to marrying you, then—"

"Oh, Ceddie, don't be absurd! Of course I have not been forced," Mary insisted, walking up to Peveril and lacing one of her hands with his. He looked down at her and she smiled radiantly up at him, immediately calming his agitation. "Pev and I will leave for Wyndham as soon as the roads are clear, which I take by your prompt arrival, they are in a fair way to being."

Cedric swallowed his ire with difficulty. "I shall accompany you, to preserve propriety. The earl would expect it of me."

"Over my dead—" the viscount began.

Mary increased the pressure of her fingers on Peveril's. "Of course, you may. When grandfather gives us his approval, you will want to wish us happy."

"That remains to be seen, Mary. I have no confidence that he will approve this highly irregular course you seem so unaccountably set on. As I have said, I stand ready to do my duty by you."

"Hallo! Sir Cedric here?" Percy exclaimed, coming into the room and looking stupefied by this turn of events. "Well, if this don't beat the Dutch! Gonna throw this dashed rasher of wind out on his ear, Pev?"

Peveril shot his friend a killing glance, but, as usual, the impervious Percy had no notion that his words only confirmed Sir Cedric's ill opinion that the viscount was prone to rash and violent actions.

"Ah, Mr. Throckmorton. I might have known I would find you here, too, to lend your scintillating wit to the occasion."

"Eh? No, how could you know such a thing? Ain't

a dashed mind reader, are you?" Percy asked, peering up at Sir Cedric owlishly.

"Where recklessness goes, there follows folly," Sir Cedric intoned self-righteously.

"I say, Pev. I don't like this fellow. Stap me, if I do. He's a devilish windbag and insultin' into the bargain. How're we gonna get rid of him?"

"We're not, Percy," Peveril admitted grudging with an exasperated look, whether for his friend or for his rival, he didn't know. "We're all going to escort Mary to Wyndham Park so that she can speak to her grandfather about our engagement."

"You're engaged?" Percy beamed at the viscount and Mary, noting for the first time their linked hands. "By Jove, can't say I'm surprised. Been making sheep's eyes at one another forever," he observed, with no thought to the embarrassment he was causing his friends.

Mary set out with the three gentlemen early the following morning, with the good wishes of the Parsnips ringing in their ears. They had all spent a most uncomfortable day at the Green Man where the tension in the air had been thick enough to cut with a knife. Mary had had the devil of a time keeping Cedric and Peveril from one another's throats, and Percy hadn't helped matters with his unthinking complaints about Sir Cedric's prosiness.

The journey to Wyndham Park would not have taken above four hours in good weather, but because the roads were far from clear, with the snow still piled high against the banks along some sections of the road, and the mud thick in other places, sucking on the horses' hooves and the coach wheels, they were slowed to a crawl. It took them all day and into the evening to accomplish the journey.

Peveril brooded during the tedious long hours in the chaise.

He hated Ledbetter with a passion. Because he was a handsome prig, heir to a wealthy earldom . . . and because what his rival had said was true. Mary would be throwing herself away on him. Much of his youth had been wasted. Now he was nothing but a frivolous ne'er-do-well.

What could he offer his Mary? A life of hard work, with not much gaiety for the first few years, that was what, putting to rights an estate brought to rack and ruin all through his own foolish neglect, and that of his feckless parents. He knew he was not being fair to Mary, asking her to share his life of penury, when she could be a countess, living a privileged life of luxury.

He watched his darling girl, who gave him an encouraging smile from time to time from her seat beside her kinsman on the opposite bench. He knew full well that he had done nothing in his life thus far to deserve such a sweet, lovely woman. If he truly loved her, Peveril thought, he would want what was best for her. She had offered him a glimpse of heaven and showed him what it would be possible to make of his life, but he was a man now, with a man's responsibilities. Unselfishly, he resolved to let her grandfather be the judge. If the Earl of Wyndham did not approve of their union, he would do the noble thing and give her up, though it would break his heart to do so.

Mary was uncomfortable with Cedric sitting beside her, but her thoughts were cheerful in the main as she dwelt on her future happiness with Peveril. She was already busy thinking of ways to get her grandfather to approve of their match and was making a mental list of things she would have to check when Pev eventually took her home to his estate as the Viscountess Lindford. She could not wait to work side by side with him in her new home, and help him set to rights the neglect of years.

She had no notion of her fiancé's gloomy thoughts. She would have been astonished and upset if she had known that he was nobly resolving to give her up. She would have been touched, too, but would immediately have set about disabusing his mind of the notion that he now had a choice in the matter.

The tired travelers arrived at Wyndham Park after nightfall.

Although there were lights burning in several downstairs windows, the large, heavy, grey stone building loomed over Peveril like a pall of doom as he descended from the old-fashioned traveling chaise Cedric had hired. He felt the house's presence and that of its imposing owner, the Earl of Wyndham, pressing down on him, mocking his pretensions to the hand of the granddaughter of the house.

He reached to hand Mary down before her relative could perform that office for her, tucking her hand under his arm after he had lifted her down and holding her close for the first time that day. He was not yet ready to relinquish her, and resolved to stay close until he was forced to give her up.

"Miss Mary! You've come home!" the earl's butler exclaimed gladly when he opened the door to the travelers. The man positively beamed upon Mary, giving Peveril, who was standing just behind her as she entered, a good idea that she was a much beloved member of the family. "Thank the good Lord, you've brought her home at last, Sir Cedric! The earl will be overjoyed."

Cedric nodded and brushed past the others to disappear down the hallway.

"Hello, Joseph. How have you been keeping?" Mary asked the butler, who was as bald as a coot and bowed with age, but whose sprightly manner and keen eyes proclaimed that he still had all his wits about him.

"Very well, Miss Mary. And even better now you've come home."

"I'm glad to hear it. I want you to meet two friends of mine, Joseph. This is Viscount Lindford and this is Mr. Throckmorton. Please see that rooms are prepared for them. In the meantime, I believe you had better put them in the library and serve them some refreshments."

"Very good, Miss Mary."

"I assume Ceddie has his regular room?" Mary asked with raised brows, indicating her kinsman who had moved off toward the back of the house without bothering to wait for the viscount and his friend.

"Yes, of course, miss."

"I would like to see my grandfather as soon as may be, Joseph. I assume he's in his dressing room at this time of evening?" She was determined to beard the old lion in his den before he could mount his defenses against her.

"Yes, miss. His habits have not changed since you left, though, if you'll pardon me saying so, miss, he's been very lonely without you."

"Hello, Grandpapa." Mary stepped into her grandfather's dressing room where a fire burned brightly in the grate and a brace of candlesticks on the mantlepiece cast a warm glow over the cluttered room.

"Eh? Wha—?" The elderly, grey-haired gentleman dozing in his chair in front of the fire woke up with a start. The multicolored woollen shawl draped over his shoulders slid off as he started up and the reading glasses perched on his forehead slipped down over his nose.

"Mary! So Cedric has brought you home at last, has he? It's about time!" the Earl of Wyndham said with a grumble in his voice as he stood to greet his granddaughter. But Mary wasn't fooled. She had seen the glad look in his eyes before he lowered his brows at her, concealing his joy.

"I am happy to see you looking as trim and fit as when I left, Grandpapa," Mary said with a smile curving up her lips and a twinkle in her eye.

"No good trying to turn me up sweet. Want to know what have you to say for yourself, miss? Your experiment at being your own mistress failed, has it? and you've come home to me. Hope you have an abject apology at the tip of your tongue," he growled sternly, "and are ready to agree to marry Cedric as soon as it can be contrived in the new year."

"Oh, Grandpapa," she said, coming forward to give him a kiss on the cheek. "You haven't changed one bit while I was away, have you? But then neither have I. I do want you to know that I love you and, however much we may disagree, that will never change," she said forthrightly, reaching down to retrieve the shawl that had slipped to the floor beside his chair and then arranging it over his shoulders to help guard against the chill that had invaded even his snug dressing room on this late December night.

"What's this you say? Not come home to marry Cedric?" The earl's grey brows shot up, but he was not really surprised. His Mary was too much like him. Too stubborn by half.

"No, but I have come home to ask your blessing on the marriage that I *do* intend to make."

"What! You think to be married, do you, miss?" He restrained himself with an effort at this unwelcome news. "Humph! Some impudent fortune hunter's latched on to you, knowing you was my granddaughter, has he? Well, if such a scoundrel thinks to get his hands on my fortune, he'll be sadly mistaken. He'll get nothing from me! As for my blessing, Granddaughter, that I'll give to your union with Cedric when it's assured that you'll be the next Countess of Wyndham, and so you know very well."

"No, Grandpapa, the man I have decided to marry is no fortune hunter. He knows that I will bring virtually no financial advantages to our marriage."

The earl bit back a sharp retort. Chewing on an oath, he restrained himself from giving vent to his feelings, fearful that he might really lose her this time. Forever. He could not bear that. It had been difficult enough these past few months. He cleared his throat. "And just who is this rapscallion who thinks he deserves you, eh?" he ground out.

"Peveril Standish, Viscount Lindford."

He stood thinking a moment. "A Standish, you say? Well," he said consideringly, one hand stroking his rough chin, "family's well enough. The name'll not shame you, at any rate. I knew his grandfather—another Peveril. Was up at Oxford together. But, by Jove, as I recollect, old Peveril had a spendthrift son. Went through the Lindford fortune in no time. You say this young jackanapes has no designs on my money?" he asked in disbelief.

"*My* Peveril knows that we shall have to manage on what his estate produces. He has no expectations from me."

"If it ain't to get his hands on my money, why does this puppy want to marry you, then?"

"Well, Grandpapa, it may surprise you to know that he loves me," Mary said with a smile curving her lips as she put her hands up to tie the shawl in a knot around his neck. She looked up into his eyes with determination. "And furthermore, I love him and know that we will have a happy future together. And though I ask for your blessing, if you refuse, I will not hesitate to marry without it."

She had put him at point-non-plus. The earl patted her busy hands and moved away to pace in front of the fire with his hands clasped behind his back under his makeshift cape.

He looked at her from under his bushy iron-grey

brows. "So, you think to get around me, do you? Think I've turned soft in my dotage? Well, let me tell you, my girl, my old bones may be decrepit, but my head ain't gone soft yet."

"No, I know you're as hardheaded as ever, Grandfather. But I'm not asking your *permission,* but your blessing," she replied with her chin up as she looked steadily across at him. "I'm old enough to marry without your consent, but I love you and want your approval, all the same."

The earl's lips twisted as he tried to control his emotion. "Always been one to speak your mind. Don't know where you get your stubbornness from!"

He didn't speak for a few moments. "Well, I'll see this importunate suitor of yours in the morning. See what young Lindford has to say for himself."

"Will you, Grandpapa?" Mary smiled thankfully, seeing that he would put up no more opposition. She ran to him and gave him an exuberant hug. "Thank you, Grandpapa. Now I will be doubly happy, knowing that you will not cast me away from you."

He patted her back awkwardly. "Humph! You're my Cassie's girl. My own flesh and blood," he said in a gruff voice. "I'm only sorry I can't leave you any of my money this way . . . Not sayin' I'll agree to this impulsive match of yours, mind, but if I find the young jackanapes will do, you'll have your mother's funds comin' to you. But I won't have you wastin' your money on young Lindford's ramshackle estate, mind. Will tie it up in a settlement, so you'll have something, should anything ever happen to him."

"Oh, it doesn't matter how you tie up the money,

Gramps. I'll have what is better than money. And Peveril and I will work hard and bring his estate back into profitability, I know. And you know how determined I can be, when I put my mind to something."

"Don't I just, my girl!"

"Well?" Peveril asked anxiously as Mary came into the library where he awaited her.

He was clenching and unclenching his hands and trying to relax the tenseness that had seized him while he waited to know his fate. After refusing the butler's invitation to join the other two gentlemen in the dining room where an impromptu meal had been served, he had been pacing nervously in the library while Mary was upstairs talking with the earl. He could not convince himself that she could stand against her grandfather. He did not doubt that the old earl would forbid the match to a penniless wastrel like himself. Now his destiny rested on her next words.

Mary leaned back against the heavy door she had just closed behind her and looked across at him, seeing the shadows in his blue eyes and the tenseness about his unsmiling mouth. He looked worried and endearingly vulnerable.

Oh, but she did love him so!

Walking toward him, she gave him a radiant smile. "It's all right, my love. He wants to speak with you in the morning, but he will agree."

"Are you sure?"

"Yes. He knows that I am determined, and though he can be a bear at times, he does love me. And now he knows that I love you and intend to marry you, no matter what. He will agree."

The shadows disappeared from the viscount's eyes and he gave her an answering smile. "Thank God!" he said a little unsteadily, coming forward to take her in his arms.

Mary met him halfway, throwing her arms up around his neck as he seized her by the waist and twirled her about. His lips found hers before he finally set her on her feet, and their mouths met in a knee-weakening kiss that had them clinging together breathlessly, holding onto one another for support.

"I had determined to give you up, if he had refused, you know," he murmured against her hair after a long, satisfying interval. His lips moved lower to the delicate spot just below her ear. He pressed his lips to her soft, fragrant skin.

A tremor ran through her at the touch of his mouth and the feel of his warm breath just there. "You didn't resolve such a thing, did you, Pev! Let me tell you, you would not have been rid of me so easily, Lord Lindford," she assured him on the breath of a laugh as she reached up to tease at his lips again with little nipping kisses.

"Was trying to be noble, but don't think I could have borne losing you. Burn it, think I would have gone to hell in a deuced handbasket without more ado, if you'd walked out of my life, my sweet darling Mary."

Her head rested in the crook between his neck and his shoulder and she looked up at him with love in her eyes. "Tell me later, love. Kiss me now," she pleaded, one hand going up to hold him about the neck, the other resting against his chest. "Kiss me!"

"Your command is ever my wish, my dear Lady Lindford to be," he whispered against her mouth.

He held her tightly as he planted kisses all over her face, her cheeks, her eyes, her nose, and back to her lips again.

"Know I'm not anywhere near good enough for you, but love you too devilish much to ever give you up!"

"There was never any chance of that, my dear," she whispered huskily, linking her arms about his waist holding him tightly.

One of his hands slipped down to the small of her back and he pressed her more tightly to him.

"I love you, Mary, my own," he said hoarsely, lifting his mouth from hers briefly. "Lord bless those footpads who put you in my way!"

"And Lord bless Belinda Ramsbottom! May she make the most beautiful Duchess of Exford ever!" Mary added with a twinkle in her eyes. "Now kiss me again, love!"

Meg-Lynn Roberts welcomes comments from her readers. You can write to her at P.O. Box 12445, Austin, TX 78711. For a reply include SASE.

ZEBRA REGENCIES
ARE
THE TALK OF THE TON!

A REFORMED RAKE (4499, $3.99)
by Jeanne Savery
After governess Harriet Cole helped her young charge flee to France—and the designs of a despicable suitor, more trouble soon arrived in the person of a London rake. Sir Frederick Carrington insisted on providing safe escort back to England. Harriet deemed Carrington more dangerous than any band of brigands, but secretly relished matching wits with him. But after being taken in his arms for a tender kiss, she found herself wondering—*could* a lady find love with an irresistible rogue?

A SCANDALOUS PROPOSAL (4504, $4.99)
by Teresa DesJardien
After only two weeks into the London season, Lady Pamela Premington has already received her first offer of marriage. If only it hadn't come from the *ton's* most notorious rake, Lord Marchmont. Pamela had already set her sights on the distinguished Lieutenant Penford, who had the heroism and honor that made him the ideal match. Now she had to keep from falling under the spell of the seductive Lord so she could pursue the man more worthy of her love. Or was he?

A LADY'S CHAMPION (4535, $3.99)
by Janice Bennett
Miss Daphne, art mistress of the Selwood Academy for Young Ladies, greeted the notion of ghosts haunting the academy with skepticism. However, to avoid rumors frightening off students, she found herself turning to Mr. Adrian Carstairs, sent by her uncle to be her "protector" against the "ghosts." Although, Daphne would accept no interference in her life, she *would* accept aid in exposing any spectral spirits. What she never expected was for Adrian to expose the secret wishes of her hidden heart . . .

CHARITY'S GAMBIT (4537, $3.99)
by Marcy Stewart
Charity Abercrombie reluctantly embarks on a London season in hopes of making a suitable match. However she cannot forget the mysterious Dominic Castille—and the kiss they shared—when he fell from a tree as she strolled through the woods. Charity does not know that the dark and dashing captain harbors a dangerous secret that will ensnare them both in its web—leaving Charity to risk certain ruin and losing the man she so passionately loves . . .

Available wherever paperbacks are sold, or order direct from the Publisher. Send cover price plus 50¢ per copy for mailing and handling to Penguin USA, P.O. Box 999, c/o Dept. 17109, Bergenfield, NJ 07621. Residents of New York and Tennessee must include sales tax. DO NOT SEND CASH.